RIDE THE ROUGH STRING

RIDE THE ROUGH STRING

—

EUGENE C. VORIES

Northwest Publishing Inc.
Salt Lake City, Utah

NPI

Ride the Rough String

All rights reserved.
Copyright © 1995 Eugene C. Vories

Reproduction in any manner, in whole or in part,
in English or in other languages, or otherwise
without written permission of the publisher is prohibited.

This is a work of fiction.
All characters and events portrayed in this book are fictional,
and any resemblance to real people or incidents is purely coincidental.
For information address: Northwest Publishing, Inc.
6906 South 300 West, Salt Lake City, Utah 84047

JAC 5.2.94

R. Larsen

PRINTING HISTORY
First Printing 1995

ISBN: 1-56901-273-3

NPI books are published by Northwest Publishing, Incorporated,
6906 South 300 West, Salt Lake City, Utah 84047.
The name "NPI" and the "NPI" logo are trademarks belonging to
Northwest Publishing, Incorporated.

PRINTED IN THE UNITED STATES OF AMERICA.
10 9 8 7 6 5 4 3 2 1

To Eunice,
my wife, best friend, and tireless proofreader

ONE

"Oh, hell, your bank don't want our ranches to run!" Ike Holland thundered in that bull voice of his. Ike never spoke in anything but a shout. "If we can't make them pay, a bank damn sure can't!"

"We don't have to make 'em pay," the round, ruddy-faced man said softly. He looked at Ike through the thick lens of his glasses, which gave him a rather owlish appearance. "All we have to do is sell them for enough to get our money back."

"You'll have to find somebody to gather our cows before you can sell them," Herm Shelly said, twisting in his chair to ease the pressure on his bad leg.

Shelly's rubbery face expressed his dislike of this whole matter. He could feel the tension in the room. They all felt it. It gripped each man like a vice around his heart.

"We keep telling you, we're losing cattle and, if we can't find out what's happening, how can you? Before you can even think of sending riders to the roundup, you'd have to pay our Pool dues, which amounts to quite a bit of money. Besides, for months now, you were supposed to find a man to help us and you ain't even done that," Shelly stated bluntly, greatly agitated at the banker.

"I've looked all over the country for the kind of man we need, but, I have to admit, I ain't found one who'd be acceptable to the bank, as well as you fellows. After all, we're not looking for just a cowboy, you know. Remember, too, you haven't done a damn bit better, either. I told you I'd consider a man if you found one, too," the bank man, Homer Reid, said honestly, not liking this any more than these ranchers did. He understood their tension and frustration. "Again, we don't have to find out what's going on. All we have to do is give instructions to whoever's in charge of the beef roundup to bring in everything he can find with your brands on it. We'll sell whatever he finds and then take whatever your land brings to maybe make up the balance. After all, you put up your land to guarantee the loans on the cattle."

"Every ranch has to send three reps to the roundup and damned if I'll pay dues and send men this year, if the bank's going to take everything I've got, anyway!" Ike shouted, folding his huge arms across his big barrel chest. "If you can't find one man to look into our problem, how the hell are you going to find the nine you'd have to send as our reps on the roundup?"

"Those men can be just average cowboys, not a real cowman, like I've been looking for. Hell, regular cowboys are a dime a dozen. Besides, if you won't cooperate with the bank, you'll just have to take whatever the bank finds without having a thing to say about it," Homer bluntly told the big man.

His round face grimaced as his bald head turned on his bull neck in his displeasure at having to talk this way. Homer liked it much better when he could joke about things. This was no longer a joking matter. And, Homer Reid did his job with pride. His first obligation was to his employer, the bank. While he sympathized with these ranchers, his first duty was to collect these loans.

"Well, fine, if that's the way you do things!" Ike bellowed. "I never should of trusted a bank in the first place!"

"Now, let's not go off half-cocked, Ike," Shelly, always the peacemaker, advised in a soothing tone. "I feel obligated to try to pay what I owe them, as I borrowed that money in good faith. What really bothers me is that I haven't been able to make a payment in the last three years. Remember, too, the bank didn't have to carry us last year, but they did, and I, for one, appreciate that. If this means sending men again this year, I'll do it and try to find every damn cow I can for them."

"Now, that's smart thinking, Mr. Shelly. That way, if there's more than enough cattle to meet your note, you can keep the extra. Maybe you'll even have enough to hang on to your ranch headquarters. If not, you can sell it and maybe save something out of all this for yourself," Homer said, sticking a stout finger in his shirt collar and running it around both sides of his neck.

He loosened his tie and unbuttoned the collar. He had never been comfortable in this kind of banking procedures.

"How about you, Mr. Hessey?" he asked. "Of course, your note's not nearly as big as the others and you did make a small payment last year. The bank's not thinking of trying to foreclose on you at this point. If a payment's not made this fall, however, it will be another matter."

Rube Hessey turned a nervous eye toward Herm Shelly. Plainly, Hessey was uneasy in any business dealing. It made him nervous to even look at the banker. He had always let his brother-in-law, Herm Shelly, do any business talking for him. The big man sat self conscious in his bib overalls, more farmer than rancher, hating even this much exposure to any type of business.

"I've already told Herm that we Hesseys will pay the bank off this next fall, no matter what," the man finally said, his voice sounding weak and out of place, coming from such a big bulk.

"From what Rube and his boys tell me, Reid, they can pay off their notes this year with just the cattle they have on their deeded land," Shelly stated. "Of course, if this storm blows up like it looks, we could still all lose a lot of calves and maybe even cows. If that happens, they'll have to rely on their range cattle, just like the rest of us." Shelly's rubbery face worked with each word he spoke. "It sure felt like a blizzard blowing up when I came in. It don't happen often, but one this late in the spring can be deadly to cows with young calves."

"Well, all right, I think you boys should plan on sending your very best men on the Pool roundup this spring," the banker said, trying to keep their attention on the problem at hand. "Let's hope they can find the cows you'll need to sell. The bank will hold off until then, if you cooperate. If not, all I'm authorized to do is start repossession and take everything I can get my hands on."

"You don't give us much choice," Ike Holland bellowed.

"Afraid that's the only choice I have," Homer stated frankly. "Do you still think someone is stealing your calves on roundup? That don't seem possible to me. I can see a few calves being misbranded, maybe, but this has to be on a pretty big scale. For the life of me, I just can't understand why you've not been able to find out who's stealing that many calves year after year. Hell, you'd think any good cowboy could catch that."

"The men I send on roundup are always ones I sure think I can trust. Last year, they all said they couldn't catch a single case of intentional misbranding a calf, at least none they could prove," Ike said loudly. "Hell, they even thought they seen lots of grown stuff with my brand on them on the spring trip, but, when the beef gather worked the country in the fall, they didn't find enough grown stuff to make a decent payment on a saddle, let alone on my note with you."

"Well, then, could somebody be stealing your stuff between the spring roundup and the beef gather?" Homer asked.

"That's what's got us baffled," Ike explained. "To get off with that many cows, there'd have to be a big outfit working the country again, during the month or so between roundups.

Surely, either the roundup crews or us ranchers and our hands would see that. No, it must be that they're branding our calves with the wrong brand so that, by the time they're grown, they've got someone else's brand on them. How they're doing it, I sure don't know."

"I feel the same way," Shelly added. "The men I sent last year are old, trusted hands, too. This year, I'm even going to let my son, Claude, go. He's kind of young, but they sure as hell can't buy him off. If he sees something wrong, he'll sure stand up and say so. I still think it has to be someone putting their brand on our calves someway, right there on the roundup. I agree, we should be able to spot anyone doing that, unless our men are in on it. If someone was re-branding them later, I'd think we'd find at least a few we could see the changed brand on. We haven't done that, either."

Shelly scratched his head as he pondered. "I've thought that it may be happening only on one wagon, as our cattle should mostly be on the west side of the Pool operation and it seems to be mostly our stuff that comes up short. The other Pool members haven't complained of missing much stock. It's hard to believe a person could buy off all the men on even one wagon, let alone on all three. Even so, all the riders on that one wagon would have to be in on it and I just can't believe that's being done."

"It's sure beyond me. Of course, I'm no cowman," Homer stated and stood up. "Well, I'll stay here in Limon a day or two, depending on what the weather does. If anything comes up you want to talk about, I'll be here at least until the next stage for Denver pulls out. Otherwise, I'll see you after the beef gather next fall. Let's hope, by then, you've found enough cows to ship and can make a good payment on your notes."

"I just wish you'd find the man you'd be satisfied with and we could send him on roundup," Shelly stated flatly, his face plainly showing the depth of his distress. "We know we're losing stuff someway. We need somebody you'll believe."

"I'll keep trying," Homer promised, then quickly added,"but I sure don't have much hope of finding a man now, in time to send him on spring roundup, anyway."

With this, the three ranchers shook his hand and left the small room, going out into the narrow hallway.

"You two staying in town?" Ike asked loudly.

"I sure ain't going home in any storm," Herm Shelly said, his face showing his dislike of such a thought. "I think I'll get a bite of supper and go right to bed. I'm not feeling too great, anyway."

"That sounds good to me," Rube Hessey said in his tight, shrill voice. "I sure don't need none of Gertie's night life at my age."

"Well, let's go get a bite then," Ike said and led the way toward the stairway. Shelly followed the others, favoring his right, misshaped foot and leaning heavily on his cane.

Back in the little room, Homer Reid laid back on the bed for some time, deep in thought. He was worried. His bank stood a good chance of losing a lot of money, if these ranchers went under. He was the one who had approved these loans, too.

He had worked for the bank for more years than he liked to remember. Most of his work, looking at ranches, cattle, and ranch people in need of loans, had always seemed the ideal job to him. He liked these ranchers, could relate to their problems and could usually help them find solutions. However, when things went sour, as they had with these loans, he certainly did not like what he had to do, threaten people and worse yet, back those threats with foreclosure on their lands and livestock. Like it or not, however, it was part of the job and Homer Reid did his job well, whatever it took. That's why he had been able to hold the respect of his bosses all those years.

He got up and washed his face in the bowl on the stand and wiped his ruddy cheeks on the towel. His bald head did not need a comb, a swipe with his damp hand put the ring of hair around the edge of his bald dome in place. He put on his hat, went out and down the stairs, but not into the dining room. At the foot of the stairs, he turned to go out into the large room holding the card games, bar and dance hall of Gertie's establishment. He did not wish to be around the three ranchers in the dining room, knowing they would not appreciate his company this evening, even if he bought their dinner.

This main room had only a dirt floor covered with several inches of fine sawdust. Several tables and chairs were scattered about, one table was filled with men playing cards. At the end of the room, an archway led to the dance floor, a raised area boasting of a wooden floor and a piano. Around its one stove sat, or stood, several of Gertie's girls awaiting the pleasure of some patron's company. Homer was not interested in either cards or women. He was happily married and had long ago given up playing cards for money.

He walked to the big outside door, thinking he might go outside to another café where he would not have to observe his customers in their present poor frame of mind. The wind almost ripped the door from his hands to force him back into the room. He quickly swung it shut again. There was a real storm raging outside and he knew a blizzard had indeed hit in full fury. He would not go outside tonight and probably would not leave for Denver for a day or two, either.

He sauntered over to the bar, where a small man with beady black eyes quickly stepped forward to wait upon his wishes. The man's round head was covered with slicked-down, black hair and a large, handlebar mustache was under his big nose. The long ends of that mustache were curled and waxed to perfection.

"Bourbon and water," Homer told the man.

The man poured a small amount of whiskey into a shot glass and sat a glass of water next to it. Homer sipped the whiskey, it was rather good for such an outpost, then took several swallows of the water. The whiskey was definitely better than the water.

For some time, he stood alone at the bar, very slowly sipping the whiskey. Finally, he saw the three ranchers come through the door from the café and turn to go up the narrow stairs to the sleeping rooms on the upper floor. They had not appeared to notice him.

Homer was about to go to the café, when the outside door flew open with a bang as the wind whipped it back on its hinges and against the wall. A shower of wind and snow gushed through the open door, setting the sawdust swirling into the air. Three men blew in with the wind and snow and now struggled manfully to shut the door against the force of the wind. As soon as they had the door secured, all three hurried to one of the large, round stoves sitting out in the center of the room, eagerly extending their hands toward the warmth, plainly happy to be out of the cold.

The appearance of one of the men caught Homer's immediate attention and he turned back to stand at the bar, watching this man. In this part of Colorado, one did not often see anyone dressed as this man. His coat was one of the East's finest, his tall beaver hat that of a city gentleman, not at all like those worn out here. Homer's glance went down the man's dress trousers to his shiny black patent leather lace shoes, again nothing like the high-heeled boots of the cowboys or even the heavy work shoes of the few farmers in the area. The man was definitely from an Eastern city and out of place here. Homer dismissed the man as a curiosity but wondered what such a man could be doing here. He decided to have another drink.

It was some time later, after the three men were warm enough to slip out of their overcoats and lay them on a chair, that the man in the Eastern clothes turned to look in Homer's direction. He had the clearest blue eyes one could imagine and Homer felt himself tense and gulp as recognition dawned on his mind. Was such a thing possible? Why, he had known this man years ago, when his appearance had been nothing like it was now.

The man also recognized Homer and a thin smile spread across the rather handsome, pale face. Even from where he stood, Homer could see the look of merriment flashing across the white face as the man now left the stove and hurried toward him, his hand outstretched.

He was a man of medium height, quite slender, with quick, easy movements. He met Homer's bone-crushing grip firmly and did not yield.

"You're as bald and ugly as ever, Homer Reid," the man greeted jovially. "My, but you're a sight for sore eyes. You're the first person I've seen since I got back that I'd ever saw before in my life."

"How do you know I'm still bald?" Homer demanded. "I ain't taken my hat off."

"You were bald five years ago and I don't think you've grown any hair on that dome, no matter how hard you've tried," the slender man said, with a friendly laugh.

Old comradeship rang in their voices and actions. Homer slapped the thin shoulder of his friend in almost bear like affection.

"Damn it, Dean, I thought they was going to learn you some manners while they had you back East," Homer said, his cherub's mouth spreading to show his white teeth in a broad smile. "As far as I can tell, you ain't improved one damn bit! What the hell are you doing back out here, anyway?"

"Just glad to be home, Homer. You'll never know how I missed this country."

However, Homer did know the hold this country could get on people. Dean was not the first cowboy he had known to go East only to return, drawn by his love of this wild country.

"How come you landed here in Limon?" Homer asked. "I'd have thought you'd have rode the train to Denver and then down to Walsenburg."

"I should have," the slender man admitted readily. "I sure should have. However, I got the stupid idea I couldn't wait to get back close to a horse, get the feel of the land again, so I've been on the stage for two days. Thought I'd go on to Colorado Springs by stage. I've always heard what a good grass country this is and wanted to see it for myself."

"Well, you certainly picked a bad time of year to look at this country," Homer informed him bluntly. "This blizzard may last several days and if it turns into a really bad one, you won't see much of anything but the inside of this room. I'm surprised the stage even got here."

"I am, too. I thought several times we might wind up in a snowdrift but the driver managed to get here, thank God. Coldest ride I ever had in my life and the most uncomfortable, too. I've decided that a stage coach is a darn poor excuse for a way to travel. But, blizzard or no, I'm so darn glad to be back in Colorado that I don't much care...especially now that I'm inside where it's warm."

"Let's have a drink and then I'll buy you the best steak this outfit has," Homer offered and turned back to the bar where the little man hurried to take their orders. "I guess you're going back to the Arrowhead?"

The slender man ordered whiskey, then turned to look at his friend thoughtfully before returning his glance to the man behind the bar. For a long moment, the man seemed in deep thought and Homer wondered what could be going through his mind. As he remembered the man, Dean Archer was not one to worry or ponder about things. He remembered Dean as a rather outgoing, friendly man who liked to see the humor in things and who never outwardly seemed to worry about anything.

"One reason I took the stage and came this way was to check on some of these ranches," the slender man said at length. "I always heard they had lots of big outfits in this part of the state, some big pool outfits, even, where a man might hire on." The man's expression drew grave, quite unlike the carefree way it had been before. "To be honest, Homer, I must have been crazy to quit Clay and go chasing a pipe dream all the way to Cincinnati. While I'd like nothing better than to go back to Arrowhead, even as just a cowhand, I'm not too sure Clay or I would ever feel the same about things. I'd always feel guilty about having left him, so...something else might be better for both of us."

"I always thought you had a pretty good job there on the Arrowhead," Homer stated. "I'll admit I was real surprised when I heard you'd left them."

"I had the best job a cowboy could ever have," the slender man stated positively. "Foreman on the Arrowhead was about as high as I could ever hope to get and I didn't realize how much I loved it until I threw it all away for a woman."

"Well, you ain't the first to do that," his friend assured him with a laugh. "I expect Clay'd understand, though—he's one fine man."

"Oh, Clay was the best—is the best—friend I ever had," Dean said softly. "I'll never know what I was thinking of, to pull out on him, and now, I'm kind of ashamed to go back."

"Did you ever marry that woman?" Homer asked.

Dean shook his head and finished his drink. The little, black-haired barman was right there to refill their glasses.

"No," Dean said, with a note of real sadness in his voice, as he seemed to stare into his glass. "No, she tried awfully hard to make it pleasant and easy for me to adjust to her way of life. Her father did, too. He even gave me a job in one of his lumber yards but everyone knew I was going to marry the boss's daughter," Dean said ruefully.

He was silent for a moment, then continued. "I guess I never really did care how many board feet of lumber there was in a pile, anyway. I'm sure it showed. They all thought I was just out to get into his bank account. After all, her dad's a very wealthy man, a state senator and director of one railroad and several other big companies. However, his wife sure never had any use for me, so what chance did a Colorado cowboy have of working into that kind of a life or family? I sure should've known better."

"I expect it was hard on a fellow, especially one with any pride," Homer sympathized.

"Well, we finally realized it just was never going to work," Dean said slowly, sad at the memories this talk was bringing to his mind. "We both gave it almost three years before we decided to call it quits. I'm sure she'll be much happier with someone from back there. I know I'm going to be a damn sight happier back out here, where I belong, even without a wife or a job."

"Well, you're sure going to have to change your clothes, if you're going to make any kind of impression on any rancher in this part of the country," Homer said, grinning at the ridiculous look the man had in those Eastern clothes, especially that tall beaver hat.

Suddenly, a thought flashed into his mind as though some outside force had brought it to his attention. He immediately wondered why he had not thought of it right off.

"By God, Dean, you're the answer to an old maid's prayer!" he exclaimed and thumped the bar solidly with his fist. "The bank's been looking all over the country for a man like you. We'd even written your old boss, Clay Hamilton, asking him to help us find one. I never dreamed that you could be available and them damn dude clothes made me forget you're was one of the best cowmen in southern Colorado."

"What the heck would a bank want with anyone like me?" Dean asked, his bright blue eyes searching Homer's face. "You can handle all their ranch business and I sure wouldn't be any good at anything else a bank does."

"Let's have one more drink," Homer said, "then, we'll talk about it over a good steak, but you've got yourself a darn good job, if you'll take it."

The two friends turned to lean their backs against the bar and looked out over the big room. Dean's eyes opened just a little wider as they watched the proprietor come from a back room to take her place for the evening. Dirty Gertie was a huge woman who lived up to her nickname in more ways than one, although no one knowing her ever used the descriptive part of her name in her presence. Gertie ran the only rooming house, dance hall, café and saloon between the Kansas line and Colorado Springs. This was the only entertainment spot in the little town of Limon or for many miles around in any direction. Rooms were cheap and most people agreed they were worth just about what they cost.

Gertie always had a number of girls working at her place who were known far and wide among the drifting cowboys. Like the rooms, they were cheap.

Gertie slopped her huge bulk into a big wooden chair not far from where the two friends stood at the end of the bar. The chair had curved arms supported by fancy wooden braces strengthened by twisted wire stays. From this reinforced chair, Gertie watched all the proceedings that took place in her establishment. Little, if anything, escaped her bright, piglike eyes. She looked at the two men at the bar, her glance showing her instant contempt for the dude's appearance.

Dean was beginning to feel almost human again after the bitter cold he had felt when entering the building. The ride through the raging blizzard in that stage coach, with the wind whipping snow around their shoulders, had been anything but pleasant. He now looked out over the room, feeling luck had been with him to even be here.

It was about this time, the card game began to break up, and for a minute, all eyes turned to these men.

"It's awfully early to quit, ain't it?" a man complained, no doubt one of the losers.

"Hell, I've been playing cards all day," a tall, well-built man replied, picking up his chips in both hands. "I've already missed one meal and damned if I'm going to miss supper, too."

This remark was greeted by a general laugh from the others. The tall, good-looking man was plainly a cowman, for he wore the wide hat, with its four block, pointed crown, and the high heeled boots of the range cowman. He seemed completely unaware of any other person in the room except those at his own table. However, Dean instantly knew, from the way the man spoke, he wanted everyone in the room to hear, his voice much louder than necessary. Automatically, Dean put the man down as a blow-hard who liked to impress others with his talk. That type person had never appealed to him and an almost instant dislike for the man formed in his mind. The cowman's hair was graying slightly at the temples. He had thick, powerful shoulders and narrow hips. His rugged good looks stood out as he walked slowly around the table with the air of a man well satisfied with his life and everything in it.

Funny, Dean thought to himself, here I've dreamed about coming back to this cow country and here the first cowman

I've seen, I don't like. I thought I'd like anybody from out here, no matter what. Life has its funny twists, for sure. For a quick moment, his mind went back to his old friend and boss, Clay Hamilton. There was little similarity between the Arrowhead owner and this cattleman.

"If this weather holds as bad as it looks," the big cowman stated loudly, "I may play cards all night tonight and all day tomorrow, too."

He now led the way to the bar, the men from his table following at his heels like well-trained sheep dogs. He noisily demanded money for his chips and the little barman jumped to do his bidding. The others stood back respectfully until his money was counted out by Gertie's husband, the little man behind the bar. The cowman had plainly been the big winner and his offer to buy drinks for all his friends was greeted with joyous shouts of approval. The men now crowded up to the bar and the two friends moved around the end to be out of their way.

After the men quickly downed their drinks, they all trooped to the door going into the café, and again as they passed him, Dean noticed how the men followed at the big man's heels.

Dean now offered to buy his friend a drink and they let the little man fill their glasses again. They were in no real hurry as the liquor tasted pretty good and they both were plainly enjoying the other's company. Dean did notice Homer's eyes were now appearing rather wide and even more owlish as he looked at him through his glasses. When the man spoke, his words were taking on a slight deliberation that was not normally there.

"You wasn't much of a drinking man, as I remember you from back in the old days," Homer said.

"I'm still not, really," Dean replied softly. "But I admit I got to where John Barleycorn and I were on pretty good terms before I left Ohio. Had to have something to take my mind off that cold, damp climate and all those people…as well as other things."

They had another drink, enjoying each other's fellowship, even though, now, not many words were spoken. They understood each other and Dean felt a thrill just to be back with his kind of people. It felt good and he let his mind think about the difference. People back East had seemed to just blend in, neither good nor bad, friendly nor hateful, just kind of in the middle some place. Out here, you understood there were good ones, like Homer, and bad ones, like Gertie. You either liked them or you didn't. It all seemed so much simpler.

Homer put his glass down and pushed away from the bar, ready to get that steak. Just as they took a step toward the stairs leading up to the rooms and the door into Gertie's eating establishment, the outside door again blew open, hitting the wall with a bang. The two men stopped to look back to see who could have been out in the storm. They could hear the wind howling, and again the air rushed through the open door, sending snow and sawdust swirling out into the large room. This time, along with the wind, came what appeared to be two cowboys.

TWO

After their first glance, the two friends were about to resume their way toward the café door. Homer had taken a step away from the bar, when he felt Dean's hand tugging on his coat sleeve. He stopped and turned his head to look blankly at his friend, then turned slowly to follow the slender man's glance. His owlish eyes blinked at what they saw. One of the newcomers was not a cowboy at all but a woman dressed in cowhands's range clothing, leather bat wing chaps over her divided riding skirt, and a short, heavy coat. Her companion was a white-haired Mexican, tall, lean and with the tough look of rawhide on his face.

As the two friends watched, a drama unfolded before their eyes, the likes of which neither had ever seen before. Dean saw Dirty Gertie struggle to heave her great bulk out of her chair for the first time that night and her heavy, stolid face took on an even more stern look than it usually held. She now waddled slowly through the sawdust to stop angrily in front of the newcomers.

Dean's eyes were drawn to the other woman. She had a strikingly pretty face. Her short, heavy coat was now thrown half open and the bright red scarf she wore at her throat contrasted sharply with the blue woolen sweater beneath it. The short coat came only to the pockets of the man's leather chaps she wore.

Jet-black hair was pulled back and rolled tightly behind her head, so it would stay up under the wool cap she had been wearing and which she now shoved into a coat pocket. As he looked more closely, Dean noticed the woman's hair was not solid black, as he had first thought, but had two tiny streaks of contrasting gray hair at each temple above her fine-featured face, now red and raw from the cold wind she had been out in.

It was the woman's eyes that held Gertie's attention. Large hazel eyes that fairly snapped with blazing anger at the huge woman. Dean thought Gertie could have made three of the slender woman and it puzzled him that such a woman would ever come into Gertie's place.

"Well, well!" Gertie gritted out in her gravel tones. "Just think of the great honor of having a missionary visit my place."

"I will not be here long, I assure you," the black-haired woman snapped curtly. "I've come for Eileen Greer."

"I thought as much." The huge Gertie belched loudly and grunted with all the emotion of an old sow. "Well, you just go on home and mind your own business, dearie. Me and Eileen have made our own arrangements."

"Not on your life!" the woman snapped defiantly, coming right back at Gertie. She squared her shoulders and stepped up to the big woman, looking her squarely in the eyes. "Eileen's only a girl and she has no business in a place like yours—she's decent!"

"Now, don't you start no name calling, missie!" big Gertie bellowed, her quick temper already pushed to its limit. "You start that and I'll learn you some names no missionary like you've ever heard before."

"Names mean nothing, I came for Eileen." The woman spoke so defiantly that Dean thought she was deliberately daring Gertie to try to stop her.

A commotion was heard from the dance hall. Dean glanced to see a slight girl being restrained by several older women as she had apparently attempted to go to the newcomers.

"You just keep her there!" Gertie ordered loudly.

Her eye briefly caught the ever roving glance of her husband behind the bar. She nodded her head ever so slightly as a signal to the little man. Immediately, he left his place at the bar and hurried toward the dance floor to assist the women holding the girl.

"Now, dearie, you ain't got no business here!" Gertie said harshly, as she returned her attention to the black-haired woman. "Now, you get the hell out of here and do your Christian work someplace else!"

"I came for Eileen!" the woman repeated with both conviction and determination in her voice. "You can't force her to stay."

"I'd like to know why the hell not!" Gertie stated bluntly. "Her own father agreed to it. He owes me over two hundred dollars and this was his way of paying it off. Of course, if you pay what he owes me, you can take her with you. Otherwise, our agreement stands and she'll just have to work it out."

"Don't make things worse!" Eileen Greer now shouted from the back room. "Papa did agree to this."

"Your life's worth far more than two hundred dollars!" the black-haired woman called over Gertie's big shoulder. "Don't be a fool! Come on, we'll take you home."

Just as the black-haired woman started past Gertie, the big cowman and his friends returned from the café. They now stopped in a group near where Homer and Dean were standing at the end of the bar. Dean's quick eyes took them all in and he wondered if these men would take part in any of this.

"I'll guarantee the two hundred dollars," the black-haired

woman stopped to tell Gertie.

"And where'd you get two hundred dollars?" Gertie demanded harshly, as another big belch rumbled from her huge body. "You got that much on you, now? Of course not. You ain't seen that kind of money in years. Everybody knows you and your pa are broke. Besides, what difference does it make if she works for me...or for you?"

"The difference would be the kind of work she does," the woman answered tartly, defiantly.

"There you go, preaching again, dearie. You shouldn't do that here in my place. Neither me or Eileen needs no self-righteous old maid to tell us how to live!"

"Don't you worry none about the girl, anyway," the big cowman now called loudly, a smile on his handsome face. "I'll personally see she's real well taken care of."

Dean saw the black-haired woman's eyes flick over to see the big cowman for the first time and he thought he could see a look of fear flash into the hazel eyes. For a moment, a heavy silence fell over the room, as if everyone was waiting for some signal to be given.

The girl now attempted to break away from those holding her. By this time, however, Gertie's husband had joined the women and he was holding the girl's arms behind her back and she was helpless. Dean saw the girl was crying but no sound passed her lips.

"Gertie, I'm going to take that girl home before you ruin her life like you did Julie Simpson's!" the black-haired woman said, with grim determination, looking Gertie straight in the eye. "You try to stop me and you'll think you've got hold of a wild cat."

"Oh, come now, dearie, you just ain't that kind."

With this, the big woman stepped forward, grabbed the lapels of the black-haired woman's coat and started pushing the smaller woman back toward the door. The woman, however, proved to be as supple and strong as the wild cat she had mentioned. She swiftly dug a spurred boot heel behind one of Gertie's thick calves and twisted her lithe body savagely.

Sawdust rose in clouds as the mighty Gertie landed on the floor, flat on her broad back. The wind was driven from her lungs, and for a moment, she lay there wondering what had happened and if she was ever going to breathe again.

The white-haired Mexican, his dark eyes flashing and his even white teeth showing in a broad smile, rushed past the fallen woman and ran toward the little man holding the girl.

"Now, hold on, Manuel!" the big cowman called and stepped out into the room as though to intercept the rider.

"You've got plenty of women already...including a wife," the Mexican said, as he evaded the big man's outstretched hand.

"By God, you'll regret that smart remark!" the big cowman threatened, his gray eyes snapping in open anger. Dean could tell the man was not used to anyone talking to him in this manner.

The tall rider did not stop but kept moving through the archway toward Gertie's man, still holding the slender girl. The little man had no stomach for this sort of thing and he let go of the girl before the tall, graceful Mexican could reach him.

"Get your things quick," Manuel instructed the girl in a kind voice. "We'll wait."

By this time, Gertie had managed to push herself up to her hands and knees, wondering if she could find in her body the tremendous amount of energy it required to raise over three hundred pounds to a standing position. It was extremely difficult and after managing the feat, she had to stop and gasp for breath, her thick legs spread wide apart to support her huge body.

Looking around, she saw Eileen had gotten a small satchel and a heavy coat and was now hurrying through the main room toward the two now waiting near the outside door. The big woman moved much faster than seemed possible for her huge bulk and managed to grab Eileen as the girl hurried past her.

"You'll not leave here 'til you're just like me!" Gertie screamed.

Quickly, she swung the slight girl around in front of her thick body and locked her heavy arms tightly around the slender waist. Immediately, the black-haired woman sprang forward, only to find herself caught from behind and pulled back by Gertie's man. The little man had slipped around behind her unnoticed. Now, as the Mexican moved swiftly forward to help, the big cowman rushed past Gertie to confront the tall rider.

Dean looked at Homer with questioning eyes. It was none of their business. He felt sure all the men with the big cowman would immediately jump them, should they attempt to go to the aid of the black-haired woman. No doubt such a move would bring every man in the room into a general free-for-all. He guessed none of them would be on their side, either.

Dean watched as his friend took off his glasses and carefully put them in the folding, steel glass case he carried and slipped this into an inside pocket. Homer's normally ruddy face carried an extra glow from the alcohol he had consumed and his German bull neck swelled out over the back of his collar. The man looked at Dean with an owlish look and a slight shrug.

"Now, Homer, I swore I'd never again do anything for a woman," Dean commented dryly, a smile twinkling brightly behind his blue eyes. He had no doubt what Homer intended doing.

"You forget—I've got a wife and two daughters," the ruddy-faced banker said softly. "I'd sure hate to think of one of them in Gertie's clutches."

"Well, for your wife and two daughters, I'll make an exception, this time," Dean commented with a wide grin. "I only hope I haven't forgotten how it's done."

One of the men with the big cowman now stepped out to go to his friend's assistance, for the man had found Manuel a very deceptive target. Something tripped this man as he stepped past the slender dude and he fell flat in the sawdust. Slowly, startled, the man pushed himself up, spitting sawdust. Homer Reid felt no pity as he kicked the man hard in the teeth. The man flipped over on his back and lay quite still. That was the way Homer Reid liked to fight. Get it over with quickly and cut down the odds against them.

Dean ran to where Gertie's man was struggling to hold the black-haired woman. The little man's beady black eyes managed to settle on the fancy dressed dude rushing at him and he quickly let go of the woman in order to protect himself. Despite his efforts, he caught Dean's knuckles with his mouth and that handlebar mustache. The blow hurt and he went down and lay still in the sawdust. He knew that was the safest place for him, as every man in the room now rushed to enter the conflict.

The big cowman was finding Manuel to be a rough opponent, for the lithe rider moved with effortless speed and hit out at him with fast, sure hands. As the cowman's friends now bore down on the dark-skinned rider, Dean managed to reach out and catch the big cowman by the shoulder, spinning him around on his heel. The blow Dean sent to the man's face was not that of a soft city dude and was completely unexpected. The big man had never dreamed anyone in the room would come against him, least of all this dude. The cowman went down heavily, though not seriously hurt.

"You'd better not do that!" a man shouted at Dean, just before Homer hit him on the side of his face.

"You don't say!" Homer shouted in a gleeful voice.

Gertie was trying hard to keep Eileen between herself and the blazing-eyed, black-haired woman. When the woman found she could not pry big Gertie's hands apart, she used a more direct approach, kicking the big woman's fat shins as hard as she could with the sharp toes of her riding boots. Gertie winced in pain. The woman kicked again and again, and at the same time, was beating at Gertie's face with her hard little fists. After a few moments of this, the big woman weakened and the girl struggled free while Gertie attempted to stand on one foot and rub her sore shin with a fat hand. The black-haired woman saw this opportunity and lowered her shoulder to hit the big woman squarely in the side, sending big Gertie again on her back in another cloud of sawdust.

The two women turned and ran quickly to the door,

opening it to let the wind whip it back against the wall. Snow and sawdust rose into the air around the swirling, fighting men. The two women turned back to watch Manuel, Dean and Homer backing slowly toward them, facing what seemed like a room full of fighting, struggling men. In the fighting, the three seemed to be giving as good or better than they were taking.

"Get out!" Homer turned to shout and shoved Manuel behind him.

"We'll play Horatio at the bridge for you!" Dean yelled, excitement plain in his voice. He was grinning broadly.

He took a hard blow on the chest from the big cowman and sent his left fist back to the man's face. It had been a long time since he had been in a fight. The two friends were forced slowly back toward the door by the superiority of the numbers against them, but they managed to make every inch cost the others in cracked ribs and bloody noses. All the while, from the background, came Gertie's curses and shouts of encouragement to her supporters.

By now, Dean was finding it hard to get the power he wanted into his blows. His arms felt heavy and the thought flashed through his mind that he had indeed grown soft in his years of city life. Maybe even old age was catching up with him! After all, he was in his mid-thirties.

He saw the big cowman's fist, looking like a sledge hammer, coming at him and he tried to dodge the blow. To his surprise, his reflexes weren't as quick and he could not move as fast he had been. He felt the blow graze the side of his head. He realized instantly, something had to be done quickly, or he would not be able to continue against such odds.

His chest was burning as his lungs struggled to draw in the air his efforts were demanding. With all the strength he could muster, he drove his shoulder under the cowman's next blow and sank it deep into the rancher's midsection, lifting the man completely off his feet. The man sat down amid another cloud of sawdust. The man's face held open-mouthed amazement that this slender dude had twice been able to knock him off his feet, something a lot of big men had never been able to do. Dean could not help but think the man would get a mouthful of sawdust if he did not close it.

By Dean's side, the ruddy-faced Homer Reid was putting up a very good account of himself. Homer looked a little soft, being on the chubby side, but he was as strong as a young bull and his nimble mind worked faster than that of most of his opponents. He seemed to know just what they would try before they struck out at him and he countered their moves in a way to get a punch in before they expected it and where it did the most good. From the expression on his face, the bald-headed banker was thoroughly enjoying himself. It had been a long time since Limon had seen two men put up the fight these two were doing tonight.

Dean managed to knock a tall, gangling man against some of the others, and for a moment, they all fell back. Upon seeing this, Homer gave a mighty shove and the men on his side also fell back. For a moment, they all stopped to look down at their fallen leader, as the cowman was still sitting where Dean had knocked him. The two friends seized this opportunity to turn and dash out the door before their surprised opponents realized what was happening.

They ran away from the building and into the raging storm which was swirling snow and dirt through the streets. A shout or two followed them, but the men inside did not seem to think the night suitable for, nor the cause worthy of, a chase.

THREE

The bitter cold air burned Dean's throat and lungs. He was still gasping for breath from the exertion of the fight as he ran to try to keep up with Homer. The wind was whipping snow and sand into his face and he could not see very far in any direction. There seemed to be no lights coming from any place except Gertie's door and that was soon shut. Dean thought, if I lose track of Homer, I could be in a bad way. He did not know anything of the town. The fight had almost exhausted him and he tried desperately to stop breathing through his mouth to lessen the burning in his throat.

It took only minutes for the cold wind to chill him to the very marrow of his bones. He felt his light, city pants slapping about his legs and wished he had on the woolen range pants and the long, heavy underwear he knew Homer was wearing.

His teeth were chattering already and he knew he did not have much time to find shelter. He had heard of people being frozen to death in these western blizzards when only a short distance from some shelter they could not see. He felt he knew now how it could happen.

"Where're we goin'?" he shouted above the noise of the storm and ran forward to grab his friend's arm.

"The stables should be around here some place!" Homer shouted back. "If we miss them, it could be a long night."

They groped their way through the endless, swirling snow for what seemed like hours but was actually only minutes. It made Dean dizzy to look at the dancing snowflakes the wind was tossing all around them. Suddenly, Homer, still in the lead, bumped into something about two feet above the ground. Both men felt along the object, trying to identify it.

"The water trough!" Homer shouted. "The stables should be about fifty feet in this direction."

"I hope you weren't on the wrong side of the trough!" Dean shouted back.

He stayed as close to Homer as he could. Both men had to fight the wind, leaning into it to keep their balance and turning their heads to one side in order to breathe. Seconds dragged into minutes and minutes could not be measured, so slowly did they pass. Suddenly, the wind lessened and Dean knew they were in the lee of some large object. Homer moved ahead, his hands outstretched in front of him.

"Part of the stables and corrals!" he shouted. "Should be a door back this way."

Without objection, Dean followed close behind his friend. His jaws chattered despite his utmost efforts to clamp them together. He jammed his hands as deeply into his pockets as he could and desperately tried to fight off the effects of the cold as it quickly stiffened his muscles. A few moments later, Homer found the door and they stepped inside a large building. Dean knew instantly it was a barn, as the movement, sounds and smells of horses came to him. He could tell their sudden entrance had caused a nervousness among the livestock.

"I'm sure this is the main barn," Homer stated, stomping his feet to keep up some circulation. "Let me light a match and we'll make sure."

A moment later, a small pinpoint of light smoked and flickered into a feeble, wavering flame. By this light, Homer ascertained they were, indeed, in the main barn of the livery.

"Hoo-ray!" Homer exclaimed. "I'm right."

"A warm fire would be more to my liking," Dean said ruefully, as horses snorted and moved about in their stalls.

"Now, don't you go giving up on Homer Reid's judgment," his friend cautioned in exaggerated seriousness.

"Oh, I'd never do that," Dean said through chattering teeth, smiling in spite of himself.

"Now, you're getting smart," Homer assured him. "Well, back outside."

Dean could have choked the man for the cheery way he spoke, as if there was nothing serious about their predicament.

"Where to?" Dean asked.

"Stable office is just north of this barn, not more than fifty feet or so. We'll go outside, turn left and just follow the side of the building right to the office door... You can't miss it, old chap."

The instant they stepped outside, the wind bit at them savagely. Dean turned to fasten the door securely behind them, not wanting to let anymore snow blow in on the animals than was already going through the cracks.

Homer did not wait, and by the time Dean had managed to secure the door, his guide had disappeared into the swirling snow and darkness. He started to follow, keeping his left hand outstretched to touch the side of the building. The fingers of that hand soon felt like sticks of wood with hardly enough feeling in them to tell the building was still there. He was sure he had gone more than the distance Homer had mentioned when he saw a faint light and suddenly felt his extended left arm caught in the grip of large, strong hands. He was jerked roughly into a small room. He stumbled, and for a moment, thought his legs would collapse underneath him. He managed to catch himself before falling all the way to the floor.

As his eyes adjusted to the dim lamp light, they now focused on the round, smiling face of his friend. Homer's eyes were twinkling and the crow's feet lines around them deepened as he stood laughing at the sight Dean made.

"You look more like Santa Claus than any big city businessman from Ohio," he said around his laugh, then added, "Last year's old wore-out Santa, that is."

There was a round stove sitting in the middle of the room on a sheet of flat metal and Dean hurried to it, his hands outstretched to seek the warmth. He didn't think he had ever been as cold in his life. As he moved, he became aware there was a man half sitting and half lying in a bunk bed which covered the back wall of the small room. The man nodded his head and forced some greeting past his lips but could force no smile upon them.

Dean could not blame the man, as this was a bad night to have unexpected company. The man's rather prominent eyes looked balefully sad as he watched his guests brush the snow from their clothing onto his floor. If he noticed Dean's city clothes, it did not appear to make any impression on him. Both Homer and Dean stood as close to the stove as they could as the man in the bunk rubbed his hand through his thinning hair and wondered what he was expected to say.

"Man, ain't this the life!" Homer Reid now exclaimed, with sudden, hearty gusto and he slapped Dean hard on the back. "Who'd trade this good life for the safe and sane life of the big city? Not us smart boys, eh? You got anything to warm a man's insides, Ron?" he asked the baleful-eyed one. "Don't be bashful…we'll reimburse you."

"Sorry, don't have a drop of what you want," the man said from the comfort of his warm blankets. He lay back and pulled the covers up around his shoulders. "Company policy that we can't keep any liquor here. There's a coffeepot yonder and coffee in that big jar on the shelf. Water's in the bucket by the door."

"Better than nothing," Homer said jovially and moved

quickly to fill the pot with water.

"Where you spending the night?" the man asked from the comfort of his bunk.

"About two feet from your stove," Homer informed him, as he sat the filled pot on top of the stove. "Think you can sleep on the floor, Dean? Maybe city life's spoiled you for such luxury."

"I'll make out," Dean told him dryly. "I always liked soft pine to sleep on."

"Try that packing box over in the corner, then," Homer said, pointing. "That sure looks like soft pine to me. Besides, that'll leave me the chair."

"Aren't you the thoughtful one," Dean said, giving his friend a knowing glance.

They made themselves as comfortable as they could, Homer on the one straight-backed chair and Dean on the battered packing box. Both moved back from the stove a little as their bodies grew warmer and began to tingle with improved circulation. When the coffee was ready, Homer got two cups from the shelf near the door and poured each a cup of the steaming brew. Their host was now snoring comfortably in the warmth of his bed.

"Wonder what happened to those people you were so darned anxious to help?" Dean asked as he sipped the hot liquid. It felt good to cup his fingers around the hot metal cup.

"I sure don't know," Homer said thoughtfully. "I never saw either of them before, but I'll bet that black-haired woman knew some place to go. Man, did you see her throw old Gertie flat on her butt? I thought we'd had an earthquake. And she did it twice!"

"Well, I hope they found their way to somebody's warm house," Dean muttered. The aroma of the boiling coffee was now strong in the air. "I even hope they had some supper, too, which is sure more than I can say for us."

"Man shall not live by bread alone," Homer quoted in his good-humored way. "You'll feel better after a cup or two of Homer Reid's coffee. If you'd rather, we can go back to

Gertie's. She might be over her mad already."

"After due consideration, I think coffee's really all I wanted, anyway," his friend told him. "Now, let's hear about this great job you've got lined up for me. If it ain't any better than your coffee, I don't think I'll be interested."

While their host slept peacefully, Homer explained about the three ranchers his bank had loaned money to and their problem with a shortage of cattle to sell the past few years. He went on to say, again, his bank had been looking all over the country for a really competent cattleman to send on the Pool roundup to determine if the ranchers were telling them the truth and, if so, find out what was happening to their cattle.

The bank would pay the salary of a top-notch ranch foreman, and if he went on the roundup as a rep for one of the three ranchers, that rancher would also have to pay him the wages of a regular hand, forty dollars or so, a month. If Dean could find enough of the ranchers' cows to make a good payment on their loans, or straighten up whatever was wrong on the roundup and stop the ranchers' losses, the bank would pay a good bonus as well.

The offer appealed to Dean. Between the salary and bonus, it might be enough to get him a little start on his own, something he had only dreamed of, up until now. Homer did his best to make the bank's offer sound good and hoped his friend was interested.

The more Dean thought about it, the more he was intrigued. It would certainly be a challenge. He was a proud man and hated to go back to his old boss with his hat in his hand, having to admit he had been a fool to have left in the first place. If he could do a good job for Homer and the bank, he could at least go back to the Arrowhead feeling he was going on his own and not like a beggar asking favors. He would have proved he was a cowman in his own right, not having to have his old outfit's help behind his success. He told Homer he would think about it and would decide for sure the next morning. With this, the two men made themselves as comfortable as they could and tried to get some sleep.

Homer's face seemed to age as he dozed off and his chin fell down onto his chest. The lines around his mouth turned down and his face lost the smile and cheery expression it normally carried. Several times during the night, he awoke to generously stoke the stove with the stable man's wood and coal. Between his cramped position on the box and his mind turning over Homer's offer, Dean slept but little.

When the stable man awoke the next morning, he cautiously pushed his head from under the warm blankets and looked out at his uninvited guests. Homer still slept with his chair tipped back against the wall, but the dude was awake on the packing crate, staring moodily at the stove. It had been a long, uncomfortable night for the man in the city clothes.

The stable man pushed back the blankets and swung his feet over the edge of the bunk, curling his toes to keep from touching the cold floor, while reaching for his pants draped ungracefully over the foot of the bed. He had slept in his long, heavy, red woolen underwear and he quickly pulled his pants on over this. After he had withdrawn his socks from his boots, he vigorously shook them out before pulling them on his feet. If he noticed the numerous holes in them, he paid no attention. Very gingerly, he put one foot into a cold boot and stomped it on, then the other. At this noise, Homer's eyes opened and he looked pleasantly out on the scene.

"Well, I trust you slept well, old boy," he said as he let the chair hit the floor with a bang and bounded quickly to his feet. He stretched elaborately and stomped around the stove several times to limber his cramped muscles. "Boy!" he exclaimed, "ain't this the life!"

Dean looked at the man and a grin slowly spread across his face at the man's boisterous attitude. He stood up, immediately feeling the stiffness of his own muscles. The fight had left him with a few aches and pains which had been aggravated by sleeping on the box. He went to the bench by the door and poured some water into the wash pan sitting beside the bucket, splashed some of this on his face and washed his hands. There was a dirty comb on the shelf above the bench and he dampened his dark wavy hair slightly before running the comb through it.

"Well, where're you going this morning?" the stable man asked as he was buttoning his shirt. As soon as this was done, he walked to the wall by the door and took the heavy buffalo coat from a hook and struggled into it. "I usually eat at Gertie's."

"Well, my good man, I'll just buy you your breakfast at that establishment in payment for the night's accommodations," Homer told him jovially. "You ready for something to eat, city man?"

"Now that you mention it," the slender man in the dude suit said with another grin. "Just one favor, though, Homer," he added in a serious tone. "Please don't start another fight until after we eat."

The storm had broken sometime during the night and they stepped out into the bitter cold of an overcast day. Dean guessed the temperature was at least twenty degrees below zero. He was immediately sorry he had put the water on his hair, for his head seemed frozen by the first gust of wind. He shivered and his teeth began to chatter before they had gone a dozen steps. At least, today, he could see several business buildings did exist in the town.

They waded through the deep drifts the wind had piled at the end of each building, to make their way up the street to the big door of Gertie's saloon. Dean wondered what to expect when they stepped inside but noticed Homer did not seem the least concerned. Gertie's man was already behind the bar and he showed no unfriendly feelings as they found their coats where they had left them. Both their hats had been flattened but were on a chair near their coats.

When they went on into the café, there were several men inside, but Dean did not recognize any as having been in the fight the night before. They found an empty table near the room's one stove and sat down.

"We really appreciate the night's accommodations," Homer told the stableman, as the cook brought them their pancakes, sausage and eggs.

"I sure agree with that," Dean added. "By the way, I never got my bag, it was storming so bad when the stage got in last night."

"I'll have it at the office as soon as I can get back there," the taciturn man promised.

The man finished his meal and left before the others had hardly taken their first bites. He had consumed his meal in a matter of seconds, for he took enormous bites with little time between them. His coffee cup was left half full as he told them he would see them later and hurriedly left the building.

The two friends took their time and enjoyed the meal. When Homer asked about his decision, Dean confirmed he had made up his mind to accept the job Homer had offered him. He had hardly gotten the words out of his mouth when the three ranchers came into the room. As usual, Herm Shelly brought up the rear, limping on that bad foot. Upon seeing Homer, they all walked slowly toward the table, uncertainty showing on all their faces.

"Good morning," Homer said jovially, waving for them to join him. "Just the men I wanted to see. Sit down and join us as I've got some good news for you, for a change. I'll even buy this morning."

The three men took chairs at the table and called their orders to the cook. Homer made no attempt to introduce them to Dean, and after briefly looking at the man's clothes, the ranchers diverted their attention elsewhere, as though dismissing something completely unimportant. Shelly could not keep his contempt for the eastern clothes from showing on his expressive face.

The little smile was again playing behind Dean's blue eyes as he watched the men's expressions. He knew how they felt about dudes. It had not been too many years ago that he would have felt the same way. He knew each man from the descriptions Homer had given him.

"Now, what's this good news you've got for us," Ike asked loudly, after their meals and coffee had been served.

"Well, I've finally located the man we've been looking for," Homer informed them almost casually. "I've known this man for lots of years. He used to be foreman of the Arrowhead Ranch near Walsenburg. If anyone can find out what's wrong on your roundup, this man can. And I know personally, he cannot be bought off. He's as honest as the day is long, I promise it."

"Naturally, we've all heard of the Arrowhead Ranch," Shelly acknowledged, his face now showing great interest. "No doubt any man capable of being foreman on that outfit could do all you say."

"All right then, let's decide on the best way to get him on that roundup," Homer said. "Where does it start from?"

"All the wagons leave from the Kincaid Ranch some fifteen miles up the Big Sandy from here," Ike said, his tone somewhat subdued at Homer's news. "There'll be a meeting of all the Resolis Pool members at Kincaid's on the first of next month. The wagons will roll out the day after that."

"There are three wagons, right?" Homer asked.

"That's right," Ike said as his voice was coming back to its normal bawl. "There are three completely separate units. Between them, they work all the country from north of the Kincaid place, east almost to the state line and all the way to the Arkansas."

"Who runs the roundup?" Homer now asked.

"Jasper Kincaid. The Kincaids keep all the wagons and equipment and winter the Pool horses at their place. We all pay dues to defray the expense of all that," Shelly explained slowly. "Normally, we send a rider or two to Kincaid's about ten days before the roundup starts and take the rest of them with us to the big meeting. This year, because of this late blizzard, we should send a man or two over there as soon as possible, as there'll be lots of extra work to get everything ready."

"How soon can your man be here?" Ike asked. "The sooner we get him here, the quicker he can start looking into what's going on."

The lines around Homer's eyes deepened and he could not

keep the smile from his ruddy face as he said, "Why, he's already here—oh, I forgot to introduce you to Dean Archer, long time foreman on the Arrowhead."

Shelly's face worked itself into several kinds of expressions, all of them showing shock and unbelief as Homer indicated the man in the dude clothes sitting at their table. No words would come to Shelly's lips, although his face showed he was trying to speak.

For an embarrassing length of time, the three ranchers looked from Dean's pale face to Homer's ruddy, round one. Dean's clear blue eyes were twinkling while Homer's hazel ones seemed to be laughing at them through his glasses. At last, Ike broke the spell.

"What the hell do you take us for, Reid?" he exploded and stood up swiftly, his big frame shaking in his anger, his unfinished meal forgotten. "This tinhorn may be a good banker, probably even knows how to read an interest table but, by God, don't try to pass him off as no cowman!"

"That's how you see it?" Homer asked almost blandly. He had to laugh now openly at the expressions on the three faces. "You don't believe me when I tell you this man ran the Arrowhead outfit?"

"Hell, no, I don't believe you!" Ike thundered. "From all I ever heard, that outfit's a real cow operation. What the hell you trying to pull, Reid?"

"We'll be the laughing stock of the territory, if we send a man like that to the Resolis Pool," Herm Shelly stated emphatically, his face still working frantically to show his disapproval of such an idea. "I can hear Kincaid now."

"Now, you're lettin' looks deceive you," Homer chided softly, his chunky body still shaking with mirth. "Didn't you ever hear you can't judge a book by its cover? All of you admitted that any man who had been foreman on the Arrowhead would have to be a good cowman. I know for a fact, Dean here was foreman on that outfit for a number of years, as my bank's done lots of business with that ranch. I must say, Dean had a good reputation, too. Now, it's true he's been away for a few years, back East for a while, but he sure as hell was foreman of that big outfit. His boss, Clay Hamilton, will tell you he's the best foreman he ever had, too."

"Is that really true, Reid?" Shelly demanded.

"As true as I'm sitting here."

"You ain't pullin' our legs?"

"No."

"And you're saying the bank will accept this man?" Ike asked in an almost whisper, for him. "Are you saying we have to accept him, too?"

"Yes to both questions," Homer said evenly. "The bank couldn't be more pleased. Now, that that's settled, how's the best way to send him?"

"God, I guess there ain't no other choice, if the bank will only play one way," Ike said, accepting defeat and slowly sinking back onto his chair. "Herm, your outfit has the reputation of taking in every stray cat, dog and rider that comes along. Maybe Jasper'll buy him as your rep."

"Are you meaning to have him go as the dude he looks?" Homer questioned, pondering this idea for a moment. "You know, that might just be the smart thing to do, at that. I'd assumed Dean would go as a regular cowhand. However, if his looks fooled all of you as badly as they seem, they might just fool this Kincaid, too. Now, if Shelly actually has the reputation you say he has of taking in strays, maybe Dean should just show up looking like he does right now. This Kincaid, or whoever's behind the crooked work, might not be as careful to cover his tracks around a dude as he would around someone who knew damn well what he was doing."

"It might just work, at that," Shelly admitted slowly, not taking his dark eyes off Dean's face. "It's sure true none of us would ever have figured this man for a cowman."

"There's one problem," Dean said, speaking for the first time. "You know how these cowboys drift from one place to another. One of them, at least, is almost sure to have seen or heard of me at some time."

"Hell, unless he knew you real good, and as long as you go

on wearing those dang city clothes, he'll never catch on until you want him to," Homer argued. "You'll have to use an assumed name, though, as I'm sure a lot of them have heard of Dean Archer. Got any ideas?"

"You say his name's Archer?" Herm suddenly asked, his face still showing plainly he liked none of this. Without a trace of humor he added, "How about Robin Hood?...He was supposed to be a great archer."

"Now, by God, that ain't a bad idea, Herm!" Homer cried enthusiastically. "Robin Hood...Robert Hood...Bob Hood? No, sir, that ain't a bit bad, Herm. You like it all right, Dean?"

"Sounds as good as any to me," the dude said softly. "It'll be kind of fun to try to run a ringer in on this Kincaid, whether it works or not. Besides, I've been away so long, I may be closer to a dude than I like to admit."

"By golly, I think it's a chance worth taking!" Homer exclaimed, his enthusiasm so great a person would think it had been his own idea. "If they do find out, which they will sooner or later, you won't be much worse off than if you went there as yourself, anyway, as I see it."

"The only thing is that, if this Kincaid finds out we've run a ringer in on him, he may be madder than heck at the man who sent me," Dean explained.

"The only one he could get mad at is me," Herm Shelly stated rather defiantly. "He's hated my guts for years, anyway, as I'm the one who's always complained about the way the Kincaids monopolize the Pool operation. It was started by Unk Kincaid in the first place and was supposed to be run democratic on everything. It was originally set up that the Pool boss would be changed every few years, and when I got enough votes to force that issue, all we got done was push old Unk out and got Mac and Jasper in. All the Kincaids have hated me ever since, even though it got Mac and Jasper what they wanted, control of the Resolis Pool. Hell, me sending a dude can't make them hate me any more than they already do."

"Now, one of you said something about thinking the dirty work was more apt to be done on just one wagon, rather than all three," Homer said, rubbing the stubble on his chin. "That makes a lot of sense to me. Now, how can we get him on that particular wagon?"

"I'd sure like to see him on the west wagon, as that one works the territory where most of our cattle should run. It even re-supplies at my ranch in June, so I'd have another chance to talk to him," Herm told them. "However, each wagon captain picks his own men, one from each ranch. There's no way of telling which captain will pick him."

"I guess we'll just have to hope he can find a way to get picked on that west wagon, then," Homer stated, thoughtfully. "You think he should just ride to Kincaid's from here and tell them Herman hired him in town and told him to get out there to help them as fast as he could…I like that."

"We'll all be at Kincaid's for the meeting and start of the roundup, so there'll be a chance for us to see if he's learned anything by then," Herm added. "We'll bring the rest of our reps and any equipment we have to furnish to that meeting. If we need to change plans, we can do it then."

"If he lasts that long," Ike grumbled loudly. "Just you remember to tell them Herm sent you, fella. Don't you ever let on I even knew about it."

"Agreed," Dean said, smiling at the big man's open apprehension. "However, you'll all have to instruct your other riders they are to take my orders in case it comes to a showdown."

"We'll do that at the meeting at Kincaid's," Ike muttered with less than enthusiasm. "I think it's cleared enough that I'm going home. I've had all of this town and meetings I can take."

"How about horses, will you bring a string to Kincaid's for me?" Dean asked Shelly.

"No, the Pool furnishes horses for all the hands, other than the one he rides in on," Herm explained. "It so happens, I have a horse at the stable I was going to take home with me. He isn't the best horse in the world but is probably better than any of the stable horses. I'll tell Hendricks to let you have him. You can ride him to Kincaid's. At least, he's got my brand on him,

2 slash S, so it'll look like you did come from my outfit."

They all shook hands and Dean watched the ranchers leave as Homer paid for the meal. Herm Shelly limped badly on his one leg and foot as he followed the others out the door and turned toward the stairs.

FOUR

    Dean spent much of the rest of the day arguing with the stableman, Hendricks, until he got the best used stock saddle, blankets and bridle the man had, for what he thought was a reasonable price. He purchased a few sets of warm underwear, a pair of five buckle overshoes and a few other things he might need at the general store. He and Homer spent some time going over the situation and discussing what would be the best way for Dean to approach things and how they would try to contact each other, if the need came up. Homer was to get word to Dean's old boss to send his saddle and other gear he had left at the Arrowhead to the Shelly Ranch, where he could pick them up when the west wagon stopped there, or if he had to go with another wagon, Shelly was to someway get them to him.
    After a quiet night's rest in one of Gertie's rooms, Dean

awoke refreshed and anxious to be on his way. It was thrilling, to him, to think he was going to once again be involved with a ranching operation back in his beloved Colorado. Despite the prospect of a cold ride, he looked forward to what this day would bring.

He and Homer ate breakfast and walked to the stable together. Dean caught the Shelly horse and put on the gear he had purchased the day before. He tied the carpet bag valise he had brought from Ohio behind the saddle. The sight of that valise should convince anyone he was a dude, no self respecting cowhand would be caught dead with one of those fancy things.

Between the valise and the overshoes, it made mounting the horse hard and awkward but, after a couple of false tries, he made it into the saddle. He leaned down to shake Homer's hand one more time and rode away from the stable. In case anyone was watching, he slumped forward in the saddle, like a dude would ride, his feet far back and slouching over the horn. The temperature had not risen much above the zero mark as he rode from the town through the drifts and under threatening skies.

In spite of the dreariness of the day, Dean's spirits were high, just to be back where he knew he belonged, on the back of a horse and with open country all around him. He had thought of little else for the past three long years and wondered again why he had ever been so foolish as to leave this country.

Once he was away from the town, he sat back in the saddle and pushed his feet ahead in the stirrups, a much more comfortable position to a man who knew how to ride. My, but it felt good to be in the saddle again. He talked to the Shelly horse and patted its neck with affection.

After crossing the Big Sandy, which was dry at that point, he turned to follow along the south bank, riding toward the west. Both Homer and the stableman had given him directions to the Kincaid Ranch.

Because the snow had drifted close to and into the creek, he had to ride out a hundred yards or more where the wind had whipped the ground somewhat free of the snow. In this manner, he could miss most of the drifts, but on occasion, where he had to cross a draw, he had to force the horse to plow its way through drifts several feet deep.

Although there was no new snow falling, high clouds kept the sun from warming the earth and the wind was still strong enough to pick up tiny particles of snow and sand from the ground and whip them into the air. When these hit his face, they stung like little needles pricking his skin.

Several times during the morning, he was forced to stop and rest the horse, for bucking the deep drifts took much of the animal's strength. By the time he had gone five miles, he decided the horse was not in much better condition for real work than he was.

He tied a knot in the bridle reins and dropped them over the saddle horn so he could keep both hands in the pockets of his heavy coat most of the time. He had purchased a pair of mittens but they still did not keep his hands as warm as his coat pockets. At best, it was not long until he had to take one hand out to guide the horse and both hands became quite stiff and numb.

He kept going until about two o'clock, when he found a small sheltered cove in the creek. He managed to swing his leg over the bulky carpet bag and dismounted. A fallen cottonwood tree furnished branches for a fire over which he warmed both himself and a can of beans. He ate the beans as soon as they were warm. He knew he had made poor time and doubted he was halfway to the Kincaid ranch. Homer had told him the ranch was on the north side of the creek but the south side gave him much more protection from the wind. He felt sure he could tell when he got to a road crossing the creek to the ranch.

Half an hour back in the saddle sapped all the warmth his body had managed to accumulate from the fire. It seemed to be getting even colder and he pulled his head into his collar as much as he could to keep his ears warmer. Even though the trees along the creek broke some of the wind, it still managed to hit him with considerable force. The wind was now whipping the snow into the air, from the ground, until it seemed it was actually snowing again. The afternoon hours dragged by as he forced the horse to keep plodding forward.

It was getting late. He hoped he would find the road leading across the creek to the Kincaid Ranch, or at least, some ranch or shelter before it became completely dark. In the darkness, he might not notice the road if he crossed it. He was about to give up and hunt shelter in the creekbed to spend the night, when he came to the two tracks of a wagon road leading across the creek. He felt sure this would lead to some ranch and he turned the horse toward the creek.

The horse cautiously felt its way down the sloping bank and onto the level of the wide streambed. At most times, the Big Sandy had more sand than water in its bed. During the winter months, however, it often had places where the water rose and flowed for some distance. At this crossing, the water spread out across much of the hundred foot wide bed and had frozen into a large ice field. The heavy covering of snow made the ice even more treacherous. Fearful the horse might slip and fall on this ice, Dean dismounted and led the animal across. The horse did not like the slippery surface under its feet and felt its way very carefully.

Once across the stream, Dean managed to mount again over the awkward valise. The road turned abruptly and left the creek, taking off toward the northwest. Here the drifts were worse than they had been on the south side, as the road was completely drifted over time after time. However, Dean noticed the horse seemed suddenly to have found a new source of energy as it fought its way through one deep drift after another. This must indicate the animal had smelled a barn or, at least, other horses not too far away. During a brief lull in the wind, Dean thought he caught the faint flickering of a light ahead. After several hundred yards, he made out the hazy outlines of buildings. A moment later, he was dismounting at the door of a large barn.

Inside, he found several horses standing in stalls, peacefully munching prairie hay. There was an empty stall at the far end of the alleyway and he led his horse there and quickly removed the valise and then the saddle. He climbed into the loft and threw down a generous feeding of hay. He found an old gunnysack hanging on the wall and used this to rub the horse down. When he felt the animal was well set for the night, he picked up the valise and stepped outside to find himself in the darkness and swirling snow of another blizzard. It took him some time to fight his way up the hill, through the drifts to the house.

His knock brought someone from the interior of the house with a light, and a moment later, the door was opened wide by a rugged-looking man in his late sixties. The man was a typical cowman as he stood there holding the lamp shoulder high and peering out at the pale face looking at him from under that ridiculous beaver hat. The man was tall and thin, with large bony wrists and gnarled hands. Dean guessed those hands had roped many a spooky critter and the faded blue eyes had looked at hundreds of prairie sunsets. Thin white hair was uncombed, and as the man stared out at this strangely dressed man trying to brush the snow from his city clothing, one gnarled hand lifted to let the stiff fingers brush through the gray locks.

"That's good enough, son," the man commented dryly, as Dean continued to try to brush the clinging snow from his pant legs. "You'll wear out them fancy pants, if you keep that up. Get out of that coat and bring it inside. You can hang it on a hook there on the wall."

"I'm looking for the Kincaid Ranch," Dean said as he followed the man inside a large ranch kitchen. His voice sounded like the dude he looked to be. "I do hope it was all right to put my horse in your barn."

"Shore it was, that's expected in this country. And, you've found the Kincaid Ranch, this is it." The old man reached out to accept the soft hand the dude extended toward him. Dean forced himself to let his hand go limp, rather than his normal, firm grip.

"Then, I'm supposed to report to a Jasper Kincaid," Dean

said, very seriously. "Is Mr. Kincaid here?"

"I think the one you want's in the parlor," the old cowman informed him gravely, his eyes never leaving the other's pale face. "You see, that happens to be my name, too, but no one ever wants to see me about anything any more...Years ago, things was different...Everyone calls me Unk, now."

Dean hung his coat on an empty hook of the rack that ran along the wall and sat the satchel below it. He unbuckled the overshoes and slipped out of them to set them beside the valise.

"It wouldn't do you no good to talk to me, nohow," the old cowman continued to grumble. "I've got as much say around here as a church mouse."

Dean grinned and hung his hat on top of the coat as his dark, wavy hair fell down around his pale face. It seemed good to be inside a ranch kitchen again and he drank in the smells that came from the room. He had forgotten how good a ranch kitchen could smell but it had been another of those things that had been lurking in the back of his mind. The north wall of this room was covered with a large kitchen range and wood box and Dean quickly moved to where he could feel the heat coming from the range.

"Go on into the parlor," the old man urged. "Go right through that door and through the dining room. Jasper's in the parlor and there's a good fire going in the fireplace, where you can warm up. I'll see if I can't rustle up some grub for you. I'll call you when it's ready. You go right on in there."

Dean went into the large dining room which opened off the kitchen. A large round table filled the center of this room, with five chairs drawn against it. He felt the room showed the definite touch of a woman's hand, a tablecloth on the table and a large buffet, neatly arranged, behind it. Another door opened off this room and he walked around the table to it.

He opened this to find himself in a large parlor with a big bay window covering the entire west wall. The north wall held a huge rock fireplace with a heavy oak mantle. On this mantle was a large vase holding a winter bouquet of sunflower stems and pods along with the lace like stems of Indian rice grass. Definitely a woman's touch, he thought. There were also several old spurs and other relics on the mantle.

In front of this fireplace, imposing itself between the cheery fire and everything else in the room, stood a large rolltop desk with a kerosene lamp sitting on its top. From where he stood, Dean could just barely make out the top of a man's head as he sat behind this desk. Dean shut the door behind him, being careful to let it make just a little noise. The man at the desk spoke gruffly, not bothering to look up.

"What do you want?" the man asked.

"Well, I'm looking for Jasper Kincaid," Dean said, trying his best to sound the way he thought a timid dude would sound. "Mr. Shelly sent me. I'm to be one of his representatives on the roundup this year."

As he was speaking, Dean walked slowly across the room toward the desk to where he could look around one corner of it at the man. The man looked up at the same instant, and for a moment, their gaze locked but neither spoke. The last time Dean had seen that face it had been surrounded by floating sawdust, for this was the big cowman from the fight at Dirty Gertie's.

FIVE

Jasper Kincaid had the rugged face and sun-tanned skin of the typical outdoor cowman. A fine straight nose separated blazing gray eyes with deep crow's feet lines in the corners. In many circles, Jasper Kincaid would be considered a very handsome man.

"You!" the big man cried out hotly but made no move to stand up.

"Yeah, me," Dean admitted dryly, his mind racing as he tried to think what he should do.

What a predicament! He knew instantly he was in a tight spot and he felt his muscles tighten, trying to ready themselves for action. He was too cold and stiff to be the least effective, should he have to fight the man.

Would the man renew their fight? Dean thought he had

best play the hand dealt him as though he had no fear of the other. After all, what else could he do? Maybe the rancher would also see the humor in the situation. Looking at Jasper, Dean saw no telltale signs of humor. The man's face remained angry and provoked.

"I doubt it'll do either of us much good, but if you want to start over where we left off, it's all right with me," Dean stated in a matter-of-fact tone. He couldn't repress the wide grin spreading across his face.

"The hell you say!" the big man thundered, standing up so violently his chair was sent scooting several feet across the floor behind him toward the fireplace.

For a brief second, Dean thought they would indeed start to fight again. For a moment, the big rancher stood looking belligerently at him. Just when Dean thought the man was going to explode into action, Kincaid seemed to think better of it and eased back somewhat. Dean could still not detect the slightest sign of humor in the man's appearance. Perhaps, the man simply did not wish to resume the fight here in his own home.

Dean thought of the woman's touch about the house and guessed the man probably did not wish the woman to know of his fight in town. This thought in itself, was enough to make Dean push the issue, knowing most any rancher would not send his worst enemy out into a night such as was howling around the house. He certainly hoped Kincaid would follow the tradition of the range in this matter. From where he stood, he could see the snow blowing past the bay window across the room. It would not be pleasant to have to go back out into that.

The big man now turned to walk back toward his chair. Dean spoke and watched the man visibly stiffen and spin back around at his words.

"Like I said, I'm ready to start over, if you are," Dean spoke in an almost pleasant voice. Jasper had to admit the dude spoke easily, and certainly had a lot of gall.

There was something frustrating about the man's cocky self-confidence and the plain laughter Jasper could see playing behind those blue eyes. Jasper had never known a dude to act this way and he immediately resented it. No dude had the right to tease a cowboy. It should be the other way around.

"Now, let me see," the slender man continued, "as I remember it, you were sitting on the floor wondering just what the hell had hit you. Are you ready to assume that position again?"

Jasper forgot his chair and rushed back and around the corner of the desk, his big hands balling into fists as he moved. Still, he stopped short and did not strike out at the dude. Dean felt he had been right, the man did not want to fight in his own home. For a full minute, the two men stood looking at each other. What a contrast they were, one so big and powerful, the other a shorter, very slender man with a thin, pale face.

When it became apparent neither was willing to start an actual battle, the big man again turned and stepped back around the desk. This time he retrieved the chair and sat down comfortably upon it. He turned his head to look up at the smiling face of the dude peering at him from the corner of the desk.

"You say Shelly sent you?" Jasper now demanded, his voice and actions suddenly all businesslike. "What's your name, anyway?"

"Bob Hood," Dean said evenly, trying to keep his tone that of a dude. "Mr. Shelly gave me a job and said I was to act as his representative on the Resolis Pool roundup, whatever that is. He said I was to come right out to your ranch and help you all I could to get the roundup started as quickly as possible."

"He what? Why that old fool! I always knew Shelly was soft in the head, but this beats anything I ever heard of him doing," Jasper said with a snort. "Hood, we sure don't have time to teach a city boy how to punch cows. Hell, Shelly knows that! A roundup's no place for a dude! I don't know what in the world he was thinkin' of, but you sure as hell ain't going on any roundup with me!"

"You might be surprised how fast some of us city folks can learn, country boy," Dean said from behind his grin. He was enjoying tormenting the man and he could tell Jasper was very annoyed. "Seems I picked up your brand of fighting pretty quick."

Had Dean been anything but a dude, Jasper would probably have seen the humor in the situation by this time. He just couldn't let a dude get the best of him.

"Do you think a lucky punch or two makes you something special?" Jasper demanded in a blustery tone. "All right, smart guy, if you've got the guts to take this job, after seeing who you'll be working for, you can try. I'll tell you right out, I'm going to give you a rough go of it. Cowpunching ain't a picnic at best, but you'll sure live to regret sticking your nose in my business the other night, Bob Hood."

"I haven't seen anything that would make me change my mind, yet," Dean told the man quite frankly.

"I just hope you don't lose your nerve, city boy," Kincaid promised calmly. "I'd kind of like to have you stick around long enough to settle a few things—away from the house, that is."

Dean was about to say something, when the door from the dining room opened and the old cowman stuck his head into the room.

"I've got some grub fixed for that young feller, Jasper," the old man said gruffly.

"All right, Unk," Jasper growled. "Why the hell didn't you just send him on to the cook shack?"

"Oh, seemed kind of good to be doing something like we used to," the man said, motioning for Dean to come with him.

While Dean ate the meal of cold roast beef, biscuits with gravy and hot coffee, the old man sat across the kitchen table from him but said very little. Dean felt he could relate to this old man, seemingly a cattleman from the old school.

After he had finished the meal, Unk told him to put on his heavy coat and overshoes before leading the way outside and through the snow to another building. Upon entering it, Dean instantly knew it to be a ranch bunkhouse and he saw men's forms lying under their blankets on the beds lined along one wall. One or two men rolled over to look, as Unk lit a lamp on the table and pointed out an empty bed for Dean to use. Several pairs of eyes watched the newcomer undress and crawl into his bed. Nothing remotely resembling this man's clothes had ever before entered their bunkhouse.

Dean was tired and stiff from the unaccustomed riding, and for some time, lay waiting for the blankets to warm enough for him to drop off to sleep. His mind went back over the meeting with Jasper, then back to their first meeting and the fight at Gertie's.

He could again see the black-haired woman's face as she struggled with big Gertie. Now, there was a strong-willed woman, he thought, and he admired her again in his mind. He remembered her strikingly pretty face and supple figure. Probably married and had five kids, he thought. The gray at her temples had told she was not any sweet young school teacher, or something like that. He did wonder who she was and if he would ever see her again. She was the last thing he thought of before dropping off to sleep, and as he did so, he wondered that he even thought of her, for he had told himself a hundred times he would never again give serious thought to any woman. After his experience with the girl in Ohio, he was definitely through with women.

He awoke the next morning with the first stirring of the men. Wishing to appear the Eastern dude they took him to be, he lay still and pretended sleep as the others got up and dressed noisily by the light of a kerosene lamp. At last, he rolled over and looked out at them.

"You might just as well get up," a man informed him dryly. "They only serve breakfast once around here."

"Oh, thank you, sir," Dean replied cheerily and politely as he swung his feet over the side of the bed. "I'll remember that."

The men turned their heads to hide the smiles this remark brought to their rough, sun-bronzed faces. They turned back to watch him dress in those fancy clothes.

He shaved quickly, and as soon as he was finished, followed the men through the deep drifts between the bunk-house and the cook shack. Not a word was spoken to him but the men did laugh and joke among themselves. He had always enjoyed the camaraderie of the cowboys and felt left out with this group.

Inside the cook shack, the men took their places on benches beside the long table and he found an empty space at one end of a bench and joined them. Few words were spoken as the men ate quickly.

Just as they were finishing, Jasper Kincaid stepped in the doorway. He quickly checked to make sure the dude was there.

"Looks like this storm'll last another day, at least," the big cowman said, speaking in a manner similar to the one Dean remembered him using at Gertie's. The man seemed to feel that the whole world had to stop and listen when he spoke. "You might just as well stay inside again today. Ben, you and Andy feed the horses in the barn and make sure they're watered. All of you make sure your tack's in good shape for when the weather breaks and the work starts."

Dean spent most of the day lying on his bed in the warm bunkhouse as the men came and went about their various chores. After the noon meal, several started a card game at the table, careful not to invite the dude to join them. Dean could not help but wonder if Jasper had instructed them to have as little to do with him as possible. He knew cowboys, or thought he did. Mostly, they were openly friendly men, if you tried to meet them halfway. None of these men acted as though they realized he even existed.

The next morning broke clear and cold, not a cloud in the blue sky. As they finished breakfast, Jasper instructed them all to saddle their horses and get ready to go look for the horses that made up the Pool remuda. He told them the first order of business for the next few days would be to get all the stock and equipment ready for the roundup wagons to roll. The man never spoke directly to Dean and he just assumed he was to go with the other men.

The last man to reach the barn, Dean went directly to the stall his horse stood in and began saddling at once. Aware some of the men were watching, he made sure to fumble with the saddle and blankets as though he was completely unused to handling them.

He was pleased with his efforts when he heard one of the men say, "I'll bet he had a fancy groom to do all that dirty work for him back where he come from."

The man who spoke was a tall, towering puncher Dean had noticed from the very first, as he was so big he stood out from the others. The man appeared to be some kind of straw boss under Jasper, as he told several men what they should be doing. The big man's shoulders slunk forward in a manner that gave him a hulking appearance and his quick temper and surly attitude did not appeal in the least to Dean. He wondered if the man was truly a straw boss, or just took it upon himself to tell others what to do.

After the men had mounted their horses, they all turned to watch the dude put the toe of his overshoe into the stirrup and swing awkwardly onto the saddle. He had to make two tries before he made it all the way on his horse. There were smiles at the way he sat there rolling forward over the saddle horn.

Jasper Kincaid, mounted on a big gray horse, led all the men away from the ranch buildings, through the deep drifts that had piled near the buildings and corrals, to the more open flats where the wind had blown most of the snow from the ground. They rode west, up the creek, for several miles and then turned north. It was hard going when they had to cross draws drifted full of snow. It was especially hard on the first horse as it broke the trail through the drifts making it a little easier for those following. Dean rode at the rear of the group, mostly ignored by the others.

Again, this seemed unusual to him, for in most ways, the men seemed typical of the cowboys he had known on the Arrowhead and he could not understand why they held themselves so much apart from him. Those Arrowhead cowboys would have made fun of the dude, all right, but they would have done it openly and probably in a friendly manner. These men just seemed to ignore him.

After they had ridden north for several miles, Jasper stopped and split the men into two groups so they could cover a larger area. He sent Dean with the big hulking puncher, Ben Shadrow, and two other riders. Dean stayed at the rear of the group so he could push his feet forward in a more comfortable position whenever he felt they weren't watching him. His soft city shoes were not very warm and were uncomfortable in the stirrups. Outside of keeping his feet a little warmer, the overshoes made riding more difficult. He wished he had gone ahead and bought a pair of boots before he left Limon. Even store-bought boots would have been better to ride with than his shoes. He thought back to the two pair of good handmade boots he had left at the Arrowhead.

They made a large circle, checking the draws and scattered watering holes for any signs of horses. They found none. They did see a very few cows and also saw the legs and parts of dead cows sticking out of some of the deep drifts in the draws. Dean knew there would be the carcasses of many cattle found in those draws when the snow melted. These late spring storms were hard on livestock caught out in them, especially those with their young at their sides.

It was the middle of the afternoon when Shadrow finally gave up the search for the day, and headed back toward the ranch. As he rode, Dean let his eyes search the landscape, trying to locate things and places for future reference. This was hard because of the sameness of the rolling prairie. The Big Sandy ran through the center of a wide, shallow valley and the trees along its banks could be seen for miles from either side, but if you rode over one of the rolling hills, you could not see even those few landmarks.

Far to the west, he could make out a long row of blue snow-topped mountains. These had to be the Front Range of the Rockies. He thought the highest one must be Pike's Peak and he guessed it to be seventy miles or more to the west of him.

As they neared the corrals on their return to the ranch, they saw that the other men had gotten in ahead of them and now stood around a fire in one of the corrals waiting to see if this group brought in any horses.

"Looks like Les and the boys got back." Dean heard Ben Shadrow mutter under his breath as he rode up near the men and dismounted. Several of the men were ones he had not seen before.

Dean was cold from the ride, and as soon as he tied his horse to a corral post, he hurried toward the fire, eagerly anticipating its warmth. He held his hands out to the blaze and unbuttoned his coat as the men silently watched him.

Jasper Kincaid watched the slender man across the fire and decided this was as good a time as any to settle the score with this dude. The big cowman slipped out of his heavy coat and tossed it to one of the punchers standing nearby. Without a word, he stepped around the fire and up beside Dean, where he suddenly struck out with a huge fist to the side of the man's pale face. The blow caught Dean completely by surprise and sent him sprawling sideways away from the fire. He rolled over a man kneeling by the fire and they fell into the deep snow together, both men struggling to get to their feet.

"What the hell!" the puncher exploded in his surprise, giving Dean a vicious shove away from himself.

"Stay out of this, Andy!" Jasper yelled savagely and pushed past the puncher to get at Dean again.

Dean was trying to get out of the burdensome topcoat but he did not have time before the big rancher rushed at him again. Dean knew it was fight or be whipped anyway and he swung out with all his strength and managed to slide his blow under Jasper's outstretched hand to catch the big man in the ribs. Jasper winced and stopped for a moment. The blow had been a good one and the big man stepped back slightly, then shaking his head, rushed in again.

Dean knew he would have to stay away from the bigger man or be crushed by the man's superior weight and strength. However, the snow, his heavy coat and the big overshoes, made it hard for him to maneuver. He tried to duck away from Jasper's vicious attack but became so entangled in his long coat and the logs near the fire that he fell heavily. The fall did not hurt, as the snow was soft and deep right there. However, before he could regain his feet, Jasper was on top of him. The big man drove both knees into Dean's chest and he thought his ribs were going to collapse. Had he not been in the soft snow, he would have been hurt much worse than he was. Even so, a deep burning pain went up the middle of his breastbone from the pit of his stomach to the bottom of his throat. Jasper's own momentum helped Dean push the man on over and away from him.

The big man rolled through the mud around the fire and stopped just short of the first burning log. Dean managed to scramble to his feet in time to run forward and drive a hard right hand to the big man's handsome face. Jasper Kincaid was a tough man, however, and he replied in kind. Dean tried his best to duck and roll with the punches Jasper was now throwing at him but could do little because of the heavy coat. It seemed he had lost his touch and timing, as well as much of his strength, when Jasper had jumped on him. He managed to get in a few good blows but they did not seem to faze the other man, as the rancher came back harder each time.

At last, the wall of punches Jasper was throwing at him became too much and Dean was forced to back up. Immediately, the big man pressed his advantage, and in a matter of seconds, Dean realized he was badly hurt. There seemed nothing he could do as one of Jasper's huge fists caught him just under his left eye and stars seemed to explode in his head. He realized the man was even then drawing back another fist, and in desperation, he tried to get his hands up to protect his face. A sudden excruciating pain hit him in the belly as the man kneed him. Even as he involuntarily doubled over, he knew the big man's fists would now find his face, and seconds later, they did.

SIX

Dean did not think he ever completely lost consciousness. However, he knew he lay quietly in the snow for some time, unable to get up. As he lay there, he kept feeling the pain ebb and flow in his stomach and chest. The thought came to him that he must get up and show these men he was no quitter. He must prove Jasper Kincaid couldn't whip him. His mind was willing but his body refused to obey his commands, so he lay there.

He finally realized men were moving about him but no one touched him or seemed to care if he were alive or dead. He could hear talking and knew they were leaving the fire, but he could not make out much of what they were saying. He finally sensed one man lean over him.

"Just leave him lay!" he heard Ben Shadrow command.

"Maybe he'll get some smarts and leave. Jasper sure don't want him around."

Perhaps he had been there longer than seemed possible, for when he finally again tried to get up, and this time his weary muscles obeyed him, none of the men were around. After he had managed to swing around to a sitting position, he could see the men had all put their horses up for the night and had gone to the bunkhouse, leaving him where he lay.

It was hard for him to accept the fact not a single one of these men would, at least see if he needed aid. He thought disgustedly to himself, and I thought I knew cowboys.

Jasper had apparently left the invitation open for him to leave, as his horse still stood tied to the corral fence. Well, why shouldn't he leave. Nothing but his pride stood in his way. His head ached, as he managed to get unsteadily to his feet and walk drunkenly to the horse. His chest and stomach still seemed on fire. Slowly, he forced his tired legs to carry him toward the barn, leading the horse.

Mud was caked on his coat and pants. His fine beaver hat was missing but he was too tired to go back and look for it. At the barn, he stopped to rest a few minutes, still breathing heavily, before he unsaddled and put the horse in a stall for the night.

Even though he could not explain it to himself, he just could not walk away from a commitment. He had told Homer and Shelly he would look into their problem. It was simply not in Dean Archer's nature to quit, once a job had been started.

He guessed Jasper would probably be at the big house. With dogged determination, he walked up the sloping ground to this house and around to the kitchen door. Here, he could see through the top glass into the big room, as Jasper and two men sat at the long table enjoying an evening drink. One of the men was big Shadrow. The other a small man Dean had not seen before.

Dean shoved the door open with a loud bang and stepped inside, trying to act as though he owned the place. The three men turned to stare at him in shocked silence, not believing their eyes. As Dean slammed the door shut, he watched Jasper try to wipe the surprised expression from his face.

Dean stood silent for a long moment, letting his mind race. Before, Kincaid had not seemed to want trouble in his own house. Perhaps, the big rancher would again not start a fight here. This appeared to be correct, as Jasper continued to sit at the end of the table nearest Dean and made no move to stand up.

Dean shook out of the muddy coat and turned as though to hang it on one of the hooks on the wall behind Kincaid. When he was almost even with Jasper, he dropped the coat to the floor and swung his left fist at Jasper's chin with all his might. His aim was just a little low and he missed the point of the big man's jaw. However, the blow was perhaps even more effective, for it caught the man squarely on the Adam's apple. Kincaid went over backward in his chair and crashed heavily to the floor. He made no effort to get up but lay where he had fallen, gagging and gasping for his breath, his eyes filled with the fear he was not going to make it. Dean watched that fear come into the man's eyes as he worked his mouth trying to draw in his breath and clear his throat. Right then, Dean did not care if the man lived or died.

"You might just as well learn one thing, Jasper Kincaid," he gritted out between clenched teeth. "You may whip me some of the time, but by God, you can't do it every time! I'll win some of them!"

Dean now swung to face the other two men still sitting at the table, the shock of what had happened plain on their faces. Big Ben Shadrow moved slightly on his chair, turning to look at Dean as the other man, a little ferret-faced man with large batlike ears sticking from his head under a large black hat, stood up quickly across the table from Ben. He seemed glad to let Ben handle this.

From the corner of his eye, Dean saw a pair of fence pliers on the shelf above the coat hooks. They would make a formidable weapon and he moved a step toward the shelf where he could reach these if needed. Both of the punchers were carrying pistols.

"You ain't got a chance of whipping me and Boyd both,"

Shadrow said slowly, his hand on the table ready to push himself to his feet.

"Just try me on for size!" the dude snarled.

The hulking Ben now lunged at Dean, his head lowered and his arms outstretched. In one sweeping motion, Dean's hand grabbed the fence pliers and brought the flat side of them down on the man's skull. The giant fell at his feet like a stunned ox in the slaughter house and did not stir.

"Next?" Dean asked the little bat-eared puncher and flipped the pliers so the sharp, staple pulling point was in position to be used as a hatchet. Boyd made no move to reach for the pistol he carried.

For a minute, the two men stood looking at each other, wondering just what the other would do. Boyd's hand was near his gun but he respected the fact the dude could probably reach out and hit him with the pliers before he could draw and level his gun. Jasper was now trying to get to a sitting position but was having a hard time of it, his legs tangled in the overturned chair. He finally kicked the fallen chair away and managed to sit up, holding on to the edge of the table with both hands. His face was pale beneath his tan and fear still shown plainly in his watering, gray eyes.

"This dude's turned into a plumb ring-tailed bear cat, Jasper," the little puncher said in the deepest voice Dean had heard in a long time. In the back of his memory it seemed he had heard that voice before, and he keenly eyed the way the little man twisted his face when talking. "Shall I use a gun on him?" Boyd asked.

Very slowly, Kincaid's head moved from side to side. Dean allowed himself to relax a little, as the little puncher now moved around the table to kneel beside big Ben's prostrate form. Dean moved past them to take a chair from the table and carried this to where he could lean it against the wall on the other side of the door. He sat down, his chest heaving, his eyes alert for any sign of trouble. His legs began shaking and he could not seem to stop them. He kept the pliers resting on his lap, ready for instant use. A moment later, a golden-haired woman came in from the dining room.

"What's happened?" the woman asked as her glance darted around the room. "Are you hurt, Jasper?" The rancher still sat on the floor next to Shadrow's body, gasping for his breath. Seeing Jasper's ashen face, the woman rushed across the room to kneel at his side. "What's wrong?" she demanded in a frightened voice.

Jasper could not speak. He pointed to Boyd and the woman turned questioning eyes to the little ferret-faced puncher still kneeling beside his friend's bulk.

"All I know is, the dude did it, Mrs. Kincaid," Boyd told her in that deep voice. "Jasper and him fought down at the corrals over something, then he came up here and started it all over again, hit Jasper in the wind pipe."

"Can't you talk, Jasper?" the woman turned to ask her husband.

"It hurts like hell," Jasper managed to rasp out in a hoarse whisper.

Dean was aware they were all now looking at him but he was too tired to care, as long as they made no move toward him. It was Mrs. Kincaid who suddenly cried out, clasping her hands over her mouth in startled surprise and excitement.

"Why, Dean Archer!" she exclaimed in open unbelief, and stood up quickly. "What in the world are you doing here?"

Dean looked up at the woman as recognition slowly dawned across his face.

"Just a job, Kate," the slender man replied evenly and sighed heavily. He thought bitterly, what rotten luck this was, but there was now no use of denying who he was. The woman knew him. "Can I ask you the same question?"

"Why, this is my home, Dean," Kate Kincaid explained in a strained voice. "My, I haven't seen you in years," she added. "What in the world did you and Jasper have such a falling out about?"

"Just rubbed each other the wrong way, I guess," Dean managed to drawl, amusement coming back into his voice.

"Well, the very idea of you coming in my own home and

causing all this trouble…hitting my husband," the woman continued in her rather quick way, her tone now also showing some genuine amusement.

Her left hand unconsciously lifted to brush back a stray lock of her lovely golden hair. She was not a pretty woman but was nice-looking and her hair was her outstanding feature. She also possessed an attractive personality with that inner vitality which automatically made most people want to know her better upon first meeting her.

"I didn't know he was your husband," Dean offered lamely.

"Well, he is. We've been married almost five years," she said, coming to stand in front of Dean.

"Well, wife, now that you've made over this tin horn dude, like a long lost relative, maybe you can answer a few questions for me, too," Jasper managed to whisper.

"Of course, dear," Kate said, turning to go back and help him onto a chair. "I do hope, for my sake, you'll both try to overcome your differences."

"Just who the hell is he?" Jasper demanded hoarsely.

"Why, Dean was foreman of the famous Arrowhead Ranch near Walsenburg, when I knew him. That was years ago, when I taught school in one of the mining camps near there. We often attended the same dances."

"His name isn't Hood?"

"Hood? I never heard that name. I knew him as Dean Archer, in those days."

"There was a fellow named Archer that was foreman on that Arrowhead outfit," Les Boyd spoke over his shoulder, as he bent over Shadrow and looked up sideways at Dean. "I rode for that outfit a few months some years ago. I never seen much of that foreman, but I remember his name was Archer and he had a big reputation as a cowman. This fellow don't look much like I remember Archer lookin', but that may just be them dude clothes."

"You don't say?" Jasper exclaimed hoarsely. "Is that right, Kate?"

"Yes, dear. Dean was known all over that area as one of the best cowmen in the country, as well as a fine man."

"So, Shelly tried to run a ringer in on us, did he?" Jasper guessed instantly.

"I don't know what you mean, Jasper," his wife said, looking in a puzzled manner from her husband to the slender man near the door. She went to the sink and dampened a towel, tossing this to Boyd who put it on Shadrow's forehead. "What are you talking about, Jasper?"

"Your good friend, Archer, here, pretended to be a dude that didn't know which end of the cow eats grass. He said Shelly sent him. Why, Archer? Did Shelly think the Kincaids weren't treating him right?"

"He says he's been missing a lot of beef the past few years," Dean admitted, knowing further deception was useless. "He didn't accuse anyone, but hoped I could find out what was happening. I thought I might find out more, if people didn't think I would know what was going on."

"Well, he must think we had something to do with it, or he wouldn't have tried to palm a spy off on us," Jasper rasped, holding his throat with both hands. "You come here claiming your name was Bob Hood and a dude. Hell, I've never had such an underhanded thing pulled on me in my entire life! By God, no man can say I don't run the Pool fair and square! I'll make Shelly crawl for this! You've got five minutes to get your gear and get your butt off this ranch, Archer!"

"I understand the ranchers have the right to assign any man they want as rep to the Pool roundup," Dean said with a wry smile. "I work for Shelly, not you."

"You may be Shelly's rep, but you won't go on my roundup!"

"I guess you can try to stop me," Dean admitted softly and stood up. "Just remember, Jasper, you ain't done too well up till now." He turned to speak politely to Mrs. Kincaid. "Nice to see you again, Kate. We'll talk about old times, one of these days."

With this, he turned, picked up his coat, tossed the pliers

on the floor, and walked out of the house. As he left, the others were working over the still prostrate Ben Shadrow.

Jasper did not say much during the evening meal, his throat still hurt when he tried to swallow or talk. His wife read the anger and hatred on his face and patiently awaited the explosion she knew was coming. His father, Mac Kincaid, also watched his son closely. Mac sat at the head of the table, a tall, thin man with a pale face and heavy mustache which he grew to try to cover a rather weak upper lip. He watched as his brother got up to leave the room, carrying dishes to the kitchen. Kate also stood up and went to get the bottle of brandy from the buffet. As was their custom, she poured three good-sized glasses, giving one to each of the men before sitting back in her chair. As she took the first sip of the liquor, Jasper could contain himself no longer.

"Shelly's the same as saying we've been stealing his beef, Dad," he said hoarsely, pounding on the table with a big fist, almost upsetting his drink. "That old man must be a complete fool to think I'd ever stand for him sending a spy in on us."

"Are you sure this man, Archer, is what you think he is?" Mac asked. He knew his son often grew upset before knowing all the facts. Jasper had always been a very poor loser. "After all, if Shelly's been losing cattle, you can't blame him for trying to find out what's happening."

"Have you seen Archer, Dad?'

"Only from a distance."

Mac watched his son intently. Mac was no cowman, as his brother had been, his dress and appearance more that of a prosperous businessman than the rough dress of a cowman. Every hair on his head was brushed neatly into place and his skin was white with care. When he spoke, his lips seemed to form each word with sanctimonious sincerity. After all, he had made money in the cattle business without ever learning anything about ranch work. He had been blessed with first a brother and then a son to take care of those details. To Mac Kincaid, the cattle business held no romance, being only another way to make and acquire money and power.

"Did Archer look like a cowboy to you?" Jasper managed to ask at last, his voice still raspy from the blow Dean had given him.

"I must say his clothes did not look like those usually worn by the average cowboy."

"Those clothes are what threw me, too. I thought old Shelly had just gone soft over another dang fool idea, like he's done before. I bit on this dude, hook, line and sinker."

"Well, I'll assure you, Dean Archer's no dude," Kate stated emphatically. "The Arrowhead Ranch is the biggest spread in that part of Colorado, and Dean was foreman there, when I knew him. If Shelly's losing cattle, I think Dean would be the best men he could possibly get to find out about it."

"I don't really give a damn about Shelly losing cattle, as long as it don't affect our operating the Resolis Pool," Mac stated bluntly. "Running that Pool has made us more money than our ranch ever thought of. It's what makes this whole operation worth while. Without it, we'd be just another ranch fighting for our life."

"Well, I don't intend for Archer to go on the roundup," Jasper declared, "and I sure don't intend to let that old fool, Shelly, upset our apple cart. I'll run Archer off, someway."

"That may be best," Mac conceded. "I'll let Shelly know what we think of all this at the Pool meeting. I sure don't want him getting any more ideas about putting us out of managing the Pool. We know he's wanted to do that for a long time."

"He can't get enough backing to ever do that. The only ones who listen to him at all are Holland and the Hesseys," Jasper said.

"I just want to keep it that way," Mac stated.

"Well, I doubt you'll have an easy time running Dean Archer off, if he don't want to be run," Kate stated emphatically. "He certainly had the reputation of doing his job well, and also that of being a man not safe to trifle with."

Jasper would have given anything to have been able to just fire Dean. However, he realized he could not fire another man's employee. Well, if he could not fire the man, he sure could make things so rough for him, he'd want to quit. Dean would not be the first man Jasper had driven from the wagons. The next morning, Jasper started putting his plan into operation.

Those first days would have been plain misery for Dean, even without Jasper's little extras. He was still not used to riding those long miles every day as the men searched the country north and west of the Kincaid Ranch for the Pool remuda horses. Jasper always sent Dean on the farthest, longest circle and when they began finding bunches of the horses, always had Dean ride on the front point where he had to keep up with the fastest horse to be in position to turn them where they wanted them to go. The two horses Jasper gave him to ride, in addition to the Shelly horse, were anything but horse running mounts and it was all Dean could do to whip them enough to keep up. How he wished he had his old saddle and even more, his boots and spurs. The riding he was asked to do was much harder than the men bringing up the rear.

At night, Dean lay exhausted on his bed and wondered why he had let Homer Reid talk him into taking this job, anyway. Yet, he had to admit to himself, he would have loved the work, had he been riding the saddle he had left at the Arrowhead and been on those good Arrowhead horses he used to have in his string.

He knew what Jasper was trying to do and this made him more determined to stay than anything else would have done. He would not allow himself to complain, no matter how many aches and pains he had. His feet hurt from riding in the soft, city shoes and, in a matter of days, his city clothes were tattered and torn and the once fancy beaver hat now resembled nothing any furrier would ever claim to have made. He forced himself to smile at the jokes Jasper and the other men made about his appearance but some of them were hard on a proud man's feelings and Dean Archer was a very proud man.

The weather was turning to more springlike days, the snow slowly melting from the draws where the deepest drifts had been. Reps from the other ranches joined the men at Kincaid's almost every day. Dean found these new riders seemed to have been well briefed on how to avoid him, for they all acted as though he had some terrible disease. Unless forced by the work to have contact with him, they avoided him completely. It was plain the men either feared or respected Jasper Kincaid immensely.

By the end of the second week, Dean found his muscles were getting a little stronger and tougher. His balance and timing were coming back to him and he knew he was riding much better. He was beginning to feel a little more familiar with the country, too. He was still unable to make any headway toward friendship with any of the men.

As the snow melted, the Big Sandy began running bank full. There were only a few safe crossings on the stream and Dean soon learned the men all went miles out of their way to one of them, for they all feared the quicksand that now filled most of the streambed. Thankfully, most of their work kept them north of the Big Sandy. One of the best crossings was about a mile above the main Kincaid Ranch buildings. Here, there was another set of corrals and some long, low sheds where a few of Jasper's regular hands worked with some young heifers having their first calves.

As the deep drifts receded from the draws, the men found mounting evidenced of the cattle that had been trapped there by the late spring blizzard. There had been heavy losses, especially among those with new born calves.

The men spent several days getting the three main chuck wagons greased and repaired, then loaded with cooking and camping supplies. In addition to the main chuck wagon, each crew had a bed wagon and another one that carried wood for fires and the ropes and steel posts for the rope corrals that were used on roundup.

Seeing all this equipment made Dean recall the roundups on the Arrowhead and he drank in the sights of the men bustling about getting ready. In spite of his trouble with Jasper, Dean found himself loving the work with the horses and equipment. This was the kind of work he understood.

There were now over four hundred horses in a fenced

pasture north of the headquarters. Many of these had to be shod before being separated into three remudas, one to go with each wagon. There would be fifteen riders, one for each member ranch, a wagon captain, a cook, a camp helper and two horse wranglers with each wagon. Each rep and each captain would be assigned eight horses, called his string, for him to ride. Dean was anxious to see which horses would be assigned to him.

Dean learned from the men's conversations that Ben Shadrow acted as captain of the west wagon and that Boyd usually went with that wagon as rep for the Kincaid Ranch.

The first of May finally came, and with it came the wagons, buggies, owners and riders of all the members of the Resolis Pool. Dean wanted to find Shelly and tell him that Jasper knew about him, but Kincaid made sure Ben Shadrow kept him busy throughout the day and away from any of the arriving ranchers.

The three roundup cooks made one large camp west of the house and all the new riders made camp around the wagons. The buggies and wagons of the ranchers were parked further to the west, somewhat away from the roundup wagons. Many of the ranchers had brought not only their riders but their families as well, and a tent city had sprung up for them.

A big barbecue was planned for the following evening and the three roundup cooks worked the entire day readying the pits they would put three half beeves in the next morning. Men worked feverishly gathering wood from the trees along the creek to have plenty of wood ready for the pit fires.

Jasper supervised the working of the horses in the corrals, separating them into three groups, one for each wagon. The three groups were then let out in separate pastures. The three wagon captains wrangled over the horses they wanted but Jasper's word was final.

The next morning, the Pool members gathered at the big house for their annual meeting. Shadrow kept Dean busy at the corrals so he never got to even see Shelly go into the house and the rancher had apparently made no attempt to locate him.

Dean wondered about this.

Later that morning, Dean saw Jasper and the three captains separating horses into one of the smaller corrals while Dean worked with one of the horse shoers as he put shoes on some of the horses. He thought, perhaps, the horses Jasper had separated were ones that were no longer suitable for the rough work on roundup and would be sold.

Just before noon, on his way to the bunkhouse, he walked alone up the sloping ground and past the buggies and wagons tied in front of the main house. He kept his eye out for sight of the crippled rancher, Shelly. As he moved around the end of one of the larger wagons, he saw a woman standing near a buggy a few yards away. The woman appeared to be searching for something in the rear of the vehicle, as she moved several articles in her effort to see behind them. He would have gone on past her, had she not turned just as he drew near. To his surprise, it was the black-haired woman from that night at Gertie's. He would have known that face anywhere, for the picture of her striking beauty and the raven-black of her hair had been deeply impressed on his mind. That face had been in his thoughts every night. He again noticed the tiny twin streaks of contrasting gray at her temples.

Today, dressed in a fine blue dress with white lace at the neck and wrists, the woman presented quite a different picture from that other time. He suddenly realized she was the most striking woman he had ever seen and wondered again who she could be. For a moment neither of them spoke, just standing and looking at each other. Neither of them could think of the words they wanted to speak, for the woman had also recognized him.

While her appearance presented a much finer picture today, his was quite the opposite. At Gertie's, he had been the proper gentleman in both his dress and appearance. Now, those same once fancy trousers carried several shapes and colors of patches and the once proud beaver hat on his head was beyond description. Dean knew he must look like a tramp to the woman.

"You!" she exclaimed at last.

"The bad penny always turns up, eh what?" Dean asked in his best imitation of a British accent. "Been in any more saloon brawls, since I seen you last, ma'am?"

Instantly, a sharp retort formed on her tongue but she then saw the smile playing behind his clear blue eyes and her angry words died unspoken. She was forced to smile, herself, at his carefree attitude and remark. She also noticed a lock of dark wavy hair protruding through a hole in that absolutely ridiculous hat. Even so, there was something about the man which seemed to set him apart from other men and she would always remember the lighthearted way he had come to her aid at Gertie's.

"Well, I'm certainly amazed to find you here," she said after eyeing him for some time. "I thought you'd have gone back to New York by now. Don't tell me you're working for the Kincaids?"

"There's one Kincaid who will not admit I work here," he said, removing his hat with polished grace.

"That does amaze me," she said, and her smile now held genuine warmth. "I never knew Jasper to forgive and forget anything. I'm amazed he's let a greenhorn like you stay for even a day."

Her voice was soft, as a lady's should be, yet he recognized a certain quality of strength in it. He knew, instantly, she was the same strong-willed person he remembered so well. The feminine clothes made it seem impossible she could be the woman he had thought so much about, the one who had thrown big Gertie on her broad backside. Had he not witnessed that event, he would never have believed this lady capable of such a thing.

"Well, now, it hasn't been easy," the slender man drawled slowly. "He's only whipped me once."

"You fought again!"

"I guess you could say we fought twice," Dean told her with a wide grin. "He whipped me once, but I guess you could say I got the best of him the second time."

"Well, I know Jasper Kincaid very well," the woman stated frankly. "He'll never give up until he whips you or runs you off."

"He can try."

With another tip of his hat, Dean hurried on toward the bunkhouse. It was not until he neared the bunkhouse door that it occurred to him he should have asked her if she knew Shelly. If he had been thinking, in place of being so pleased to see her again, he could have asked her to get word to the rancher for him. Now, that this thought had come to him, he was angry with himself. He turned back, thinking it might still not be too late for him to ask her but, as he left the bunkhouse, he could see the woman going inside Kincaid's front door. He turned back and entered the building.

A few minutes later, Shadrow came looking for him. Jasper wanted to see him at the corrals at once. Instantly, Dean became aware of a feeling of apprehension coming over him. Without a word, he brushed past the big man and strode quickly toward the corrals.

He found the big cowman in one of the large rear corrals with several of the men who had been separating the horses. Leisurely, Dean climbed the pole fence closest to Jasper.

"You want me, Kincaid?" he asked as insolently as he could, a thin smile on his lips. He really enjoyed tormenting the big man, although he knew it was a dangerous thing to do.

"I'd not have sent for you, if I didn't," Kincaid told him curtly, always ready to flare back at this slender man. "You still say you're going on roundup as Shelly's rep?"

"Mr. Shelly hasn't told me otherwise."

"All right. I've decided not to argue the point," Kincaid said and Dean felt his apprehension heighten. "Years ago, Archer, each rancher furnished his riders with mounts for the roundup. However, for the last five or six years, the Pool's furnished the horses for every man." Kincaid was speaking loud enough for all the men to hear plainly. "You see the horses in that next pen there? Well, that's your string. Make sure you can recognize them."

"Fine," Dean said dryly. However, the feeling of apprehension would not leave him.

"You'll think fine, after you try to saddle one of them," the rancher assured him, his tone too pleasant. "I'm real proud of the job I've done picking that string for you. We usually hire a special bronc rider to ride them, but this year, I decided to let you have them. That's the rough string on this outfit, Archer, and…they're all yours."

"Gee, thanks," Dean managed to say, trying to keep the smile from fading from his lips.

It took great effort, for he knew instantly what this meant. In any group of horses as big as the remudas for the Resolis Pool, there was certain to be a few really bad horses, no doubt some real outlaws, who hated man with a passion. If these horses were indeed the worst in the entire remuda, it could be almost the same as signing his own death warrant to try to ride them.

"I didn't sign on to ride any rough string," Dean said evenly.

"Afraid?"

"Could be," Dean admitted ruefully, honestly.

"Well, you should've checked on some of the rules before you signed on this outfit, smart boy. Pool rules state each man is to ride the horses assigned him," Jasper told him bluntly, looking Dean squarely in the eye. "Now, if you're half as smart as you think you are, you'll go find Shelly and tell him you've just quit."

Dean met the eyes of the big cowman, as he let his mind race over the situation he was now faced with. It had been a serious mistake not to make sure he would get a fair draw on the horses. He well knew the risks of doing cow work on even a good horse, let alone the added risk of trying to ride a horse that was more interested in trying to kill you than do the work. Men who rode the rough string were usually young men who loved to ride and fight mean horses, men who were proud of the fact they thought they could ride any animal with four legs, and usually could. Such a man had to like doing this kind of thing and did little else.

Dean had known such men. They grew old before their time, if they survived at all. Even then, they started at it young and were good at what they did. Dean was now thirty-five years old, an age when even good bronc riders began looking for gentler horses to ride and quit even thinking about riding the rough strings.

Dean had always been considered a good rider. He had always prided himself in his ability to get the most cow work possible from his mounts. Having a horse pitch with him once in a while did not bother him too much. However, it had been many long years since he had attempted to ride a really mean horse. In fact, as foreman on the Arrowhead, he had gotten his pick of a lot of good horses to ride. Now, at this stage of his life, he knew it would be almost suicide to attempt to ride the kind of horse that made up a real rough string.

A lot of cowboys were good riders. A few were even excellent horsemen, but only a very few of these would qualify to ride a big outfit's rough string. In fact, most progressive ranchers were no longer keeping such animals, finding it cheaper to sell the bad horses than to replace good men.

Jasper awaited the man's reply to his challenge, feeling sure the slender man would have to admit this was something he could not do, and walk away. Never had Jasper Kincaid wanted more to break a man's spirit than he did this man.

Dean frowned, as the thought flashed through his mind that Jasper must be desperate to keep him off the roundup. Kincaid must be behind Shelly's trouble. Why else would he go to such lengths to keep him from going on the roundup? He wanted now, more than ever, to find out what was going on. He heard himself telling himself that it would do him no good to find Shelly's missing cattle, if he did not live to tell what he had found.

"Well?" Jasper asked at last.

"Are you crazy, Kincaid?" Dean smiled, knowing only a complete fool would accept such a challenge. He had surely walked right into Jasper's clutches on this one. He had to give the man credit for setting a slick trap for him.

"I told you he had it real soft on that Arrowhead outfit," Les Boyd spoke from where he sat on the top rail of the corral not far from Dean. His deep voice vibrating in his narrow chest.

"So you admit you ain't man enough to ride those horses, Archer?" Jasper sneered and pulled his horse around, as though to leave. "Go draw your time from Shelly."

"Now, just hold on a minute," Dean said, knowing even as he spoke, he was being a fool. He shrugged his thin shoulders and his old devil-may-care attitude sprang to the surface. "You'll have to do better than that to get rid of me, Kincaid. I'll ride your damn horses and you too, if you get in my way."

Jasper jerked his horse to a stop, unable to believe what he had heard.

"Well, I'll be damned!" exclaimed Boyd.

Jasper swung his horse back around to let his eyes search the slender man's face, shaking his own head slowly in his unbelief.

"You're a fool, Archer," he said bluntly. "Shelly can't be paying you enough to take that chance."

SEVEN

For a few minutes, Dean sat on the fence watching Jasper ride off through the corrals. He knew he was being a fool. He had no obligation to risk his neck to find what was happening to Shelly's cows. He doubted if Shelly, Homer, or anyone else would respect him any less if he were to just ride on out of here. In fact, most would agree he had only used good judgment.

Yet, something deep within his inner being told him that he could never go back to Arrowhead and hold his head high, like he used to, if he ran out on a job just because things got tough. His respect for the feelings of those friends he had left at Arrowhead just would not let him quit and walk away. It was very important to him, that if he ever went back to the Arrowhead, it would be with his pride, his head high, a winner.

"I'd not let Jasper hooraw me into somethin' that could get

me killed," a voice said from behind him.

Dean looked around to see Unk Kincaid looking through the corral poles at the horses of the rough string. Beneath a battered, sweat-stained old hat, the man's gaunt face showed with real concern.

"I've heard of you, Archer," the old cowman went on. "I've heard you was a good cowman, but from the looks of your hands, I'd say you ain't been riding them kind of horses for a long time…. if ever. I'd not let anyone push me into somethin' I couldn't handle."

"Thanks, old timer. I'm glad to know there's one Kincaid who can talk like he had some sense," Dean said as he climbed slowly from the fence. "By the way, does the ranch have any good hackamores or bridles with bits I can use on those horses?" Dean asked the old man. "I'm sure the bit on my bridle's too light to stop most of them."

"Use anything you can find in the little tack room off the east end of the barn," the old man told him. "Everything in there's Pool equipment."

The old man looked closely again at the younger man, then turned to walk slowly toward the house, bent slightly at the waist and leaning forward on his bowed legs.

Dean found the tack room the old cowman had mentioned. Here, he went through the equipment hanging on the walls and piled about in no order, until he found a headstall with a heavy, high-curbed Spade bit and two hackamores with their heavy braided bosals, or nose bands, and rope reins. Such hackamores were used mainly when breaking young horses, but Dean felt some of the outlaws might still work better in those than with a bit in their mouths. He would not normally have used a bridle with such a cruel Spade bit as the one he had found, for it could cut a horse's tongue to shreds, but he also knew he would need every advantage he could get on some of those horses.

He also remembered something he had seen Chet Warren, the best bronc rider he had ever known, do when riding an especially rough horse. He found a discarded old jumper, rolled this into a tight roll and tied it across the fork of his saddle with leather thongs he cut from an old bridle rein. This would give his knees extra grip on the fork of the saddle. He found a good pair of leather hobbles and a short, braided, rawhide whip, called a quirt, and added these to his equipment.

After a quick meal at the cook shack with some of the regular Kincaid hands, he returned to the barn to get the equipment he had selected and carried this, with his saddle, to the corrals. As he walked, his thoughts were on the problems he knew he would have with these horses. He had grown up around horses and had spent years on the Arrowhead where he had many good mounts to ride. He knew there was a vast difference between a horse that would buck on occasion, when spooked, and one that fought all authority of man until it would buck and fight every time it was ridden.

He had known such horses and some of the men who rode them, but he had never attempted to do it himself. The men that rode such outlaws were fierce competitors, willing to gamble their life on their ability against that of the horse. He had a healthy respect for both the outlaw horses and the men who could ride them.

Although he had never had any desire to ride such mounts, he had a basic belief he had the physical ability to ride almost anything he put his mind to. This was challenging him in a way nothing else had ever done. This would be testing every bit of riding ability he ever had, as well as his pride in himself as a rider. He had been thrown many times, so that would be nothing new, when it happened, although, at his age, he knew his body could not absorb the jolts as it once had and he did not look forward with any relish to being thrown.

Most western horses bucked when first broken to the saddle, in fact, in his younger days, Dean had broken quite a few himself. He knew some horses continued to buck all their lives, on occasion. However, if properly handled and trained from the start, few horses continued to buck after their initial training, unless badly spooked or frightened.

It was the few that continued to fight all authority, which developed such an art to their bucking that they could throw all but the very best riders, and sometimes even those. These horses were then put into the rough strings of the big ranches of the west who hired special bronc riders to ride them, or in later years, were sold to the rodeo producers. Out of the rough strings of the big outfits of the west, came a very few real outlaw horses that would deliberately kill a man, if they ever got the opportunity.

All these thoughts were going through Dean's mind as he carried his equipment to a round corral next to the corral containing the horses he was to ride.

This corral was about forty feet in diameter, made in a circle of upright posts set deep in the ground next to each other. An inch-thick steel cable ran around the outside of the corral near the tops of the posts and was anchored to each gate post. The only part not a circle was the pole gate leading from the other corrals.

In the center of this round corral was a snubbing post sticking about four feet out of the ground, having over half its length buried in the earth. This post was worn slick and smooth from many ropes sliding around it. He carried his saddle and the other equipment to lay them near this post.

He knew postponing the moment he would try to ride one of his mounts would only make it worse. It was a sure thing, if he couldn't ride them here in the corrals, he would never be able to ride them out on the open range.

Someway, word had gotten out, that the dude was going to try to ride a member of the rough string, for men now gathered around the corrals and peered between the posts to watch what he was doing. He would have just as soon not had an audience for that first attempt but knew there was nothing he could do about it.

"I'll bet that dude never rides one of them horses," he heard a man say.

"Hell, you've got to give him credit for having guts, if he even gets on one," another said. "I wouldn't do it."

"Well, I've got five bucks that says he can't ride old Brownie," Les Boyd's deep voice said. "I don't think anybody ever rode him the first time out in the spring."

Dean opened the gate into the corral containing his mounts. For several minutes, he stood looking closely at the horses who were, in turn, watching him just as closely. They milled about, afraid of what the man was going to do to them. Dean's long experience gave him an insight as to the disposition of most of the horses, from their looks, the way they carried themselves, the shape of their heads and the look they had in their eyes. One glance was all he needed to convince him he was going to be in for a rough time on any of them.

Never in his life, had he seen eight meaner-looking and acting horses, and his heart sank at the thought of having to ride such animals. Being a cowman, he doubted he would ever be able to do much cow work on any of them. But, the first and biggest challenge was simply to ride them.

Only three animals in the entire group appealed to him in the least. Two were buckskins that looked so much alike he guessed them to be brothers or half brothers. The other horse was an exceptionally well-built, stout, yet trim gray gelding with good action. This horse had a roman nose and eyes that seemed to glare at the man with hatred. The gray bit and kicked at any horse that came near it. The other horses were just mean-looking animals.

Dean had known a very few ranchers who considered the horses in their rough string to be some of the best-working cow horses the outfit owned. They were just too much horse for the average cowboy to handle, but were top cow horses under a real bronc rider. The horses Jasper had picked for him did not strike him as being what any rancher would consider their best working cow horses. He immediately had the feeling he would be do very little work of any kind on these horses, even if he could ride them.

He remembered Les Boyd's remark about a horse called Brownie. There was one large brown horse in the bunch with a big head and a pronounced roman nose. He assumed this was the animal Les had in mind and it was a good bet this horse was the worst in the bunch, or Les would not have known him by name. After some maneuvering, he managed to run this horse away from the others and through the gate into the round corral.

Dean closed the gate and stood watching the horse for a few minutes. The animal ran back and forth across the opposite side of the corral in a very nervous manner, its head high and letting loud snorts roll out through its nostrils, as its eyes watched only the man. As he looked at that big powerful animal, Dean knew again he was being a fool to even think of trying to ride such a horse after his years away from even good, gentle mounts. Any way you looked at it, he was playing right into Jasper's hands. If he quit, he would not find out what was happening to Shelly's cattle. If he stayed, there was a good chance he would be crippled or even killed by one of these horses. Either way, Jasper would be rid of him and any knowledge he may have gained would be of no benefit to Shelly, if it died with him.

He walked slowly to the snubbing post and picked up the new lariat rope he had purchased in Limon and idly shook out a rather large loop, constantly watching the big horse's every move. The horse had bright piglike eyes set close to the front of its head and these also watched everything the man was doing. Those bright little eyes showed plainly their hatred for the man.

Roping had once been a highly developed skill in this slender man but the years of inactivity had dulled the reflexes and timing necessary to send a loop accurately where he wanted it to go. Having a new rope did not help either, as it was stiff and not broken in for roping. It took him three throws before the loop settled over the big brown's roman nose as the horse raced around the corral. Dean ran quickly to the snubbing post where the rope made a snapping sound as he made two fast dallies around it.

As the rope tightened on its neck, the big brown whirled to face the man, pulling back on the rope with all its great strength. The horse reared high in the air, striking out with both front feet in its blind hatred of the man, even though Dean was far out of its reach. When its hooves returned to the earth, the rope slackened slightly and Dean quickly took up that slack with his dallies. Each time the horse struggled, it came a little closer to the post and the man took up the slack. With each struggle, the rope also drew a little tighter around the animal's neck. By now, the horse's breath was being cut off by the noose and it was actually choking itself with its struggles.

Dean tried to talk calmly to the horse, but his own breath was now coming in short quick gasps. Again, he was aware of his poor condition for this kind of work. The years of city life had left his body softer than he had even realized. The animal seemed to have no interest in anything he was saying, anyway. He couldn't help but wonder how he would ever saddle this horse out on roundup, where there would be no round corral or snubbing post.

At last, the horse stood still, its feet braced against the pull of the rope, its wild eyes dull and its sides heaving as it tried to suck air past the noose and into its lungs. What little air was going down its windpipe made a loud rattling noise.

Still holding the rope tight, Dean went slowly around the post toward the quivering animal. Carefully, he lifted his left hand and extended it, palm down, toward the horse's nose. When his hand had gotten within a foot of the animal, the brown again tried to rear and strike out at the man with its front feet. The rope was too short for the horse to get much height and Dean had been looking for this and jumped out of danger. He again took whatever slack the horse gave him.

Time and again, Dean tried to work up close to the horse but each time his hand came near the animal, it would throw itself into another desperate attempt to fight. At last, the horse could stand the pain no longer, completely choked down. The big brown's eyes went glassy as its legs buckled under it. Dean felt the temptation to just keep the rope so tight it would choke the horse to death. That would be one way of not having to ride it. However, he loosened the rope until the horse could again get its breath.

As the horse lay on its side, loudly sucking air into its tortured lungs, the man quickly slipped the stoutest hackamore over the horse's head and adjusted it in place. He took a large red handkerchief from his pocket and tied this to both sides of the headstall above the horse's eyes. He also formed a half hitch with the rope and put this through the throat loop and over the animal's nose. In this way, not all the pressure would be on the animal's throat, should it again fight the rope. He let the horse lay for a few minutes while he searched around the corrals until he found a piece of wire about four feet long. This he brought back and laid by his saddle.

When the big brown had gotten enough of its wind back, it struggled to its feet and again fought back against the rope. This time, however, the rope's pressure was on its nose as well as its throat, and while the struggle was fierce, it did not last nearly as long as had the first one. At last, the horse gave up and let Dean touch its neck and side. Dean slid the bandanna down over the horse's eyes, blinding it. The horse now stood quivering but not fighting as Dean tied it solidly to the post with just enough slack to let the horse stand.

The horse shook as the man slid the saddle blanket on its back and then the saddle. Dean straightened the saddle slightly and then reached down to pick up the wire. He quickly formed a hook in one end of this and used it to reach under the horse's belly for the cinch ring. At all times, he was careful to stand well up toward the horse's shoulder, never getting close to the animal's hind feet. A moment later, the saddle was cinched tightly on the animal's back.

Dean let the horse stand a few more minutes while he stood back looking at the animal. Both man and horse were breathing deeply, as Dean mentally told himself what a fool he was not to find Shelly and walk out of this mess. He took the beaver hat from his head and wiped the sweat from his forehead and face with his shirt sleeve.

"Well, by golly, you got farther with old Brownie than Jasper ever dreamed you would," a voice said behind him and Dean turned to see several men peering between the upright posts of the round corral.

"You make out your will, Archer?" Les Boyd called

softly, his deep voice vibrating in his chest. "Anybody got any money to bet?"

"Bet on what?" a man asked. "You bettin' on the dude or Brownie?"

"On Brownie, of course," Boyd said and most of the men laughed. None offered to back the man.

While Dean was regaining his strength, he knew the horse was doing the same. The man did not want to wait too long and give the big brown any greater advantage than it already had. He removed the rope from the horse's head, carefully coiled it and dropped it near the snubbing post, not wanting it on the saddle where he might become entangled in it.

As the big horse stood quivering, he made final adjustments on the hackamore, making sure the big knot of the adjusting ropes was right under the horse's jaw where it would give him the most leverage with the reins. He could not help but feel the tightening of his heart in his chest, as he now put the right rein over the animal's neck. The moment of truth was at hand.

Holding both reins and some of the horse's mane in his left hand, he reached back with his right hand to twist the stirrup around so it was facing him. In this way, he could reach the stirrup with his left toe and still remain near the horse's shoulder, hopefully out of reach of the animal's hind feet.

Reaching for the saddle horn with his right hand, he swung swiftly into the saddle. After making sure only his toes were in the stirrups and the rope reins were the right length, he leaned forward cautiously and jerked the blind from the headstall, dropping it to the ground. He straightened quickly in the saddle, grabbing the saddle horn with his right hand.

For a fleeting moment, all was calm as the horse seemed dazed by the sudden return of its sight. The next instant, Dean thought the devil himself had broken loose. He expected the horse to try to put its head down between its front legs and buck forward. He was braced to try to hold the horse's head up all he could. Instead, the horse moved backward for several quick steps, then reared violently on its hind legs. Instinctively, the man leaned forward in an attempt not to pull the horse over on top of him.

As Dean leaned forward, however, the horse suddenly threw its head back, catching the man squarely in the center of his forehead with the top of its head, stunning him. The horse stopped its rearing before going all the way over backwards and returned its front feet to the ground. Dean was too groggy to even think what he was doing.

Dropping its head between its front legs, the horse now began bucking in great high leaps, violently twisting and shaking its body with each buck. When its front feet hit the ground, its back legs kicked up viciously, snapping Dean's head on his neck as though it were on the end of a whip.

The blow to his head had all but knocked Dean unconscious in the saddle. He realized the horse was now bucking wildly with him but there seemed nothing he could do about it. Only his instincts keep him in the saddle at all. Desperately, he tried to clear his thinking and locate the horse's head through the fog which now seemed to cover his vision and his mind seemed far away from his body. He needed to know where the horse's head was in order to give himself a sense of direction, enabling him to try to anticipate the animal's next buck.

The next thing he was clearly aware of, was being flat on his back on the ground and the horse bucking wildly around the corral with an empty saddle, the stirrups flapping up and meeting over its back, making a loud popping sound each time they came together.

"Let him lay right there," Dean heard Ben Shadrow's voice telling the others. "When he hit me with them fence pliers, he didn't offer to help me none. I've been waiting to see how he'd like a dose of the same medicine."

It was several minutes before Dean could force himself to a sitting position. He sat and watched the horse continue to buck and bellow around the corral. It was several more minutes before his head cleared. He felt the lump forming in the center of his forehead with gentle fingers. His head ached dully but he had no other pain and decided he had received no other serious injury.

He tried to pay no attention to the stream of remarks coming from the other side of the fence. Very slowly and deliberately, he got to his feet and went to the snubbing post for the rope.

The instant the loop settled over the horse's head, the battle started all over again. Having definitely won the first round, the horse was more determined than ever not to be ridden. Again, Dean had to choke the animal completely down before it would let him put the blind back over its eyes. Dean again tied the horse solidly to the snubbing post. While the horse stood shivering and sucking in its breath, Dean searched around the corrals until he found a short stout stick about eighteen inches long and two inches in diameter. When he finally remounted the horse, he held this club in his right hand.

Again, Dean jerked the blind off and sat quickly back in the saddle, holding the club poised and ready. The horse took the same few quick steps backwards and reared. Instead of leaning forward this time, Dean brought the club down solidly between the horse's ears with all his might. The force of the blow momentarily stunned the big horse and it fell to its knees before it could catch its balance. When the animal managed to get back on its feet, it did not attempt to rear again but went right to bucking in earnest.

Dean dropped the club and grabbed the saddle horn. He was not riding for prizes and there was no point in making a fancy ride. Just to stay on the horse was his entire ambition. Without the extra grip the rolled jumper across the fork of the saddle gave him, he would never have been able to stay with the horse through those first high hard pitches.

Dean tried to get in rhythm with the horse, feeling its muscles bulging under the saddle. He tried to keep his feet well forward to take as much of the jar as possible each time the horse hit the ground. How he wished he had his boots and spurs, for they would have felt so much safer and the spurs would have given him extra grip against the horse's sides on its upward heaves. His greatest fear was that, without high-heeled boots, he would get a foot through a stirrup and be dragged. However, he could already tell he was getting better at anticipating the horse's actions.

Luckily, the big brown was somewhat tired and winded from its first efforts. When the horse discovered it could not dislodge the kicking human from its back, it stopped bucking and threw up its head. There was an audible sigh of amazement from those watching around the corral fence.

"By God, I never thought he could ride him!" Boyd said in his unbelief. "Now, I'm glad none of you took my bet."

Although the horse had stopped bucking, it still would not do what the man wanted. The horse had bucked until it could buck no more, but it had not surrendered and refused to walk forward, no matter how much Dean kicked and whipped the horse with the ends of the rope reins. For some minutes, the horse stood there, its head drooping, its front legs spread wide apart and its sides heaving.

Dean let the animal rest a few minutes, thinking the horse would then accept his authority and walk forward. This did not prove to be the case, however, for Brownie was a complete outlaw. As soon as the horse got its wind back, it suddenly began bucking again, not as hard or as high as the other times, but still bucking its very best. Around and around the corral they went, the horse wasting none of its energy on bellowing or other useless noise. Now, the only sounds were the popping of the saddle leathers and the grunts of the horse as its hooves thudded to the ground.

Suddenly, the horse cut straight across the corral, barely missing the snubbing post. Dean felt the horse, in its desperation, make one more great high leap. This time, it was headed straight for the corral fence, making no attempt to turn and buck around the corral as it had been doing. The rider was helpless to do anything, although he saw the fence looming ahead of them.

The horse hit the upper portion of the corral posts head on. The force of the crash was so great that Dean was thrown not only out of the saddle but all the way over the fence, where he landed hard on his left shoulder. Tiny fingers of pain shot throughout his entire left side as he felt his shoulder blade grate under his weight.

He managed to roll over onto his back but lay where he had fallen. This was the second time this horse, the first of his string he had tried to ride, had not only thrown him but had hurt him. He wondered if any of the men would come to see how badly he was hurt, as he lay trying to clear his mind.

At length, he heard the sounds of someone running toward him and he turned his head to see the black-haired woman coming toward him as fast as she could run, holding her long skirts high to keep from tripping on them. Even in his condition, he could not help but notice her trim ankles.

The thought flashed through his mind to fake his condition to see what she would do. Then, he knew he wasn't that cheap and sat up. When his eyes met hers, as she hurried to him, she could see again the little smile playing across his face.

"What in the world happened?" she exclaimed, out of breath from running. "Someone at the house said Jasper had given you the rough string to ride. Is that true?"

"It seems as though," he said lightly.

"Did you get thrown all the way over that fence?"

"Oh, no, I just flew over it," he said ruefully, as a grin spread slowly across his thin face. "I think I went plenty high but I've got to improve my landings."

"Well, I never!" she exclaimed as he slowly stood up, gingerly moving his left shoulder.

He tried to hold his left arm still and close to his body to ease the pain.

"Why don't some of you men help him?" the woman turned to demand of the men still standing near the fence. "Don't tell me Jasper Kincaid has made such cowards out of all you men, that you won't even help another human being."

"No, ma'am, Miss Shelly," a rider said sheepishly and stepped forward and began brushing the dirt from Dean's shirt and pants. "We just didn't know which needed help the most—this dude or the horse."

"Why, what happened to the horse?" she asked.

"I think old Brownie broke his neck when they hit that fence. He hasn't moved since."

"Good," Dean said calmly. "That'll be one ride he won't forget…and I won't have to ride him again."

"Then, you were actually thrown over that fence?" the woman asked incredulously.

"I sure never jumped that high," the man said with his dry humor. "I remember I was still on him when he hit that fence."

"You, sir, are an idiot!" the woman exclaimed harshly. "Why in the world did you let Jasper push you into this?"

"Did I hear that man call you, Miss Shelly?"

"Yes, I'm Marian Shelly."

"Is Herman Shelly your father?"

"Yes, why?"

"Then I guess you know why I'm doing this," Dean said lightly, walking back toward the corral.

"Not in the least, sir. Should I?" she followed him to ask.

"Well, I work for your daddy," he turned back to tell her. "My name's Dean Archer and I signed on to try to find out what has been happening to the Shelly cattle. I also work for the bank in Denver. Didn't your daddy tell you? That's why Jasper's trying so hard to get rid of me."

"So you're the one Mac jumped Dad about in the meeting this morning?" the woman exclaimed and eyed Dean closely, trying to piece together what this all meant. It was not like her father not to tell her everything he was doing. "They had a violent argument about Dad sending someone to spy on the Kincaids, but I didn't know what it was all about. Dad told me he had hired a man named Hood to go as a rep, but nothing more. He and Mac are always arguing over something, anyway," the woman stated in her rather abrupt manner. "Well, we certainly need to know what's been happening to our cattle, but that don't mean we want you risking your life on those horses. No, Shelly would never ask that. I'll go tell Jasper I fired you, or whatever you want, but he certainly can't force you to ride the rough string."

"Now, you just hold on a minute, Miss Shelly," the man said as bluntly as she would have done. Although the smile was still on his lips, Marian instantly realized this man was someone to be reckoned with, despite the appearance those clothes gave him. Perhaps his will was even as strong as her own, for he added, "I'll let you know when I want anybody to tell Jasper anything for me."

"Very well," she said tartly.

"One thing for sure," the cowboy beside Dean said. "You've ridden the worst horse in the remuda, that's for sure, and we all seen you do it, too. Just wait till Jasper hears you not only rode old Brownie but that you killed him. He'll be fit to be tied."

EIGHT

Dean made his way around the upright posts of the round corral to where he could climb over the horizontal poles of the regular corral fence. His left shoulder hurt badly when he tried to use his left arm to pull himself to the top pole. He tried to hide any sign of the pain from those watching.

"Help that man get his saddle off that dead horse!" Marian Shelly commanded from outside the corral, her tone left no doubt she intended the men to obey her order.

Without a word, several of the men jumped forward to follow Dean over the fence and inside the round corral where they helped pull the saddle and hackamore from the dead horse. By the time his gear was free, four mounted men arrived to place their ropes around the neck of the dead animal and drag the lifeless form from the corrals.

It was all Dean could do to force himself to carry his saddle and gear to the barn and hang it all up. Strong habit made him put the saddle over a saddle pole rather than just dumping it on the floor, as was his first temptation. He walked stiffly to the bunkhouse, which he found deserted, and threw himself on his bed.

After a few minutes, he was so stiff he could hardly move or roll over. Pain throbbed dully throughout his left shoulder and side. All his muscles complained from lack of condition and the strain he had put them through.

One thought kept running through his mind. He would be absolutely crazy to attempt to ride another member of the rough string. He told himself several times, that pride or no pride, he would just have to tell Shelly he was quitting.

Ever so slowly, the memories of his friends at the Arrowhead came into his mind and they again replaced the thoughts about quitting. If he ever returned to those friends, he wanted to be able to look them all in the eye, knowing he had done his best. No, he would not allow Jasper to force him to leave because of some bad horses.

He heard the bunkhouse door open. Dean made no attempt to look around to see who had come in. He guessed it would be Jasper, upset upon hearing of what had happened. Someone came inside making a queer dragging sound. The person came close to the bed where he lay and stopped.

"I hope you ain't hurt too bad, son," Herman Shelly said kindly. His dark eyes searched the face of the man on the bed. The lump in the center of Dean's forehead was already becoming discolored. Shelly grimaced at the horrible-looking lump. "I sure never thought I was getting you into anything like this, when I agreed with your friend, Reid, to hire you."

Dean forced himself to roll over very carefully to where he could look up at the man standing above him. Herm Shelly's bad leg caused the man to stand bent to one side. His rubbery face worked in his concern for the man on the bed. He could not hide that concern and Dean felt appreciation for the man showing his feelings so plainly.

"It wasn't your fault, Mr. Shelly," the man on the bed said softly and moved his legs to allow Shelly to sit on the edge of the bed beside him. "I played the fool, right into Jasper's hands. It was partly rotten luck, too, for I never dreamed Jasper would have married a woman I knew years ago."

"Well, we might just as well admit we're licked, I guess," the crippled man said, his expressive face working with his thoughts. "I'll give you credit, though, you've got guts. You tried, too, but no job's worth risking your life on those horses. I'd be the first one to say it's not worth it, my leg's plenty proof of that."

"You're sure right, no job's worth it," Dean admitted ruefully. "But, one thing is. Jasper must be trying to hide something, or he wouldn't be so anxious to keep me off that roundup."

"If he is hiding anything, he'll sure never let you close enough to know what's going on, now he knows why you're here," Shelly said with disgust.

"I still think I can find it, if he's doing anything crooked, but I can't unless I go with the wagons," Dean said, stubbornly. "After all, there're only so many brands used by the Pool. Surely a man can see if someone is misbranding calves."

"A man may not live to see what's happening, if he has to ride the horses Jasper gave you," Shelly scoffed. "Be sensible, man. Jasper, or whoever is doing this, has fooled some of the best cowboys around this part of the country. Now he's on to you, he'll keep you so far away from what he's doing, you'll never even get a smell of it."

"You still think it is more apt to be done on the west wagon?" Dean asked.

"Almost has to be, if the Kincaids are behind this. The other two captains are old time men who have always been known for their honesty. Shadrow works for Kincaids in the winter and is in their debt, I'm sure. He's only been captain the last few years, too, about the same length of time we've been missing cattle. Besides, that wagon works most of the territory my cattle should be in."

"If that's the case, Jasper will do everything he can to keep me off that west wagon. How do you find out what wagon you'll be on?" Dean asked.

"The captains will choose their riders right after the big barbecue this evening. They're not supposed to discuss who they'll take before then, but they have to have one man from each outfit with each wagon. I sometimes wonder if Jasper don't tell them what men to take, but he ain't supposed to. I hear you met my daughter, Marian, too," Shelly said with a grimace. "Now, I'll catch hell from her for not telling her all about hiring you."

"After meeting her, I'd say she could give you a rough going over," Dean observed mildly, the smile coming back to his lips and blue eyes.

"She can be as rough as any horse in that rough string, when she gets riled," Herm admitted.

Dean wondered if the man knew his daughter had been in Limon the night of the big storm and had fought with Gertie while her father was asleep upstairs. He did not mention this, thinking Shelly might not be the only one who hadn't told all. If so, Dean did not want to be the one who gave away the woman's secret.

"Well," Shelly said with a long sigh, grimacing again as he pulled himself to his feet. "Let's just forget this whole thing, Archer. I'll give you a month's pay for your efforts and you can tell Reid to sic the bank on me, if he wants to."

"I'm not quitting, and I don't think I've done anything you can fire me for," Dean said, moving to try to ease the pain in his shoulder.

"You mean that, son?"

"That's still the way I see it," Dean said slowly, firmly. "What men can I trust?"

"The only ones we can be sure of are the men Holland sends and the Hessey boys. I understand the three boys are all going this year, so there will be no hired rider as their rep. The Hesseys are a tough outfit, any of them will fight at the drop of a hat, even old Rube, although he'll run from a pencil or a book. My son, Claude, is going this year. He's too young, but he's sure honest. He can't be on the same wagon with you. You'll have to find out which Hessey, as well as which of Ike's men, will be on your wagon. Outside of those, you'll have to sure be careful who you say anything to. I never really knew any of the riders to be dishonest, but it sure looks like some of them has to be in on this stealing."

"Well, we've gone too far to back out now," Dean said simply. "One thing, though, Homer was to get word to the Arrowhead to send my saddle and things to you. I'd appreciate you getting them to me as soon as you can."

"If you can get on the west wagon, you can get them right at my ranch, as it normally stops for a rest and fresh supplies at my outfit, which is about forty miles southeast of here. If you don't get on that wagon, I'll arrange to bring them to you, wherever you are. I'll want to see you and see if you've found out anything, anyway," Shelly said, walking to the door, dragging that one foot with each step he took. "Are you coming out for the big feed?"

"I'll be out a little later," Dean told him and lay back on the bed.

After the rancher had gone, Dean forced himself to get off the bed. Every movement brought more pain. He went to the cook shack where he sat several buckets of water on the big stove to heat. As soon as the water was quite hot, he carried it, bucket by bucket, to the bunkhouse and poured it into the galvanized round tub the men all used for their bathing. By the time he had carried the last bucket and got undressed, the water was cool enough for him to get into the tub. The tub was quite small, so all he could do was sit in it and scoop handfuls of the hot water up over his shoulder. The hot water seemed to soothe many of his aches and pains.

After his bath, he put on the cleanest of his clothes and felt better. He knew much of the stiffness would be back in his muscles by morning. When he left the bunkhouse, the remains of the beaver hat sat at a jaunty angle on the side of his head. This was not altogether due to the highness of his spirits but partly because of the size of the lump in the middle of his forehead.

He thought back to the parties he had attended while on Arrowhead Ranch and he would have given a lot to be able to look tonight as he had back in those former days. He hoped he would not see Marian Shelly again while he looked like this, a tramp. Why should this woman bother him? When he had left the girl in Ohio, he had promised himself he would never again let any woman control his thoughts. Now, practically the first woman he had seen since returning to Colorado was bothering him. She was such a pretty lady.

He knew if Marian Shelly had any interest in men, she would not be waiting around for someone like him to come along. He guessed her age to be about his own, middle thirties. Any woman who had reached that advanced age alone in this woman short country had reached it by design, not from lack of opportunity.

He walked alone in his thoughts toward the big fires now burning in a large grassy area west of the barn and corrals. He could see women and the roundup cooks scurrying about several long wooden tables while the men stood around the fires, talking in small groups as men always do. As Dean now walked near the fires, not a man spoke to him. Never had he felt so alone or such an outsider among a group of cattle people. This still surprised him. He had never known any man who could keep independent cowboys from talking to whomever they wished. He thought it was most likely his clothes that kept the others at a distance, for he knew cowboys distrusted anyone in city clothes.

The evening air was quickly turning cooler and he felt its chill through the light jacket he wore. He walked around the edge of the last fire to where he could be close to it and yet alone, away from any of the others. The soft breeze kept most of the smoke away from him. He watched the women working over the meal at the tables as he enjoyed the warmth of the fire.

Three other men had come to this fire but Dean had not noticed them, so deep was he in his own thoughts. When he glanced up to see them, he found they were all strangers to him. Two were tall while one was short and stout. All carried pistols with full cartridge belts around their hips and all wore new black hats and jumpers. The jumper on the shorter man fit him snugly across his muscular shoulders. A moment later, Dean saw the shorter man turn and look at him with eyes of blue ice. Not an ounce of friendship was in those eyes. The man's eyes took in his shabby appearance before he dropped his gaze.

"Evenin'," Dean said softly, at last.

The chunky man nodded his head curtly and turned back to speak to the others. Dean could not hear what was said but saw the other two turn to look at him with the same cold blue eyes. Dean now looked past the men and recognized Marian Shelly hurrying toward them.

"Eben, Tony!" the woman called and Dean saw the chunky man turn toward her with the quickness and grace of a wild animal.

"Hello, Marian," the chunky man greeted her in a high, tight voice. "How's our favorite cousin?"

"I'm fine," the woman said, smiling at the three men, coming forward to extend her slender hand to each. "We're so glad you're all going on roundup this year, as that means more we can count on."

"If we lost as many cows out on the range as we did close to home in that late storm, we'll all be lucky to find anything worth shipping," the chunky man said evenly.

"That's what Dad and Claude think, too," she said seriously, then added in a much lighter tone, "By the way, I want you Hesseys to meet a man you owe a lot to, especially you, Tony." The woman now took one of the taller men by the arm and led him around the fire toward Dean. "Mr. Archer, meet the Hesseys, Tony, Adam and Eben."

The three men drew closer to Dean but made no motion to shake his hand or recognize him in anyway. Dean wasn't too sure what he should do, either, or what the woman could have meant by them owing him something. For a moment, they stood looking at each other in silence.

"Tony, this is Dean Archer. He's riding for us, as well as working for the bank in Denver. I'm sure your dad told you about him. He's also the man who helped me get Eileen out of Gertie's," Marian said rather gayly. "In fact, if it had not been for him and his friend, I don't think we would have gotten her out of there."

"Well, by God, I'm glad to know you, Archer," Tony Hessey, one of the taller men said and now stepped forward to shake Dean's hand. His grip was firm and strong. "Eileen and I were married a few days ago and I sure do thank you for helping Marian get her out of that place."

"Glad I came along at the right time," Dean said gravely, feeling the strength in the man's long fingers.

"Marian told us some dude helped them get Eileen out of there," Eben, the chunky man, said and also stepped forward to shake Dean's hand. "Dad told us we was to find a man named Hood who was supposed to be working with Herm and the bank."

"Well, that's me," Dean said. "Had to drop the name Hood as Mrs. Kincaid recognized me."

"Well, we sure hope you can spot whatever's happening to our cows," Eben Hessey told him in that high, tight voice that reminded Dean of the way Rube Hessey had spoken. "We'll back you any way we can, if you find anything."

As they were speaking, Dean noticed the line of men now beginning to form at one of the serving tables. He saw Eben Hessey turn and also observe this.

"I'm going to go get in line," the chunky man said and his brothers turned to follow him. "We'll see you around, Archer."

"Can you tell me how I can get assigned to a certain wagon, Hessey?" Dean asked, as the men started away.

"Why, what wagon do you want on?" Eben Hessey turned and hesitated to ask.

"Shadrow's west wagon."

The chunky man's cold blue eyes again went over Dean from the top of his ridiculous hat to the flat soles of his shoes.

"I really don't know how anything like that could be done, Archer, but I'll think on it."

With this, the man turned and hurried to catch up with his brothers.

"Friendly cusses," Dean commented dryly to the woman who still stood there. "Would you care to dine with me, Miss Shelly?"

"Oh, I'd love to, Mr. Archer, but I have to help wait tables," the woman said, meeting his eyes squarely and he thought there was genuine disappointment in the expression on her pretty face. "Tell me, why do you want to be on the west wagon?"

"Your dad thinks that's the most likely one doing any dirty work," Dean told her frankly. "If it is, and the Kincaids are behind your problem, Jasper sure won't want me on it."

"That's true. If he's behind our trouble, he'll probably get my brother, Claude, put on that wagon. Claude's just a boy and would be the easiest to fool."

As they were talking, they walked slowly up the gentle slope toward the tables. It gave him a queer feeling to be walking beside the woman, so neat and pretty in her dark dress. He was aware of the glances some of the women were giving them.

"I do wish you luck, Mr. Archer," she told him, as they neared the first table, where the women were beginning to serve the food. She left him to take her post at one of the tables and he turned to start walking down the long line of men now waiting to be served.

As he walked, his eyes searched the faces in the line and not a man smiled at him. He again felt completely alone.

"Don't try to crowd in, Archer," Les Boyd's familiar deep voice said from the line ahead of him. "The line forms way back there, for you."

"You don't say," Dean commented dryly, stopping as though thinking of challenging the man.

"Just keep on movin'," Ben Shadrow sneered from behind Boyd, his hulking figure looming high above the others in the line. "You won't crowd in here without a fight."

"Step right up here, Archer," Eben Hessey's high, tight voice called from a few places in front of Boyd. Dean had not noticed the three Hesseys there in the line. "We've been savin' a place for you."

Dean smiled thinly and turned to walk past the Kincaid men to where Eben Hessey was indeed holding up the line for him to step in front of the chunky rider. Dean wondered if the others would try to prevent this, knowing the Kincaid men would instantly resent this. He could hear muttering from those now behind him but no man made a move to stop him. Plainly, the men either respected or feared the Hesseys too much to start trouble with them. He remembered Shelly saying the Hesseys would fight at the drop of a hat. No doubt the men all knew of this reputation.

"Thanks, Hessey," Dean said gravely.

"Plumb my pleasure," the chunky rider said coldly. "I've got little use for that bunch."

Their plates were soon filled with a variety of good foods, barbecued beef, potatoes and several types of home-canned vegetables. Dean carried his filled plate and coffee cup back to the fire he had left and found a log to sit on while he ate. The Hesseys had disappeared and Dean now ate in silence and alone, as other riders came to the fire but stayed some distance away from him.

For some time after he had finished eating, he sat looking moodily into the fire thinking about having to ride another member of the rough string in the morning. He looked up to see Jasper Kincaid coming toward him. The big cowman stalked up to stop beside the man still sitting on the log.

"I hear you killed a Pool horse this afternoon," the big man said in a grave tone.

"He killed himself," Dean looked up to tell the man.

"Well, he's coming out of your pay, anyway," Jasper stated bluntly.

"You can try," Dean told him quietly.

"Oh, I'll do it, you can count on that. I'll have a replacement assigned you in the morning," Jasper said and turned to walk away. He seemed satisfied with himself in the matter. "I'd be careful not to kill any more," the man said loudly over his shoulder. "I doubt you can afford it."

Dean turned his gaze back to the fire. He heard women talking now. They were through with the serving of the men and children and were now fixing plates for themselves. Dean looked up to see Marian Shelly coming toward his fire with plate and cup in her hands. He stood up quickly to offer her a seat on the log and to take the plate and cup from her hands while she sat down. When she took the plate back from him, he sat back down on the log next to her.

"This is an unexpected pleasure," he said, a friendly smile on his pale face.

"Oh, fiddlesticks! No one gets any pleasure out of the company of an old maid," the black-haired woman said in her straight forward, abrupt, forceful manner.

"Well, now, you might just be surprised at what gives me pleasure," Dean said and laughed quietly at the quick look she gave him.

"Well, I must admit every time I've seen you, something exciting's happened," she said and her lips parted in a smile. "What do you have planned for tonight?"

"Nothing I've done since meeting you has been really planned," he said ruefully. "I'd like to take you to some social function, just to show you what I can do when following a well-laid-out plan."

Marian Shelly seldom blushed these days, but her cheeks turned pink at his remark. It had been years since a man had spoken to her in this manner.

"Why, Mr. Archer, are you asking me out?"

"I sure am, ma'am. When's the next party or dance we could go to?" Dean asked while inwardly asking himself why in the world was he talking this way to this woman? Hadn't he promised himself he was through with women?

"I don't dance," she said rather defiantly. "That eliminates most functions around here."

"Oh, I can teach you in no time," he assured her.

"Never!" she cried hotly, for dancing was strictly against her very strong religious beliefs.

"Oh, now, it wouldn't take me that long," he protested, a wide smile now on his thin face.

In spite of herself, she laughed heartily.

"I'm sure it wouldn't take you long, if I were to try to learn. They say, however, you can't teach an old dog new tricks."

"Well, then, when's the next box supper or other social?" he insisted, not really knowing why he persisted.

A mischievous gleam came into her eyes as she looked sideways at the man. That certainly was a bad-looking bruise on his forehead.

"Well...there's going to be a quilting at...."

"Boy, if you think it would take a long time to teach you how to dance, just you wait till you see how long it would take you to teach me to quilt," he interrupted quickly, finding himself more fascinated by this woman all the time. "Let's think of somethin' else."

"I'm afraid I don't attend the type functions most of you cowboys enjoy," she said softly.

"Do you like horses, Miss Shelly?" he asked suddenly.

"Of course, very much. Who doesn't, in this country?"

"I thought as much. Well, that's one interest we have in common. Perhaps we can go riding some day."

"Well...perhaps."

"Fine. We'll go for a nice ride, the next time I see you."

"You are a very persuasive talker, sir. We'll see about that and what all has happened by the next time we meet," she told him demurely. "Perhaps we will."

"I'll remember that and hold you to your promise," he said.

"Speaking of remembering, thanks for not telling Dad about our first meeting," she said, again looking at him from the corner of her eye. "He didn't know I came to town that night and knows nothing about that brawl in the saloon. He'd die, if he knew I took part in such a thing. I guess I do owe you something for that night, as well as not telling Dad. I'll look forward to that horseback ride."

After she had eaten, he walked with her back up to where the women and some of the younger girls were starting to wash the big pile of dishes. He left her there and walked slowly back toward the fire as the three wagon captains were now getting ready to choose their riders. Most of the men seemed in a jolly mood and Dean guessed there were several bottles passing among them. He was tempted to see if he could find someone who would share a bottle with him, then quickly discarded that as a bad idea. Riding one of the rough string sober would be hard enough, let alone after a few drinks made him careless.

He had also gotten the idea his new friend, Marian Shelly, would surely not approve of a man drinking. Why should he care about what she would think? Women always fogged up a man's mind. His mind had sure been in a fog for three years back in Ohio. There was definitely nothing to be gained by going into another fog over Marian Shelly. She sure was a pretty woman, though, and so different from the girl he had left in Cincinnati.

Even though he felt much alone among the men, he still could not help but feel good at being back in Colorado. The smell of the night air, the clean smell of green grass and spring time, made him feel good again, in spite of his loneliness. This was a heck of a lot better country than what he had left back in Ohio. No matter how most of these riders treated him, he was glad to be back here among people he understood. He liked these cowboys, even though they would not associate with him. He never doubted the fact they would someday come around to accepting him as one of them.

To hell with it, he thought. He would look forward to trying another member of the rough string in the morning. He was home, wasn't he? Well, not completely. Arrowhead Ranch still seemed like home, but this was a whole lot closer than Ohio had ever been.

NINE

Jasper Kincaid stomped about the open space between the big fires and the ranch buildings, followed by the three silent wagon captains. Jasper assigned each man his spot before stepping away from them and coming somewhat closer to the large group of men awaiting his instructions. There was considerable milling about, as the men from each ranch tried to get together and still be apart from the big group. Dean found Manuel, the Mexican who had been with Marian that night at Gertie's, was to be the third rider for the Shelly outfit. The man's smile lighted up his dark face at recognizing Dean. Marian's brother, Claude, was a young man feeling his pride at going on his first roundup. The three shook hands, after introducing themselves. Dean saw Claude's eyes going over his appearance. The young rider seemed somewhat disappointed at what he saw.

"All right! All right!" Jasper yelled. "Let's have it a little quiet!"

Immediately, the men near the fire grew silent. Again, Dean was amazed at the power Jasper seemed to have over these normally rowdy cowboys. He also kept asking himself, how he could possibly get on Shadrow's west wagon and wondered if Eben Hessey was indeed thinking on it. There seemed little chance either of them could influence the selection at all.

"As I call off the ranches, the riders representing that outfit this year kind of step out in front where the captains can see you," Jasper instructed loudly. "You ranchers and home guards stay back out of the way. If you get mixed up with the reps, some poor wagon boss might make a terrible mistake and pick one of you."

There was a general good-natured laugh at this remark and more shifting around among the men as the ranchers moved further away from their reps.

"Masterman will start, Summers will follow and Shadrow will pick last on this first go round," Jasper continued. "When your name's called, line up behind your captain. Let's start with the Hardy outfit."

Three men stepped forward and split apart a little ways to give the captains a chance to recognize each man.

"Smitty!" the short, bullet-headed Masterman called loudly.

A short, blonde cowboy left the others and walked swiftly toward Masterman. As he walked, the man let out a loud yell of delight. Plainly, he had been chosen by the man he wanted to go with.

"Johnson!" Summers, a tall taciturn man, called and the second man walked toward him.

This left the third man to go with Shadrow without choice and he walked slowly to stand behind the big man.

"This time, Shadrow goes first!" Kincaid yelled. "Let the DZ men step out!"

Three more men stepped away from the others. They were quickly chosen by the captains and Kincaid called for riders from the Croft Ranch. This time, Summers had first pick and the man he chose let out a war whoop you could have heard a mile away, he was so glad to have been chosen for the center wagon.

Dean watched closely as the men were called and the line behind each captain grew longer. He became aware Jasper had called for the Hessey reps and turned to see the three Hessey brothers step out from the others, their cold indifference showed plainly in their manner as they waited to be called. Adam went with Summers, Tony with Masterman and Eben went to Shadrow.

Dean watched as the chunky man did not go to the end of the line behind the big wagon boss, as had all the others. Eben stopped and pushed his way in right behind the hulking captain. Again, Dean noticed none of the men seemed to want to contest the man's actions. It was plain none of the men wanted to challenge a Hessey.

"Holland outfit!" Jasper called.

Three men, one an exceptionally tall puncher, stepped forward. The tall one went to Shadrow's wagon and Dean mentally made note to contact this man as soon as feasible. Dean realized it would be Shadrow's first pick in the next go round, as Jasper called for the Shelly reps to step out. Where would he go? Claude and Manuel joined him in stepping away from the thinning crowd.

"I've got a message for you, Ben," Eben Hessey whispered to Shadrow in his high tight voice. "You take Archer!"

"What?" Ben snapped in surprise and turned his head quickly to look around into the cold, hard eyes of the chunky rider behind him. "He's going on Summer's wagon."

"He goes on this wagon, if you want to stay in one piece!" Hessey hissed and jabbed a stubby finger into the small of the captain's back. "You call Archer's name, or I'll blow a hole in your guts they can drive the chuck wagon through!"

"Go ahead, Ben, it's your turn!" Jasper called impatiently.

For a moment, big Ben Shadrow bowed his head as though in prayer. He called out Archer's name, his voice no longer loud but the sound carried to the waiting men.

Jasper swallowed hard as he peered in unbelief toward the hulking shape of Ben Shadrow. In the darkness, it was hard for him to read anything in the big captain's face. Ben must have lost his mind. All the captains had been told that this man was to go on Summer's middle wagon. Jasper made that wagon his headquarters and he wanted the man where he could watch him as closely as possible. It was his hope the horses he had given Dean would force the man to quit, but one way or another, he intended to get rid of Archer and he thought it would be easier, if Dean was on the wagon he spent most of his time with. He almost stopped the choosing to ask Ben why he had picked this man. Then, he realized to do so would let all the ranchers know he had told a captain who to pick, and that was strictly against Pool rules. There was no point in giving Shelly any more reason to question his leadership of the Pool.

"You can take your pistol out of my back, now," Shadrow told Hessey, as Dean walked silently past them to the end of the line.

"Hell, I never had a pistol on you, Ben," Eben told the big man and lifted his stubby finger to his lips to blow away imaginary smoke. "You sure scare easy."

"I'll see if I can't make both of you regret having mixed in my business!" Shadrow said angrily. "I'll not forget this."

"I won't either," the chunky rider assured him. "You want me to call out to everybody that you was told who to take? Hell, that might just be enough to get you and Jasper both thrown out on your butts."

"Just let it lay," Ben said softly, realizing all the advantages lay with the other man. "I'll take care of you some other way."

"Just you remember, it may be me taking care of you, Ben," Hessey advised the big man softly, his cold eyes meeting the big man's squarely without any sign of fear. "As long as you do your job as wagon captain, we'll get along. You try to push me and it'll only happen once!"

After all the men had been chosen, the wagon captains made their lists and gathered around the roundup boss to finalize plans, as the men drifted away toward their camps. Shadrow hated to have to tell Kincaid why he had taken the man he was not supposed to take, but knew he would have to face the man and his anger sooner or later.

Dean walked by the cold-eyed chunky rider on his way to the bunkhouse. "Thanks, Hessey," he said easily.

Hessey said softly, "We're even, Archer."

"We sure are," Dean agreed.

Without another word, Hessey moved off toward the wagons and Dean walked up the sloping ground toward the bunkhouse. He would not move his things to Shadrow's bed wagon until morning, so would have one more night in a bed. As he walked past the main house, he heard the voices of young people talking on the front porch. He thought he could make out Claude Shelly there with a blonde-haired girl.

He was awake long before daylight the next morning. His muscles complained bitterly with every move he made as he crawled out of his bed. He very tenderly touched the lump on his forehead and found it was extremely sore. Since he did not have one of the canvas war sacks used by the cowboys to carry their belongings in when on roundup, he had to be content to put all his things in the carpet bag valise.

Before packing it, he withdrew the heavy bone-handled Colt .45 in its holster and strapped this around his waist. He took the gun out and made sure it contained only five bullets and the hammer was resting on the empty hole in the cylinder. He did not want it to go off accidentally by hitting the ground when he was thrown from another horse. He had not wanted to give away his dude appearance by carrying the gun, but now it made no difference. He had decided that if he was going to have to ride the rough string, he should carry the gun. He might be lucky and kill a horse before it could kill him.

After shaving, he took the valise to Shadrow's bed wagon and put it alongside the war sacks other riders were now putting in the wagon. At sight of the fancy flowered valise, several of the men smiled and tried to hold back their laughter.

He went to the barn and carried his spare hackamore, two bridles, the wire and club he had used and placed these items in the wagon. Just as he threw these over the side, Shelly arrived, along with Manual, who carried a canvas-covered bedroll and a new slicker for him. The rancher did not say much that morning. He wished Dean good luck and held out his hand. Dean shook the man's hand firmly and the rancher turned to leave.

"Get in touch when you can," he said over his shoulder.

Dean went to where the women had again set up the tables for serving breakfast. He saw Marian only from a distance while he was eating. As soon as he finished, he walked swiftly to the corrals where his rough string had been kept up for the night. He got his saddle and gear and carried this to lay it by the snubbing post. Taking the rope, he went into the corral where the horses were nervously waiting.

Dean again looked over the members of his string, making sure he would know each of them. Again, he thought only the two buckskins and the gray to be horses that could amount to anything. He wondered which horse would be the worst, now that Brownie was gone. After some study, he selected a big black. This horse was a heavier horse than Brownie had been, with large hard hooves and muscular legs. It had a mean look in its eye and snorted its defiance at the man. Dean ran this horse into the round corral.

He roped the horse on his second attempt. To his surprise, this horse did not fight back against the rope, as Brownie had done, but whirled to face the man as soon as the noose tightened around its neck and stood rigidly still. It even allowed Dean to lead it close to the snubbing post. The big horse stood nervously, but not flinching, as Dean slipped the heavy hackamore on its head and swung the blankets and then the saddle onto its back. From the saddle marks on the horse's withers, Dean knew the horse had been ridden many miles. To still be in the rough string, the horse must be a hard bucker.

As a precaution, he again used his red bandanna to blind

the horse when he mounted. For a moment, before putting his toe in the stirrup, he stood in thought. Damn it, he hated the thought of mounting this horse. He felt his stomach tighten into a large knot. It took all the courage he could muster to force himself to reach for the stirrup and swing up. His left shoulder hurt so badly he knew he would not be able to use his left hand on the reins, as would be normal for him. He tested to make sure only his toes were in the stirrups. Slowly, although it was about all he could do with his left arm, he leaned forward and jerked the blind from the horse's eyes.

Instantly, the black bowed its powerful neck and leaped high into the air. It was a terrifically high twisting buck that had the rider all but out of the saddle from the start. Dean desperately dug his knees under the jumper roll for that extra grip so important to him and managed to stay with the horse, despite the fact he was already unbalanced. He grabbed the horn with his left hand, and in spite of the pain, held on for dear life.

They were now coming back to earth and he pushed his feet forward to take the jolt of the landing. Dean was jarred to the very marrow of his bones as the horse shook the ground, hitting it with the force of a pile driver. Never had he been on a horse that could go as high, or hit the ground as hard as this horse was doing. No wonder the average cowboy could not ride the animal.

He felt his head snap on his neck, and for a split second, thought he was going to black out as his head flew forward from the force of the landing. He realized the horse was even then going up in another pitch. Again, he desperately dug his knees against the fork of the saddle, under the jumper roll. Without the extra grip that old jumper gave him, he could never have stayed with that horse.

The big horse reached the peak of its pitch, shook itself violently and started down. His head snapped back and his hat flew off. There was a sudden sickening sensation in Dean's stomach as he felt the jumper give way. Before he could react, he was sailing off over the horse's head. Never had he been thrown as high as he was this time and he desperately tried to locate the ground before he landed. He managed to twist himself so that he lit more or less on his feet in a crumpled heap. He sat there for some time, thankful he had not hurt his shoulder again and watched the big horse buck and run around the corral, the stirrups flapping loudly with each jump the horse made. Looking along the fence, he saw he again had an audience.

As soon as he caught the horse, the black stopped and stood nervously, but not fighting him, as he examined the jumper, now hanging by one thong from the fork of the saddle. It had been no accident. Both thongs had been cut part way through with a sharp knife. Someone had deliberately done this to try to get him thrown, perhaps even killed.

With savage determination, Dean rolled the jumper and retied it securely to the fork of the old saddle. As he did so, he made a promise to himself never to mount another horse without first thoroughly checking his gear. He had been careless.

With the old jumper again fixed to his satisfaction, he put the blind on the horse and again twisted the stirrup and swung into the saddle. When the blind was removed, the horse again leaped high into the air. This time, however, the rider was expecting the mighty effort and by gripping the saddle fork beneath the jumper with all his might, he stayed in better position in the saddle. Automatically, he swung his feet forward to take the terrific jar of the landing. How he missed having his high-heeled cowboy boots.

The horse seemed to go even higher on its next buck. By now, Dean's brain was somewhat foggy from the hard jolt of each landing, but he managed to keep track of the horse's head, giving him that all-important sense of direction, until the horse's leaps became slower and less jarring. At last, the horse gave up, throwing its head up in defeat and going around the corral in a stiff-legged jarring trot.

Dean found he could now turn the horse to each side and make it stop when he wanted to. He worked the horse for several minutes and then rode it up close to the snubbing post.

He was so glad to be getting off the horse under his own power, that he got a little careless and dismounted without twisting around to land near the horse's shoulder. He was about in the center of the animal. Instantly, the horse humped up and kicked viciously at his leg, giving his shin a glancing blow. Fortunately, the hoof did not hit his leg squarely or he would probably have received a broken bone.

To say the least, it was very painful and he jumped back to stand on one foot and hold his bruised leg in both hands. When he could again put his weight on the injured leg, he limped to the fence to lean wearily against it. He lifted his arm to wipe the perspiration from his face and his shirt sleeve came away red with his own blood. The terrific pounding the black had given him had caused him to have a gushing nose bleed.

"That was a good ride, amigo," Manuel Vigil called softly from the other side of the fence. "I think you have rode the worse one. Yes, I am sure Poncho is the worse, after Brownie. I, myself, have rode that horse and he is a good horse, if you can stay on him. Always watch him close, though, for he will buck with you again at the most not wanted time."

Dean turned his head to look between the posts to see the tall Mexican peering at him. He could tell there were others lined around the fence but none of the others spoke. Manuel probably knew what he was talking about, and if the black was the worst left in the bunch, and if he could last those first few days, he might just live to ride the rough string in spite of Jasper Kincaid.

A short time later, Dean's extra horses plus a new one Jasper had added to replace Brownie were turned out with the herd going with Shadrow's wagon. Dean put the blind on the black horse and carefully mounted. This time, the horse did not attempt to buck when he pulled the blind and he had no trouble when a man swung the gate open into the other corrals. He rode out to help take his string to the remuda.

Both of the other wagons were going east and north from the Kincaid ranch and these pulled out first, Masterman's some little time before Summers', in order to keep their horse herds separated. About the time Summers started his outfit down the creek, sudden loud shouts were heard from the main creek crossing. Dean and several men rode toward the crossing, leaving the remuda with the others.

Most of the ranchers had gone up the creek to cross at the safe crossing but one buggy had attempted to cross where the main road normally crossed when the creek was dry. The driver had let the team get too far downstream in the two feet of swift water flowing down the creek. The Big Sandy often became quite "quicky" when large amounts of water churned up the soft sand. That's why most people would not attempt to cross the Big Sandy in flood stage except at those certain safe crossings.

Dean watched as a man rode out into the current and swung off his horse. Standing thigh deep in the muck, he and the driver, also now out of the vehicle, managed to unhook the team from the buggy. The freed animals floundered in the sand but finally made their way across the stream and up the opposite bank. The men now looped the rider's lariat rope around the back axle of the buggy and he remounted his horse, dallying the rope around his saddle horn.

The one horse could not move the vehicle in the sucking sand. Several more men now rode out into the stream to put more ropes on the buggy. They stayed a rope's length from the buggy to be on more solid footing. Still, they were unsuccessful in moving the vehicle. After several futile attempts, they gave up, gathered up what articles they could from the buggy and brought them to shore. Even as they watched, the vehicle slowly sank deeper and deeper into the sand until it disappeared under the water, leaving a slight riffle the only sign of it.

"Lucky old Judd got out when he did," a man said.

"Hell, he ought to have knowed better'n that and gone up to the safe crossin'," another said, with little pity. "The Big Sandy don't forgive many mistakes."

They all now rode back to the main remuda and Shadrow had them start the horses up country, toward the west. Once the remuda was strung out in the right direction, the men left them in charge of the wrangler and dropped back to ride in a loose group behind the chuck wagon with its trotting team. They worked no cattle that first morning, as this was too close to the Kincaid ranch itself and the regular hands would take care of any cattle this near the ranch. Most of the range cattle would have been driven farther south by the late storm, anyway.

They crossed the Big Sandy at the safe crossing above the ranch, near a set of working pens and the long, low calving shed. They turned more west than south, as they would go to the extreme western edge of their country before starting their part of the actual roundup. At noon, they stopped to eat a cold lunch of the leftovers from the barbecue, which the cook had managed to bring along. Immediately after lunch, they mounted, and when Dean mounted the big black, Poncho bucked, but this time only halfheartedly, and Dean had no real trouble in riding the horse.

They now rode in a northwesterly direction, the Big Sandy having turned more toward the northwest. Dean realized they had come far enough west of Kincaid's so he could make out the blue and white top of Pikes Peak more plainly than he could from the ranch. He guessed it still had to be sixty miles or more to the west.

Later in the afternoon, Shadrow split the men up to make a big circle looking for cattle. The big captain assigned Dean the farthest, widest circle of all. The big black worked for Dean pretty well most of the afternoon, but did break into a bucking fit when he tried to make the horse cross a very steep draw. Dean managed to ride the horse and felt much better about his riding ability.

He found few cattle and no calves old enough to brand, so he finally turned to ride back toward the center until he caught up with some of the other men driving a few cows toward where the wagon would be camped. When they caught up with the wagon captain, the big man rode through their herd and decided there were no calves big enough to brand and so had them drive the entire bunch toward the north and let them go.

Several riders, besides Dean, reported they had seen the carcasses of many cattle where the late blizzard had covered them in the deep draws. Whenever you rode close to one of those draws, the smell seemed to permeate the air for a long ways around each draw.

That night, they made their first camp on the open prairie. It was a calm evening, the grass was turning green and the weather was mild. The cook fed them the last of the barbecued beef and hot sourdough biscuits. Dean ate with relish, enjoying the open air and being back on the range.

As soon as he had eaten, he took his bedroll some ways away from any of the others and unrolled it. Tonight, he was too tired to do anything but crawl into the bed. For a while he lay relaxing in the blankets, content to look up into the sky as the stars were coming out. He thought back to other roundups he had been on. The smell of the prairie seemed good and clean and from somewhere out in the gathering darkness came the soft sound of the bell the wranglers had put on one of the horses, and in the distance, the howl of coyotes. He listened to some of the men as they started a game of cards near the fire. That game would go on every night as long as the wagon was out.

All these sights, smells and sounds seemed good to him as he lay there. Just before he dropped off to sleep, he thought about Marian Shelly and wondered if she would be thinking of him. Probably not. She had no reason to. He let himself imagine that he had found their missing cattle and how proudly he would announce it to her. Then, she might have a reason to think of him.

TEN

The next thing he knew, the cook was rousting them all out with the noise he was making as he prepared breakfast. The sun was just turning the eastern sky a soft pink as the men rolled out and dressed.

The camp had been made near a small spring and all the men went to wash and those that wanted, shaved along the small stream that flowed a short distance from its source, before disappearing again into the ground.

They ate their breakfast of sourdough biscuits, bacon, fried potatoes and coffee. There was also a pot of oatmeal for any who wanted it; canned milk was used for cream. They would have bacon and pork the first few days, then a beef would be killed and they would eat beef three times a day from then on.

There were two cardinal rules of any well-run roundup. Every man was to have any personal chores finished before he ate breakfast and the night hawk, as the night wrangler was called, was to have the remuda in the rope corrals by the time breakfast was finished.

The horses were mostly ones that were used to the rope corral and would stand quietly with their shoulders just touching the rope, their heads out over the rope and pointing away from the center of the corral. Each man roped his own horse as quietly as he could and led the animal outside the corral to saddle. The men all saddled quickly and mounted, to wait and watch the man riding the rough string top off his horse for the morning. Usually, this was the most exciting thing that happened each morning.

Today, however, there were several other riders who had to top off their mounts. Since it had been several months from their last saddling, several horses bucked with their riders that morning. There was much shouting and good-natured joking during this excitement. When the men were all safely mounted, they dropped back some little distance from the corral to wait and watch the rider of the rough string top off his mount for the morning.

"Just tell Les what horse you want, Archer," Ben instructed Dean, as he entered the corral. "Some of them rough string horses are mean to handle inside the corral and I sure don't want them tearing it down or causin' a stampede. Hugh," he called to a tall young rider mounted just outside the corral, "you go on in there and be ready to snub his horse if we need to."

The captain let the gate down and the man rode inside and placed himself behind the roper, holding back just enough so that his horse should not spook when Les threw his loop.

"What horse you want, Archer?" Les Boyd asked between his crooked lips.

"That solid buckskin," Dean said, pointing to the rangier of the two dun horses in his string.

"Going to try old Wrangler, are you?" Les asked, eyeing

the horse closely. "Be ready, Hugh, he's mean to catch."

A man had to be a good roper to catch horses in the rope corral without exciting the ones he did not want. There were almost two hundred head of horses in that flimsy corral and the little bat-eared rider, Les Boyd, walked softly behind the line of horses until he was in the right position to make his throw. Dean watched the little man closely, for he could tell much about the man's ability from the way he would throw his loop.

It turned out that Les Boyd was an expert with a rope. The little man glanced over his shoulder to make sure Hugh was properly placed with the snubbing horse and sent a rather large loop streaking out to settle over the buckskin's head. The man had not whirled the rope but had held it low beside his leg and then just flipped it out smoothly. He instantly jerked the slack and with the continuation of the motion of his arm, gave the end of the rope to the man on the horse who quickly grabbed it and dallied it around his saddle horn.

"Open the gate!" Shadrow yelled. "Let the rest of them out before trouble starts."

The loose horses saw the gate instantly and made a run for it. Hugh was watching carefully, trying to keep his rope from becoming tangled around any of the free horses before pulling it back to hold the buckskin, who was also making a run for the open gate. Les Boyd tried to stop the horse by waving his hat in its face before ducking out of the way.

The horse hit the end of the rope and snapped around, stayed on its feet, and began fighting the rope. The mounted cowboy held his horse in check and several of the men now rode up to try to drive the buckskin closer to the mounted man. They finally got the horse close enough for Hugh to take enough slack to hold the horse's head about three feet from his saddle horn. While Hugh held the horse, Dean put on the hackamore and blind. He hobbled the animal before removing Hugh's rope.

Dean quickly saddled the horse and stood a moment looking at it, before removing the hobbles. Well, this would be the acid test. This would be the first time he had mounted one of his charges out on the open prairie. There would be no corral to keep the horse, should it buck Dean off. Gritting his teeth and feeling the knot in his stomach, Dean forced himself to twist the stirrup and swing up. The horse humped nervously but did not attempt to buck with the blind on. Dean made sure he was ready and that only his toes were in the stirrups.

The instant the blind was jerked off, the horse bogged its head and began bucking viciously. This horse bucked straight ahead in high hard pitches and Dean soon found he was in rhythm with the horse and was riding him. Although he lost his right stirrup after several jumps, Dean managed to stay with the animal until it finally quit its pitching. Dean found this animal now reined rather well and turned it to ride back to where the others waited. The roundup had really started and he sighed in relief.

"Nice ride, Archer," Eben Hessey said coldly in his high shrill voice, as Ben Shadrow mounted his horse to lead the men from camp.

The cook, wranglers and flunky were already busily breaking camp. They took down the picket line and the rope corral, piling the ropes and pegs in the wood wagon. The cook would lead the way to their new camp, some five miles away at another watering hole. The men would have the camp set up by the noon break. The wrangler would have the horses in the rope corral so the men could change horses for the afternoon work.

Again, Dean was given the farthest circle to make to the west. Once he was alone, he found Wrangler to be a responsive horse, reining well and seemed to have exceptional athletic ability, exceptionally quick on its feet. As long as he kept the horse moving, there was no problem. However, when he attempted to hold the horse at a stand for a few minutes in order to study the lay of the land before him, the buckskin immediately began twisting and turning and in a moment was bucking. Again, the horse bucked hard but straight and Dean managed to ride it. From then on, if he wanted to look at the country, he let the horse circle slowly, always moving, as he looked for cattle and the lay of the land.

He found cattle that morning, and after circling them, headed them toward the wagon. Once he was behind cattle and working them, he again found Wrangler was responding and working the cattle well for him. It seemed the horse simply did not want to stop its constant motion.

By the time he joined the other riders, they had a fairly sizable herd to work. Dean found that despite the fact this was the first time the buckskin had been ridden in many months, it never quit nor acted as though it were not already toughened into working condition. Of all the horses he had ever ridden, he had never known one with more energy and spirit. Dean was even a little sorry when he got off the horse to turn it loose for the afternoon.

This time, Eben Hessey snubbed the other buckskin, called Buttons because of the dapples in its coat, and Dean had no real problem in saddling. This horse also bucked with him and bucked hard. Dean again lost a stirrup because of his fear to put more than his toe in the stirrup, and despite hanging on for all he was worth, was thrown. The fall did him no real damage but caused some delay before one of the men roped the free horse and brought it back to Dean. This delay caused Shadrow to curse and storm as they waited for the man to return with Dean's horse. Dean eyed the man quietly and said nothing.

On the second try, Dean rode the buckskin to a standstill. He found this horse to be a much quieter horse than Wrangler, not as nervous and would stand for short periods without bucking. That afternoon, Dean was assigned the job of watching the herd and keeping it gathered in a loose bunch while two men, the tall Holland rep and Les Boyd roped the calves and drug them to men on the ground who threw and held them for Shadrow to brand. The roper called the brand of the mother of the calf he had roped and the wagon captain put that brand on the calf.

From where he had to operate, some distance from the action at the branding fire, Dean could not tell too much about the brands of the cows. However, riding around the edge of the herd, he was able to see many of the freshly branded calves, now back with their mothers, and every one he checked carried the same brand as the mother. If there was any attempt to brand a calf with the wrong brand, he could see no evidence of it. Perhaps, whoever was doing it, was waiting until things settled down more, when people might not be watching as closely.

Even from where he was, Dean could tell that Ed Ward, the Holland rep, and Boyd were both very good ropers. They seldom missed their calf and kept the flankers near the fire busy all afternoon. After all the calves had been branded, the riders drove the cattle several miles north and turned them loose. By the time they returned to the camp, the cook had the evening meal ready and the men quickly unsaddled and turned their horses loose. Only the Wagon captain and the night hawk kept horses up, tied at the long picket line.

After supper that night, Dean made himself acquainted with Ed Ward. Holland had told the tall man to back any move Dean made and he assured Dean he would certainly do so.

"Hell, I'd back you anyway," the tall rider said honestly. "I'd back any man with the guts to try to ride them horses they give you."

"I don't know how Ben works the ropers," Dean said, appreciating the man's open remark. It was the first time any of the men had shown the slightest friendliness toward him. "You and Les seem to be good at that job, and you ropers would be the first ones to know if Ben's putting the wrong brand on a calf. I hope you'll rope most of the time, and if so, keep your eyes open, not only on your calves but also on what Boyd's doing, as well. He and Shadrow are thick as thieves, anyway, and I can't bring myself to trust either one."

"You've got them both pegged right. This is the first year I ever rode with the west wagon, and the first time I ever roped with Boyd," Ed said dryly. "Have to admit, he's sure slick with that rope, as good as I've saw, but you can bet I'll keep an eye on him and I won't be bashful about hollerin', if I think he's pullin' anything. I've rode with several of these other fellers and I don't know any of them that I think would cheat."

"Well, let me know if you suspect anything," Dean told him.

"I sure will, Archer," the tall rider drawled and moved away toward his bedroll. "You're the one who'd best watch out. A lot more men have been killed out here by bad horses, than ever was by bad men, injuns and outlaws combined."

Again that night, Dean went right to bed. He found he was not quite as stiff as he had been the first night. He lay quietly for a while before dozing off, his thoughts on what he had learned that day. There certainly had been no sign of any wrong doing. Wouldn't he feel foolish, if he had worked so hard to get on this west wagon and it turned out to be one of the others that was changing brands?

Before he dropped off, he again let his mind bring up the picture of the black-haired Marian Shelly. How pretty her face was in his mind's eye. Funny, he never thought about the girl in Ohio anymore.

ELEVEN

Dean awoke with a start. He had been dreaming he was again riding Brownie and the horse had just hit the fence head-on and he was again sailing out over the horse's head. He seemed to glance down and see the tops of the corral fence posts plainly below him.

He sat up in a cold sweat, as the rest of the camp was beginning to stir. His left shoulder was still sore but much better than it had been and he could tell his other muscles were beginning to toughen. He could remember when condition had been no problem to him.

He pulled on his clothes, again thinking how miserable they looked, and reached for his shoes. He could not help but wonder how much longer his body would be able to take the kind of punishment the rough string was giving it.

As he laced the shoes, he let his eyes rove around the camp. Most of the men slept fairly close to the chuck wagon. Men were now up and in various stages of dressing, all having put their hats on first, and one man was already heading toward the rope corral. It was Ben, his hulking gate plain in the early morning light.

The big man stopped near the saddles and other equipment piled near the corral gate. He turned to look furtively back at the camp. When he saw Dean was still beside his bed, he turned quickly to the saddles, looking for Dean's. Watching the camp closely, he kneeled to roll the saddle over, reaching in his pocket for his knife. At the roar of the .45, the ground seemed to explode in a shower of dirt to his face and he turned his startled face to find Eben Hessey standing between him and the corral, a smoking Colt in his hand.

"What you doing, Ben?" the cold-eyed man asked lazily. "You think Archer needs another fall?"

"Of course not, Eben!" the man exclaimed, his eyes plainly showing his surprise but he was not about to show fear. He pulled his hand from his pocket. It held nothing deadly, only a leather thong. "I was just going to put this by Archer's saddle, in case he needed it."

With this, the big man dropped the thong and stood up to turn and stalk back toward camp, trying hard not to show his anger and knowing he had almost been caught in the act. He had not noticed where Hessey had bedded down the night before, but the man was apparently sleeping near the saddles and had been behind a small mound between the saddles and the corral. Shadrow would make sure the next time.

The gunshot brought Dean and several of the other men to find out what happened. Hessey showed Dean the leather thong and told him what the wagon captain was doing.

"I always sleep near our equipment," the chunky man explained in his cold manner. Dean noticed how the man's eyes were like blue ice as he spoke. "I noticed how careful you was to check your equipment over the other day and guessed someone had caused you a problem and might try something with mine. Neither of us is liked too well by the bosses of this outfit."

"Should have done that myself, Hessey," Dean said frankly. "Somebody did cut the strings holding that old jumper to my saddle fork and caused me a hard fall. I owe you one, Hessey."

The man eyed him with those cold eyes and moved off toward camp. There was no sign of friendship, as the man was a complete loner.

That morning, Dean had Boyd rope the gray horse someone had told him was called Ute. This animal acted completely peaceful as Boyd led it away from the herd to the gate where Dean slipped the hackamore over the gray head. The horse continued to act indifferently about the whole procedure. This made Dean even more cautious, for he remembered how this horse had bit and kicked at all the other horses.

He led the horse to where his saddle lay, the horse standing quietly as he reached for the blankets. Without warning, the horse reached out, its teeth flashing as it attempted to bite Dean in the middle of the back. Luckily, the man had been watching and ducked away, dropping the blankets and twisting to avoid those flashing teeth. Instinctively, he brought the rope reins down across the horse's nose in a slashing blow. "Damn you, that was close," he said as the horse now pulled back, its eyes watching the man closely.

Keeping his glance on the horse at all times, the rider hobbled the horse and proceeded to saddle it, as it again stood quietly. Once saddled, Dean pulled out his bandanna and put it over the horse's eyes, before removing the hobbles. He was about to mount the horse when a scream of pain shattered the clear morning air. It came from the camp. He stood back to see what had caused it, as several men now ran toward the chuck wagon, some trying to lead frightened horses behind them. Dean quickly put the hobbles back on the gray, and left it to run toward the knot of milling men near the chuck wagon.

"Those damn fool kids! They was wrestling and the flunky fell and cut his back bad," a man said, as Dean neared the men. "God, it's bad! Must have slid across a tent peg or somethin'!"

Dean eased between men until he could make out the form of the flunky on the ground. The boy lay on his stomach as men lifted his shirt until they could all see the terrible cut across the boy's back. It was deep, wide, and bled profusely.

"We've got to get that blood stopped!" the cook shouted. "He'll bleed to death sure, if we don't!"

"Damn them kids, anyway," Shadrow growled, as he now knelt beside the boy. "You're always playing around when you should be workin'. Your damn foolishness is going to cost us a lot of time."

The big wagon captain stood up and walked a few steps away. Dean could see all the men were watching more than trying to help. He quickly ran to the chuck wagon and drew open the flour bin. He forced the whole drawer out and carried this quickly to where the boy lay, and sat it down next to the cook.

"What the hell you doin' with my flour, Archer?" the cook demanded hotly, looking up at the slender rider through watery eyes.

"Spread that over the cut," Dean instructed calmly. "It may stop the bleeding."

He dropped to his knees and began scooping the flour onto the boy's back. As the blood soaked into the flour, he added more. Ed Ward dropped to his knees beside Dean and began adding more flour. They tried to press the flesh together over the flour.

"Does anyone have a needle and thread?" Dean asked, looking up at the men standing around. The big wagon captain now seemed indifferent to the whole affair. Dean did not hesitate and said, "There should be a harness needle in some of the repair equipment. See if you can find one and some thread. Bart, get some water boiling in a hurry."

"Who the hell you think you are, Archer?" Ben demanded, coming back to stand at the edge of the group. "You ain't the boss here."

"You take over, then, Ben," Dean told the man sharply. "This kid's back has got to be sewed up, or he'll never make it to a doctor."

"You ever done any such sewing before?" a man asked.

"Not on a human, but I've sewed up a cut horse or two," Dean said evenly, as the cook got up and ran to put a small pot of water on the fire.

Ed Ward lumbered to his feet and ran toward the wood wagon, which also held the few leather repair items carried on the roundup. Hugh Loring, the DZ rep, knelt to take his place, helping Dean sift flour over the soaking blood. His eyes met Dean's across the boy's back.

"I think it's beginning to slow down," he said slowly, his big hand letting the flour trickle between his fingers. "Either we're slowing it, or he's runnin' out of blood."

"I guess you know you've ruined a bin of flour," Bart grumbled, letting his gnarled old hand rub his whiskered face. He went to the fire where the small pot of water was already boiling. "I guess if it saves that boy's life, though, it's worth it," he added gruffly.

Ed came running back from the wagon carrying a long curved harness needle and some waxed thread for sewing leather.

"Boil the hell out of that thread and needle," Dean told him. Ed turned on his heel and hurried to the fire to drop the items into the pot of boiling water. Dean looked up at the others. "Some of you'll have to hold him down while I do this, as we have no ether to put him to sleep with."

Several of the men now held the boy helpless and still. They all watched, as Dean used a fork to pick the hot needle out of the pot. As soon as he could touch the needle, he threaded it. Slowly, he forced the curved needle through the flesh on one side of the wound and back up through the other side. He pulled the thread through as gently as he could, as the boy screamed in pain. Dean cut the thread and tied the flesh together as best he could. He had to put in ten stitches to close the wound. Between pulling the flesh together and the flour, the wound was now only seeping a small amount of blood.

"I don't know how much muscle damage was done, or if infection will set in and kill him," Dean said gravely, "but he may make it to a doctor. One of you get his horse."

"Make sure you get his personal horse, Les," Shadrow called, as the little ferret-faced man now hurried toward the corral. "He can't take a Pool horse."

"He can't make it by himself," the young day wrangler said, feeling guilty about the whole situation, as he had been the one roughing with the flunky when the accident happened. "I think I'd better go with him."

"Hell, no!" Shadrow exploded. "We're already short one hand. You stay here and do your job!"

"He can never make it to Limon on his own, Shadrow," Dean objected softly. "I'd say, let the wrangler go with him. We can get by, somehow."

"I keep telling you, Archer, you ain't running this wagon!" the big man thundered. "Hell, he hurt himself, let him take care of himself!"

Dean looked from the white face of the wrangler to the flushed one of the wagon captain.

"I'm not going to let a kid die just to salve your ego, Ben," he said softly and turned to the wrangler. "You don't want your friend to die, do you?"

"Of course not."

"Then get your horse."

With this, the kid spun around and ran toward the corral. He was back in a few minutes with two saddled horses. Ed Ward helped Dean lift the flunky onto his saddle. The boy sat sloppily, swaying and holding the horn with both hands, his eyes filled with tears of pain. Dean watched the wrangler mount his horse and handed the young man the reins of the flunky's horse.

"You know where Limon is from here?" he asked. The wrangler nodded. "You'll have to go at a slow walk all the way," Dean cautioned. "He can't take any trotting. Just keep moving and get him there as fast as you can. You may have to tie him in the saddle, he's lost so much blood, but you get him to a doctor...understand?"

As the two horses left camp, the wrangler looked back past

the slack figure on the lead horse to where the men were now starting to move back to the day's work. Several men turned often to look at the departing riders. They were hard men, but they were all hoping the kid made it.

"That was a good job, Archer," Ed Ward said gravely and looked at the big wagon captain. "You ain't got no feeling for anyone, have you, Ben?"

"Hell, I've got a wagon to run and we're already over an hour late," Ben growled, with no emotion showing on his face. "I got no time for feelings. Come on, Archer, top off that horse and all you men mount up. We ain't got time for this foolishness."

"Sure too bad it wasn't you that got hurt, Ben," Hugh Loring drawled loudly. "I'll bet you'd be singing a different tune, if it'd been you."

"Hell, I learned a long time ago how to take care of myself," Ben growled over his shoulder as he walked to his horse. He did not like it that some of the men seemed to be more on Archer's side today than on his. "Bart, have the night hawk take over the horses. The two of you'll have to move camp by yourselves. Slim can drive one wagon for you and lead his horse."

"Don't expect dinner to be on time!" the cook growled as he dumped the balance of the flour out of the wooden drawer. He would have to get a fresh supply.

Dean now walked to where the gray horse had stood quietly, hobbled and blinded. He knelt down to remove the hobbles and the horse again tried to bite him. Even though it could not see because of the blind, it instinctively tried to grab Dean in the back. Dean was watching and again jerked away from the horse, but not before his shirt was torn by the flashing teeth. Again, he brought the rope reins down across the horse's nose as hard as he could. The animal tried to pull away but then calmed down and stood quietly as the man removed the hobbles and put the rein over its neck. Dean was watching, as he reached for the stirrup and was ready when the horse tried to nip his butt. This time, he struck the horse savagely on its nose with his fist.

On the next try, he swung into the saddle. When he was ready, he pulled the blind. To his surprise, the horse made no attempt to buck but walked calmly ahead, like a well-broken old cow horse would have done. It was when Dean tried to pull the horse to a stop that it happened. The gray suddenly sprang into its top speed and ran away from camp. Ben Shadrow turned to smile at Les Boyd, as they both knew the horse and were expecting this to happen. Neither had mentioned this to Dean.

Dean found he was helpless to do anything but ride, for the horse did not respond to any of his pulling on the reins. Luckily, it was fairly flat prairie country with no fences. The horse seemed to run blind, without seeing anything in front of it, just running or stampeding, as the cowboys called it. Dean had seen a horse or two do this but had never before been on one when it happened.

Never, had he felt so helpless. It was frightening, for he had no control whatsoever. He felt the horse would have blindly gone over a cliff, had there been one in front of them. Miles went by, before the horse began to tire, but it continued to run. Dean tried to watch the country ahead, ready to jump, should the horse hit a draw or hole, or stumble for any reason. The way the animal was running, Dean would not have been surprised had the horse fallen over the unevenness of the ground. He did not want to be caught under the horse.

They had gone several miles before the horse began to slow and show a little response to the man's pulling on the reins. Then, as suddenly as it had begun, the horse slid to a stop and immediately began to buck. The gray was tired from the run but it could still buck. Now, it pitched wildly, twisting and bawling with each jump. The man had been caught somewhat off guard and now fought to stay in the saddle, pulling on reins, saddle horn and jumper roll as best he could. By some miracle, he managed to ride the horse, until at last, completely worn out, it stopped from sheer exhaustion, not from any desire to behave.

Dean let the horse stand and breathe heavily for several minutes, then pulled the horse's head around and urged it to move ahead. The horse now seemed completely docile, just as it had back at the corral. It now moved ahead at a swift walk and seemed under complete control, stopping or turning whenever Dean lifted the reins.

Not a man had followed him to see if he made it and Dean knew that Shadrow had insisted all the men go on about the business of making the morning circle. The gray had run in the opposite direction from the way the men were going, and Dean now had to ride back those miles to where the camp had been. After what had happened at camp that morning, Dean knew he had better learn to ride these horses, knowing that if he were hurt by one of them, the wagon captain would show him no pity.

He had never known a man like Shadrow, nor had he ever felt so alone among a group of men. Even the worst man he had ever ridden with, would never have let the kid go on his own to find a doctor, as Shadrow had wanted. He knew, too, he had done nothing to help his position with the man by stepping in and helping the boy. He knew the big wagon captain definitely resented any challenge to his authority.

The wagons had already left camp by the time he got back to where they had been. There was nothing to do but ride toward the west until he found some of the men. It was past noon when he caught up with some of the riders now driving cattle toward the bunch grounds. He fell in behind the herd and a moment later, the big wagon captain rode up to him.

"Archer, you made us late twice today," the big man growled, as though it had all been Dean's fault. "I had to send someone else on your circle, besides making us late pampering that damn kid. I won't put up with that kind of stuff. You try to take over again and you'll regret it!"

"Fine! Give me some decent horses to ride and I'll even try to help you," Dean told the man bluntly, meeting the big man's eyes squarely.

"By God, you learn to ride the horses you're given, damn it," Shadrow snapped. "We ain't babyin' you or any more kids, either. I'll tell you one more time, you ain't the boss here—I am!"

Dean shrugged his thin shoulders and turned the gray to the work of pushing the cattle along. It was midafternoon when they reached the bunch ground about a half mile from the wagons. Dean helped bunch the herd, Ute now seeming to work pretty well for him.

An old cow suddenly broke away from the bunch at a run and Dean turned the gray after her, kicking his heels against the horse's sides as he did so. The horse took right out after the cow and was fast enough to head her, turning her back toward the herd and Dean pulled the horse down to an easy lope. As they drew near the herd, he pulled back on the reins to slow the horse further and found the horse would no longer respond to the reins as it had been doing. Instead, it now loped easily right through the herd, scattering cattle before it in all directions and the man was completely unable to do anything about it.

Men shouted at him and rode quickly to try to stop the cattle from scattering further over the prairie. They could tell Dean was unable to do anything with the horse. Ute went all the way through the herd as cattle ran to get away from the charging horse.

Finally out of the herd, on the other side, the gray would still not respond to the reins, but loped steadily toward the camp. The horse loped right up to the gate of the rope corral. There, the gray stiffened its front legs and crow hopped to a stop, jarring the rider as much as it could. Dean swung down, watching the horse closely in case it tried to bite him. The horse stood there like an old gentle plow horse and calmly waited for the man to pull the saddle and turn it into the corral with its mates.

"Next time, we'll try that spade bit on you and see how you like it," Dean promised the horse.

As Dean was closing the corral gate, Shadrow and about half the men rode in for dinner and fresh horses. Each man caught a fresh horse and tied it to the picket line before going to the chuck wagon. Dean watched silently as the men caught their horses and led them away, waiting for Shadrow to say something or tell one of the men to rope a horse for him. At last, the big man came by him, leading his horse toward the picket line.

"You won't need a horse this afternoon, Archer," the man said gruffly. "You can flank calves."

Dean shrugged and walked to the chuck wagon, where he grabbed a plate and got his meal. Since he would be on foot wrestling the calves all afternoon, he took off his pistol and laid it with his bedroll on the bed wagon.

Ed and Les again roped. There were two teams of flankers. Eben Hessey was to work with Dean and they were soon busy as the ropers brought the calves close to the branding fire. Here, one of them would grab the rope with his right hand and go down it to the calf, reach across and place his left hand over the calf's back to catch the lose flesh of the calf's flank. He would then lift the calf against his legs and throw it to the ground with the left side up, while the other man ran to grab the hind feet.

This man dropped to the ground and pushed the bottom leg forward with his feet, while pulling the top leg back against his stomach. The front man placed a knee on the calf's neck and put his weight on the calf's shoulder. Between the men, they held the calf helpless while the work was done.

Again, how Dean wished he had his boots, for the heels of his shoes often slipped and let the calves kick with the bottom leg. Dean took quick note that the chunky Hessey had not left his pistol in camp as the flankers usually did, but wore the heavy belt and holster throughout the work.

The ropers were often the only ones who saw the mother of the calves and Dean could not tell if they were calling out the right brands or not. He did note that Shadrow always put on the brand the roper had called.

Dean also had to admit the big, hulking captain worked hard, castrating the bull calves and then branding each calf. The man drove himself at a fast pace and did not seem to slack the work. He was not the best man with a running iron that Dean had ever seen, but he managed to get a brand burned on a calf in a hurry. As he watched the men, Dean thought back to when he had run the Arrowhead wagon. In those days, he had done much of the branding but had always been much more particular about the way the brands had looked, than Shadrow was doing. Of course, there had not been nearly as many brands to use, and he had to admit that would have made a difference.

Whenever a cow followed her calf close to the fire where he could see her brand, Dean watched closely to make sure the roper called the brand on her side. Never did he catch one calling the wrong brand. He had the feeling Ed Ward was an honest puncher but he could not bring himself to trust Boyd.

After one particularly sloppy job of branding a Hessey X bar X calf, the big wagon captain shook his head in disgust and angrily tossed the iron back toward the fire.

"We got some damn poor irons this year," he grumbled. "And, not having that damn flunky to keep up the fire, sure don't help. Hell, I've got to do everything." He put more wood on the fire as he talked.

"I'll have to admit that last brand wasn't too neat," Dean observed dryly, knowing any remark he made would irritate the big man.

"It's them damn irons!" Ben snapped irritably, stooping to pick up the iron he had thrown and stuff it into the fire. "Hell, I can make as good a X bar X as anybody."

"Is that what that was?" Dean asked innocently, his blue eyes snapping as he winked at Hessey. "I thought sure that was a blotch, bar, scab."

Eben Hessey snickered openly and the other two flankers looked away quickly as they held their calf. Shadrow's face turned dark with anger. He stooped quickly to pick up a red-hot iron from the fire and turned to rush at the slender man in the patched clothing and wilted beaver hat. Reaching out with his left hand, the big man roughly caught Dean's shirt and pulled the smaller man close to him. Dean's shirt spread at the back where Ute had grabbed a piece of it, showing the whiteness of the man's skin.

"Damn you, Archer, I'll take no more of your insults!"

Ben bellowed, holding the hot iron so Dean could feel the terrific heat on his face. "You make one more smart remark and I'll brand you!"

Dean met the man's glance squarely. To show fear here would be a disaster. The big man's brown eyes glared their hatred at him and he knew the man would make good on his threat at the slightest provocation. Without his gun, he was pretty helpless, knowing that to grab the man's arm would probably get at least one of them badly burned. He held his gaze on the man's face but said nothing.

"How many men can you afford to lose today, Ben?" Hessey's shrill voice cut through the silence. "You brand that man, and you lose two more, 'cause I'll blow your brains out."

Shadrow's glance went to where Hessey stood with his hand on the butt of his pistol. He did not question that a Hessey would shoot. He believed those stories about how a Hessey would as soon shoot a man as talk. Slowly, he let go of Dean's shirt and let his hand with the hot iron fall, holding it away from his leg.

"Just you remember, Archer, I'll take no more off you!" he snarled.

"Ain't this been one hell of a day?" one of the other flankers said softly.

It was at that moment that a call came from the ropers.

"Get somebody to rope the mother of the calf Les's bringing in!" Ed Ward yelled, as he drug a calf toward the fire. "We can't neither one make out what her brand is."

Shadrow turned to holler loudly to some of the men guarding the herd. A moment later, two of them rode through the cattle to where the two ropers now sat their horses, each holding a calf at the end of his rope.

"Clyde, you catch that cow followin' Les's calf," Ben instructed. "Baldy, you can heel her and we'll see who she belongs to."

The two riders rode closer to the cow, who was now standing close to her calf and bawling at it with motherly protective instincts, as it struggled against the pull of the rope.

"Tie hard and fast, Clyde," Baldy called, as both men shook lopes in their ropes. "If you can hold her, I'll throw her in a hurry."

The flankers stood silently watching, as Clyde circled a little closer to the cow, swinging his loop over his head. He caught the cow's head and started backing his horse to tighten the rope. Immediately, Baldy jumped his horse forward, his loop swinging, and as he went past the cow's rear end, he swung the rope under her in an attempt to catch her back legs. He missed, but his efforts spooked the cow, which now ran past Clyde's horse, heading toward the other cattle. Clyde pulled his horse around away from the cow.

Dean knew instinctively that the rider had turned his horse the wrong way. The man was in trouble. He should have turned the horse toward the cow, Dean thought! Dean watched as the man continued to turn the horse to the right, the wrong way. The horse now headed directly away from the direction the cow was running.

The rope went down under the horse's front legs, as the cow, now going full speed, hit the end of the rope. The force jerked the front legs out from under the horse and the rider was driven to the ground alongside his horse's head. As the men watched in horror, the horse went on over in a somersault, its hips crashing down on the helpless rider. It seemed the horse struggled to right itself, but because of the rope and the way it had fallen, could not roll on over. The horse lay there with its hind quarters squarely on the man's head and shoulders, its hind legs helplessly kicking in the air.

Dean grabbed the hot branding iron from Shadrow's limp hand and ran toward the fallen horse. As he neared the animal, he stopped to put the iron on the rope. The rope flared and flamed as it snapped in two.

He and Eben reached the horse at about the same time. Each man immediately grabbed a hind leg and rolled the animal off the man. Now that it was right side up again, the horse struggled to its feet, standing to look dumbly down at the man on the ground.

They rolled the cowboy over onto his back. There was no sign of life. The weight of the horse had probably crushed his chest. Eben put his face down near the man's nose.

"He ain't breathin'!" he shouted.

Dean put his ear on the man's chest. He could hear nothing. He lifted the man's hand and felt his wrist. There was no pulse. Shadrow and the other flankers hurried up beside them. No one spoke but merely looked at each other.

"Never knew what hit him," Ed Ward said at last, from where he still sat on his horse. "Damn, Clyde should have knowed to have turned his horse the other way. He should never have turned against the rope."

"Hell, anybody can make a mistake...but I think this one cost him his life," Eben Hessey observed in that high, tight voice he had.

The flankers ran to take the ropes off the calves and Shadrow told the herders to let the herd drift back west. They would work these cows again tomorrow. All the men then gathered around the still figure on the prairie sod.

"Hell of a note," Les Boyd said in his deep voice. "Clyde was a good man. We'll miss him."

"It was my fault," the cowboy, Baldy, said sadly. "I should never have told him to tie hard and fast. Had he dallied, he could of let go."

The others said nothing, even though they all felt the same way. The man should have dallied and never turned away from the cow. But, it was done.

"You flankers get shovels from the wagon," Shadrow said stiffly. "All we can do is bury him. I'll have Bart make some kind of a marker so we can find him, if any of his kin folk want to bury him again, later."

"Don't you have to report such accidents to the legal authorities?" Dean asked.

"Not on roundup. We're kind of our own law on these wagons," Shadrow said angrily, thinking Dean might be trying to take over again. "These things happen once in a while. I'll tell Jasper and he'll tell whoever needs to know and send for another rider to rep for the Hardy outfit."

The big man turned away and walked to where his horse stood hobbled near the fire. Without looking back, he unhobbled the horse, mounted and rode toward camp. The men followed in silence. The four men on the flanking crew got shovels and went back to dig the grave. After putting the body in and filling the shallow grave, they shoveled dirt over the remains of the branding fire and walked to camp.

The men were quiet that night. There was no card game. Clyde had been one of the regular players. When Dean crawled into his bedroll, it was not missing calves he was thinking about. What a day this had been. One boy had been seriously hurt and one man killed.

A person never knew what would happen on roundup. It was always dangerous work, but someway, you never thought about it happening to you or your group. He had hardly gotten acquainted with Clyde. He had no way of knowing what kind of a man he had been, but you someway felt closer to him now than when he had been alive. For a little while, Dean lay looking up at the moon as it rose in the sky. Tonight, it seemed as red as the blood that had run from the flunky's wound. He finally dropped off to a fitful sleep. He was soon dreaming, he was again on Ute, hanging on for dear life as the horse ran over one cliff after another. Then, the horse was stomping on Clyde's dead body and he was unable to make the animal stop. When he awoke, he found he was as tired as when he had gone to bed. That was no way to begin another morning on the rough string. Again, he called himself a complete fool to stay on this roundup but wondered what else he could do after he had gone this far. Were the risks he was taking worth it? Hell, no! But, he knew he would not quit.

TWELVE

The morning after Clyde's death was one Dean would long remember. The men were all in a somber mood as Boyd roped a small bay member of the rough string for Dean. He had originally thought this animal would be an easier one to ride. This, however, turned out to be wishful thinking. The horse was small, only weighing about nine hundred pounds, but was as wiry and tough as they came. The animal was sneaky quick and had developed the habit of bucking forward, then drawing himself backward and ducking back under the rider's leg. It took an exceptionally quick rider to catch the horse's movements in time to keep his balance when the horse did that trick. The horse threw Dean three times that morning before he finally managed to ride the animal away from camp. The falls were bad enough but forcing himself to get up and back on the horse was even worse.

As usual, Shadrow gave Dean the furthest circle away from camp, making him ride many more miles than the other men. At about the western most edge of his ride, Dean was dropping down a long slope of the rolling prairie when the little bay suddenly put its head down and began bucking. Dean was rapidly becoming so accustomed to a horse breaking in two with him that his instincts took over instantly. However, the little horse again managed, after bucking forward, to suck himself backwards and duck under the man's leg. Dean was thrown hard, his foot barely coming free of the stirrup. It took him a few minutes to clear his head.

When he stood up, he could see the horse disappearing over the top of the little swell. There was nothing he could do but walk. Soon, his feet were hurting from the light shoes and he found he was limping slightly. He cussed the little bay horse with every step. He walked several miles before he could make out the dust of the cattle gather moving far in front of him.

It was close to a ten mile hike to the bunch grounds from where he had started walking. He guessed he had covered almost half the distance to the wagon when he saw a rider loping toward him, leading his horse. It was Hugh Loring.

"Lose something?" the DZ rep asked, with a smile, as he drew up near the man on foot.

"One of us lost. Thanks, Hugh," Dean said, reaching for the rope hackamore reins of the horse. "You may have to snub him for me to get a blind on him."

"I've been going to tell you about the blind I seen a good bronc rider use on his bridle," the tall lanky rider said, holding the horse tight for Dean to put the bandanna over its eyes. "It was sure slick. I think you and me can rig one up that would be a whole lot better than doin' it the way you are."

"I'm game to learn something new," Dean said evenly, after the horse was blindfolded.

He swung on the horse, checked his stirrups and reached forward to jerk the blind off. The horse instantly sucked backwards. Dean managed to stay with the horse and he whipped the animal sharply across its rump with the rope reins. He wished he had his quirt, for he would have used it on this horse with a vengeance.

"A quirt would help this horse a lot, too," he managed to shout to the lanky cowboy, when the horse decided to go ahead and not continue its bucking.

Before they reached the bunch grounds, which Shadrow had moved a mile or so north of Clyde's grave, they saw the cow Clyde had roped, still dragging the dead man's rope around her neck. As soon as they had the cattle bunched, Ed Ward roped this cow and Les Boyd expertly caught her hind legs and stretched her out on her side where Ben and another rider clipped hair enough to make out her brand. Ironically, it was the brand of the Hardy outfit, the ranch Clyde had ridden for.

Jasper Kincaid rode up as the first crew were eating dinner. He dismounted and tied his horse on the picket line and walked to the wagon. His gray eyes went over the faces of the men scattered about eating their lunch. Upon seeing Dean, the eyes stopped and Dean felt sure the man's disappointment at seeing him still there could plainly be seen in those eyes. Dean smiled indifferently and went on with his eating.

After the men had finished their meal and Dean had managed to ride another member of the rough string off toward the herd, Jasper called Ben aside and the two talked for some time about the slender man in what was left of his once fine city clothes. Neither man was happy Dean was still there and both expressed their bitterness at his grit and determination. They had both felt sure the rough string would finish him, one way or the other. When Ben told the Pool boss about the flunky and Clyde, the man seemed to blame all of this on the slender man now riding toward the herd.

"Well, you get rid of him," Jasper instructed tersely. "I don't care how you do it, either, just get rid of him."

Jasper watched the work that afternoon and discussed the territory they were covering with Shadrow. It was plain to all the men that the roundup boss was not too happy with the amount of territory they had covered in those first days.

The next morning, Dean again found where someone had cut the thongs holding the old jumper on his saddle. Without a word, he retied the jumper roll and made ready to ride Poncho, the big black. That morning, he rode the horse the first time, but had a gushing nose bleed for an hour or more afterward, from the beating the horse gave him. At least, he had the satisfaction of riding past Jasper Kincaid with his head held high, partly to hold back the nose bleed, but proud to still be in the middle of that big black horse.

There were several times during the next days that he thought he would just have to give up, for those horses were pounding him unmercifully. Each time he was thrown, and this still happened with some regularity, from somewhere deep inside himself came the determination that drove him to get up and get back on the horse that had thrown him.

The other riders, although they knew Shadrow hated them for it, were beginning to be drawn more and more toward Dean for they could not help but admire his nerve and determination. Besides, the man was a likable fellow, always cheery and had a friendly smile whenever they met during their work.

The young day wrangler returned with the news he had gotten the flunky to the doctor in Limon and he thought the boy's back would heal. Jasper also brought another kid to act as flunky and another rider came to take Clyde's place.

Hugh Loring was as good as his word. He worked several nights with Dean to make sliding rawhide blinds that they fastened on the hackamore headstalls and the light riding bridle. These blinds slid up and down on loops on the headstall and Hugh added his own touch by tying a long leather thong to the top center of each blind. This thong ran under the top of the headstall and back through a strap around the horse's neck so that Dean could grab it without getting out of position in the saddle. A pull on the thong, lifted the blind up over the horse's eyes. This left the rider in a much better position to either ride or dismount. The rider sometimes still had to lean forward to push the blind down, when he wanted the horse to see but it was much easier and more permanent than the bandanna, which Dean often dropped and someone had to retrieve for him.

He tried the Spade bit on Ute the next time he rode the gray horse and found he had somewhat better control over the animal, but Ute still managed to stampede once with him, and no matter how badly he cut the horse's mouth, he could not control the animal. The bit was so cruel and cut the horse's tongue so badly that Dean hated to use it, but felt he someway had to get control over the horse.

Dean found a couple of the horses would work better with the light riding bit in the bridle he had bought in Limon than with the hackamores but most of the horses still worked best with those. By now, the two buckskins were working fairly well for him. He used them when he could for the long outside circles. These horses were two of the toughest he had ever ridden and would cover those extra miles with effortless ease and come back to camp ready for more. Button was even bucking less, and some mornings, did not buck much at all. Dean was afraid to say anything, for fear Jasper would take the horse away from him and find him something that would be harder to ride.

"I seen that bronc buster I was telling you about, do one other thing that might help you with Ute," Hugh told Dean one night, after Ute had again stampeded with him. Hugh was now becoming quite friendly toward Dean and Dean enjoyed the man's company. He found they had similar ideas and opinions on many subjects.

That night, the two men worked on the lighter hackamore. Hugh got several pieces of wire from one of the wagons. He took the longest piece and wound this around the nose band of the hackamore, leaving a small space between each loop of wire. Two shorter pieces, he worked into the big knot the adjusting ropes made under the horse's jaw and worked them around until they were sticking about a quarter of an inch out of the knot. He placed these sharp ends where they would dig into the horse's jaw when the rider pulled hard on the reins.

The first time Dean rode Ute with this rig was the first time he felt he had any real control over the horse. The wire wrapping on the nose band cut deeply into the top of the horse's nose and Ute soon had to give in to the pressure. Then, when the horse tried to run and Dean jerked the knot up under its chin, the wire points began digging into its lower jaw, as well. The gray horse threw up its head and slid to a quick stop. Each time it tried to run, Dean jerked up on the reins hard and the horse immediately stopped and threw up its head. It seemed the horse was gaining some respect for what the man could do, and although it quit trying to stampede so much, it would still buck each morning when first mounted.

The days passed quickly, although the work was hard and the hours long. Dean slowly was riding better and thrown less often. He began to feel more at home with the men and his love for the country. The animals, birds and other wildlife made him glad he was back where he felt he belonged, in spite of the horses he was expected to ride. He took his regular turn as a flanker but was very careful to say little to Shadrow.

Now, he knew there were at least four honest men watching for any sign of misbranding. They had found none and he was about to decide there was none being done, or that whoever was doing it was waiting until after they passed the Shelly Ranch. They were now in the area where the Shelly cattle normally ran. Every day he saw many Shelly cows with calves, quite a few dry cows that had probably lost their calves in the spring storms and quite a few grown steers as well as numerous yearlings. He could see no reason why there would not be a goodly number of cattle ready for market on the fall roundup.

He wondered if he was missing something. Could something be happening to the cattle between the two roundups or was the misbranding being done on the other wagons? As soon as this spring roundup was over, he would about have to try to cover as much territory as he could to find out about these other possibilities.

One other observation made a big impression on Dean.

The slender man was a cowman. He knew cattle and had worked long and hard with the owner of Arrowhead Ranch to build up their herds. The bulls used by the members of the Pool were not what he considered good bulls. He guessed that each member turned out bulls which did not cost too much, on the theory that he did not know whose cows they would breed, anyway. It seemed to Dean the ranchers were all defeating themselves in not improving their herds by using good bulls. He mentioned this to some of the other riders, but for the most part, they were merely cowboys and simply shrugged their shoulders for this was their bosses' business, not theirs.

One morning dawned cool, with a light rain falling. It was Ute's turn to be ridden and Dean wondered if his luck with the hackamore would hold for this ride. All the horses in the rough string were more apt to buck when the weather was damp and cool.

He led the horse out of the rope corral to where his saddle lay. After checking it over thoroughly, he saddled the horse, his quirt in hand ready to hit the horse should it try to bite him. He now carried the short whip on his saddle at all times. If a horse needed it and he was in a position he could use it, he did. He found the little bay and a few others soon respected the whip as much as anything he could use on them. Still, he never used it needlessly but only when that seemed the only thing a horse respected.

This morning, Dean had a little trouble mounting the horse in his slicker, but he finally managed it and leaned forward to push the rawhide blind down below its eyes. Because of the dampness, the blind was hard to push down. Immediately, Ute tried to stampede, running toward the camp.

Dean jerked hard on the reins and the horse slid to a stop and threw its head up, remembering the hated hackamore. Ute tried two more times to run, each time getting closer to the camp and, each time, Dean jerked the horse up short. He tried to turn the horse toward open country, but Ute now refused to turn.

It seemed the horse had now decided that, if it could not

run, it would buck. The gray bogged its head and bucked straight toward camp. Men now began to move away from him, wanting to be far enough away from the bucking horse that they would not get in trouble with their own mounts.

"Watch out!" a man shouted, trying to lead his horse out of the way. He had dismounted to get something from one of the wagons.

"They're coming right into camp!" Les Boyd yelled. "Turn him!"

The crooked-faced rider rode as close as he dared to the bucking gray and threw his hat in front of Ute in a vain attempt to turn the horse away from camp. Ute did not change his direction but trampled the hat, crushing it into the soft, wet dirt.

"Turn that horse! Turn that horse!" Shadrow now commanded. However, he was unable to force his own mount closer to the commotion because of the noise the cook was now making by banging away on his dishpan with a big wooden spoon.

"Turn him, turn him!" the cook yelled as the horse was now nearing the camp fire.

Ute paid no attention to their yells but bucked through the fire, scattering coals and ashes, knocking the iron bar holding a pot of beans flying in one direction, the coffeepot in another and a lid to a dutch oven in yet another.

Dean had to smile in spite of himself. He was having no real difficulty in riding the horse that morning and his wild yells and flapping slicker only seemed to make the horse buck harder. The horse was now bucking alongside the chuck wagon, as the cook dropped the pan and scrambled under the wagon for protection. Ute stomped the dishpan, putting several deep dents in it. The horse was now so close to the side of the wagon that its shoulder struck the emergency water barrel strapped to the side. The force of the blow lifted one rear wagon wheel off the ground before a strap broke from the impact, tipping the barrel over to give the startled cook an unexpected bath.

Dean was about to throw himself off the horse onto the wagon to avoid being scrapped off on the side, when the horse bucked away from the side and Dean managed to pull himself back into the center of the saddle.

Ute continued to buck, turning in front of the wagon to buck across the wagon tongue and back along the other side. At the rear of the wagon, the horse turned in just enough to let its shoulder strike the extended end gate which was also the lid of the chuck box, and when down, formed a working table for the cook. The supporting leg collapsed, pulling the entire chuck box out of the wagon bed. This crashed to the ground sending dishes, pots, pans and provisions flying into the air. A tin cup hit Dean in the face and he yelled, kicking the horse in the sides with his heels. Ute now bucked away from camp, leaving a scene of utter destruction, milling and yelling men including a wet and bedraggled cook who cursed the rider and the horse with vengeful vigor.

A few more bucks and the horse threw up its head and trotted forward like a gentle old kid's horse who would never think of doing anything wrong. Dean looked back over his shoulder to observe the camp. The cook was trying to find his things among the wet flour, beans and other supplies. Other men were trying to right the chuck box and get it upright and back on the wagon.

"By God, you sure made a hell of a mess of camp!" Les Boyd yelled, stooping to pick up his battered hat.

"If you think you can do a better job with these horses, I'll sure trade strings with you," Dean called back.

That was one morning the rough string rider had to wait for the rest of the men, in place of them waiting for him. He had to admit he rather enjoyed it. Most of the men cursed the gray horse but Dean noticed Hugh, Ed Ward and Eben openly laughed and joked about the mess. Those three were beginning to become more Dean's friends each day.

Jasper visited the wagon each week, staying a day or two to observe the work and to see the territory each wagon covered did not leave any gaps and miss any cattle. At each visit, Jasper was frustrated to find Dean still there and still riding the rough string. It seemed impossible to him that a man, soft from years in the city, could possibly ride those animals. At the conclusion of each visit, Jasper again instructed Ben to someway get rid of the man.

THIRTEEN

It was the day after one of Jasper's visits that Dean first noticed an uneasy feeling in his stomach, shortly after eating breakfast. Perhaps it was just the thought of having to ride Poncho, for it was the big black's turn to be ridden and this horse was still the worst one to ride.

Diarrhea hit him in the middle of the morning circle. Dean did not want to get off the big black out alone on the prairie, but at last, he could hold it no longer. He pulled the blind up and swung down. Poncho fussed and fumed and jerked back while Dean was relieving himself. He saw that the blind had worked down to where the horse could see and knew he was in trouble for Poncho probably would not let him walk up to him out on the prairie. He should have hobbled the horse but had been in too much of a hurry.

As soon as he could pull his pants up, Dean tried to walk up to the horse, so he could slide the blind up over the horse's eyes. The horse would have none of it, backing away from him no matter how hard he pulled on the reins. Dean was afraid to try too long, for fear the horse would jerk away from him. Finally, he gave up and turned to begin walking toward the bunch ground, leading the horse behind him. As luck would have it, he did not meet another rider and had to walk all the way to the wagon. Diarrhea hit him twice on the way and he felt both sick and weak when he walked into camp. It was well past the noon dinnertime. He noticed Ben had again not sent anyone to look for him.

"What happened to you?" the grizzled cook demanded, as Dean walked up to the chuck wagon. "You know Ben won't allow me to hold grub for anybody who ain't here on time."

"I'm not interested in anything to eat, but I could sure use some coffee," Dean said. "I've got a bad case of the Mexican quick step. Had to get off this damn horse and couldn't get back on him without someone to snub him up for me. I've walked a hell of a long ways."

"Well, Ben must have seen you, as I see he's coming in, now. He'll no doubt help you back on your horse. I'll get you a cup of coffee, though. Sorry about your problem. I'd fix you a plate of grub if I could."

"Thanks," Dean said and realized this was the first time Bart had ever shown any friendliness toward him. In fact, it was the first time the man had spoken to him since Ute had torn up the camp.

Dean turned to watch the wagon captain ride up, dismount and tie his horse to the picket line and walk swiftly toward the wagon.

"What the hell happened to you?" Ben demanded sharply, striding up in his hulking gate. His voice carried disgust but no concern. "Get yourself throwed again?"

"No, but it had the same results. Had to get off and I couldn't get back on with no one to snub for me," Dean explained. "I had to walk a hell of a ways."

"That's too damn bad," the captain said in mock sympathy. "I'll snub him for you so you can get right out to the herd. We don't have time for you to change. I don't like for the others to have to do your work, either."

Dean started to make a sharp retort, when the cook cut in before he could say anything.

"Don't be too hard on him, Ben," old Bart said, handing Dean a filled cup of coffee. "He's got a bad case of the runs and you know what a hell of a job it would be to have to ride those horses with the runs."

"That's too damn bad, Archer. We've got no time to wait for some waddy who can't take care of those chores, first thing in the morning. Let's go."

Dean took a swallow of the coffee as the big man turned to walk toward his horse.

"God, that's awful coffee, Bart. Worst you ever made."

The old man smiled, he was used to the men talking about his coffee this way.

"It's just your taste is upset with your miseries," he said.

Dean drank what coffee he could as Ben had now gotten his horse and rode up, his rope ready. Dean threw out the balance and tossed the empty cup to the cook.

"Thanks, Bart."

"Sorry I couldn't do more," the cook told him and turned back to his pots and pans.

Shadrow flipped his rope over the black's head and snubbed the horse close to his for Dean to slide the blind up over the horse's eyes. The horse now stood for Dean to mount. Shadrow pulled the blind down without asking Dean if he was ready and the horse leaped as high in the air as it had that morning. Dean fought to stay in the saddle, woozy and weak from the diarrhea. Had the black bucked as long as usual, Dean would not have been able to stay in the saddle. As it was, his nose again bled for the better part of an hour.

He was in misery all afternoon, as he helped hold the herd. He was thankful to be riding and not on the flanking crew. Twice, he had Hugh snub the black and hold him while he dismounted to relieve himself.

"Have any of you other fellows had this Mexican quick step?" Dean asked the cowboy, when he had again mounted.

"You're the only one, far as I know."

"Funny, usually hits the whole camp. I've been eating and drinking the same as the rest of you."

"Hadn't thought about that, but you're right. Does seem a little strange. I'll ask around and see if any of the others have been hit with it."

That evening, Dean sat near the fire, feeling chilled and not hungry. He was surprised when Bart brought him his supper. This was extremely unusual, for the cook never waited on any of the men, not even the wagon captain or the Pool boss. Maybe the cook was finally coming around to liking him, as were most of the other men, and he felt a little good about that. He didn't feel like eating much but managed to get a little food down and drank several cups of coffee. It tasted queer, but he again assumed it was because of the way he was feeling.

As he sat by the fire for some time, he kept thinking he could see Marian Shelly's pretty face in the coals. He thought about the woman for some time before he finally went to bed. He wondered if she would be thinking about seeing him as much as he looked forward to seeing her?

The next morning, it was Wrangler's turn to be ridden. Dean was certainly not looking forward to trying to ride the horse, as it was still one of the hardest buckers of them all. Besides, he was both sore and galled from the diarrhea and it would be painful to just sit on a saddle, let alone take the punishment of a bucking horse. He also felt extremely weak. Hugh led the buckskin out of the corral and snubbed it to his horse for Dean to put hobbles and blind on it.

"I've asked every man on the crew, but no one else has had any of your problem, Dean," Hugh told him. "I can't figure that out, either. If it was something you ate, we should all have it."

Dean wondered about this as he saddled the horse. He made a last trip behind a bush and made ready to mount the horse, after leading the animal up a little, hoping to take some of the buck out of it. It did not work, for Wrangler was always ready to buck the first thing in the morning.

Dean twisted the stirrup and put his toe in it to swing up. Once in the saddle, he rested a moment, feeling the horses's muscles knotting under the saddle in anticipation of its morning fun. Dean also felt the raw places in his crotch. His seat was already on fire. He was thankful he did not have to lean forward, for the blind slid down on its own when he loosened the thong. Wrangler was bucking instantly. It hurt like raw fire and tears came to his eyes as he fought to stay on the horse. He lost a stirrup but still managed to ride the horse by shear determination and will power.

He was in misery all morning, between the cramps and the raw places inside his crotch. Twice, he had to dismount while alone on his outer circle but, with the aid of the blind and making sure it stayed up over the horse's eyes, he managed to remount Wrangler both times with no real problem and the horse bucked but a little each time. He now had a bunch of cattle headed toward the bunch ground and Wrangler went to work behind them like the good cow horse he should have been.

Noon found a larger than usual herd and Dean was on the first shift for lunch. He turned Wrangler loose and did not catch another horse, for it was his turn on the branding crew. He had hardly reached the wagon when the cook met him carrying a plate of food and a cup of coffee. For the first time, Dean's quick glance caught what he thought was a slight smirk at the corner of the cook's mouth, mostly hidden by the man's drooping mustache.

"Nice of you, Bart," Dean observed, watching the cook closely now. "You've sure been nice to me lately."

"Well, you deserve it," the man said, turning away.

"By golly, maybe you deserve a little service, too, Bart," Dean drawled easily, his suspicions now fully aroused. "It just don't seem right to have you waiting on me this way, when you don't do it for anyone else, not even Ben. Here, you sit down and eat this. I'll get some more for me."

The cook snorted in disgust and started to walk away. "Hell, nobody ever waits on a cook," he added.

"Well, let's just change that. Here, Bart, now you sit down and eat this."

Dean sat the plate down and grabbed the old man's arm. The cook's face now held a startled expression as his watery eyes searched the thin face under the floppy beaver hat.

"No, I can't! Ben won't stand for that."

"Let's not worry about what Ben'll stand for. It's time you got a little of the attention you deserve around here," Dean insisted, picking up the plate and holding it out to the man.

"You know I can't!" the cook wailed, seemingly in real fear.

Dean's voice now took on a tone of command.

"Eat this, Bart...and drink this coffee, too. I've thought it tasted extra funny the last few days. Have you been putting something in it?"

"Of course not! It's just coffee, like always! Nobody else's complained about it tasting any different than usual. Hell, you all gripe about it all the time."

"No one else has had this Mexican quick step I've been having, either. I thought it was funny your being so nice to me all of a sudden."

"Hell, I just thought you got a raw deal and tried to help. I guess that's the thanks I get."

"Well, you're going to eat that plate of food and drink that coffee, if I have to ram it down your throat," Dean snapped savagely.

"Ben's coming, Archer," Ed Ward warned from where he and several of the other riders had been watching the exchange between Dean and the cook.

"Let him come," Dean said, not turning his attention from the cook. "Either eat this plate of food and drink this coffee, Bart, or I'll whip you within an inch of your life. If you live, I'll tie you on Poncho and see how you like getting your guts beaten out of you!"

He shoved the plate toward the cook. Bart's watery eyes met his and he took the plate with trembling hands. "If you insist. There ain't nothing wrong with this grub. It's just like everybody else gets."

"Fine! Eat it!"

The cook took several bites of the food. "Tastes all right to me," he said.

"Take a drink of that coffee and be damn careful you don't spill any of it," Dean said.

"What's going on here?" Ben demanded, as he walked up to the men. "Why're you standing around here? You know we've got men to relieve at the herd. Bart, what the hell are you doin', eatin'? You know better'n that!"

The wagon captain moved to where he could glare down at the whiskery face of the old man, his own face flushed with his anger.

"Bart ain't going anywhere until he eats that food and drinks that cup of coffee," Dean said evenly.

"What the hell are you up to now, Archer?" Shadrow whirled to demand hotly.

"You heard me, Ben. Bart eats this stuff he's been giving me, and which I think he put something in to make me sick."

"Don't be ridiculous, Archer. We've all been eating the same grub and nobody else's sick."

"You want to drink this coffee, Ben?" Dean asked. "I think it's in the coffee, anyway, not the food."

"I ain't gonna drink your damn coffee!" the big man almost shouted. "And Bart ain't either! We've got work to do and no time for any of your personal arguments."

Dean's face was calm but his hand was on the butt of his pistol. "One of you's going to drink that coffee, one way or another," the man said, evenly, coldly. "I've had all I'm going to take. Bart, drink that, or by God, I'll shoot you both!"

"Les," Ben said, quickly looking over his shoulder at the little men.

"Les ain't moving, Ben," Ed Ward said evenly, his hand already on the little man's shoulder. "The rest of us would like to see one of you eat that grub. Something's sure been making Archer sick."

"That's right, Ben," Hugh Loring added, now stepping up beside Dean and his big hand was also on his pistol.

"What's this? Mutiny? Are all of you disobeying my orders?"

"As far as roundup goes, Ben, we'll take your orders," Hugh said quietly. "But, if Bart's been putting something in Archer's food or drink, we've all got a right to know about it. Hell, he might put it in ours."

Shadrow now turned to the cook. "Did you put something in Archer's coffee, Bart?"

"Hell no!"

Dean's pistol seemed to jump out of his holster and was now pointed at Bart's foot.

"Drink that coffee, or I'll blow a toe off to start with!" Dean told the man. "Bart, you drop that coffee and you're a dead man."

"All right, all right. I did put some stuff in Archer's coffee. After all, he let his horse tear up my camp. It served him right," Bart said tersely.

"Kincaid or Shadrow in on this?" Dean demanded.

"No. I was just getting even with you, myself."

"Where's the stuff and where'd you get it?"

"It's in a little bottle in the chuck box. I've kept a bottle of it for years as protection in case you guys get too funny with me."

"Get it!" Dean told him. "I'm going right with you, too, so don't try anything. Hugh, keep an eye on Shadrow for me."

"Hell, Archer, what do you want from me?" the big captain demanded. "Bart told you, I'm not in on this. If he's actually been putting something in your coffee, hell, I don't blame you for being mad." Shadrow stomped away from the group to go to the Dutch ovens where he began filling his plate. "This is between Archer and Bart, men. Finish your grub and get your horses. We've got work to do."

Dean looked at the little bottle the cook was holding out to him. It had no label and contained a clear colorless liquid.

"I don't know what it is, but it sure works every time," Bart insisted. "I got it from the druggist in Limon. That's the only weapon a cook has to fight back with. That's all I've got. Throw it away and I can't do you any more harm."

"Throw it away? Hell, no, you're going to drink it," Dean said savagely. "Then, you're going to get on a horse and ride the hell out of here and see how you feel. I hope it makes you half as sick as I've been!"

"No, I won't drink it!"

Again, the pistol seemed to leap into Dean's hand.

"Damn you, Bart. I'd ought to just kill you for what you did to me," Dean said, taking the top off the bottle and holding it out to the cook. "Drink it right out of the bottle, and by God, you're going to drink it all."

With these words, he held the pistol next to Bart's stomach and eared the hammer back with his thumb. The cook gulped and swallowed, took the bottle and tipped it to his lips. Dean watched to make sure he drank it all. He took the empty bottle from the cook's trembling hand, to smash it savagely against the iron rim of a wagon wheel.

"Now, catch your horse and ride on out of here and don't come back while I'm on this wagon."

Dean turned to walk back to where the men were finishing their lunch. He picked up a tin plate and cup and went to the fire. The cook hurried past him to go directly to Shadrow. A moment later, the big captain walked over to where Dean was now sitting on the grass holding his plate on his crossed legs.

"What the hell you mean, telling Bart to leave?" the big man demanded.

"That's what I meant. I'd not feel safe around here, as long as he's doing the cooking."

"How many times do I have to tell you, Archer, that you ain't running this wagon?" Shadrow demanded, his feet wide apart, his big hand now resting on the butt of his own pistol. "You don't tell anyone to leave."

"I suggest you get one of the wranglers to act as cook until you can get a new one in here," the man on the ground said, almost pleasantly. "Bart sure ain't staying with this wagon."

"I keep telling you, you ain't the boss!"

"Oh, I know that, Ben," Dean said lazily. "If I was, you'd be going with him. I'd still not be surprised if you or Jasper wasn't in on this with him. You've both tried hard enough to get rid of me."

"Well, Bart ain't going anywhere, until I say so," Ben said stubbornly.

"Then say so, Ben," Eben Hessey's high, tight voice said from behind the big man. "If he did that to Archer, you'd better not let me catch him in this camp tonight."

The big man looked over his shoulder at the chunky rider behind him. Hessey's hand was on his pistol and those ice blue eyes told the man he had no choice.

"Aw, a cook ain't worth shootin' somebody over," the big captain said, with a heavy sigh and turned away. "Forget it. Les, go catch a horse for Bart. He can find Summers' wagon and explain this to Jasper. Jasper can decide what to do. Hank, you see if you can't cook up some supper for us of some kind. Saddle up, men, we've got work to do."

FOURTEEN

Marian Shelly bustled about the large kitchen as she went over all the items she planned to have ready for the wagon crew when it arrived for the noon meal. As she checked on the hams cooking in the oven and the pans of rolls ready to go in, her thoughts kept turning to the man her father had hired to try to find out what was happening to their cattle. She wondered if he had found anything. As she remembered the way the man had looked the last time she saw him, persistent doubts that such a man could help them kept unsettling her mind.

Marian was a ranchwoman, had spent most of her life right here on this ranch and she knew the hardships of ranch life. She had lost two sisters and one brother to disease. Her mother had died years ago, a woman worn out ahead of her time by the trials she had endured. Her father had been a cripple from an accident with a horse for almost as long as she could remember. She knew the odds Dean faced and she remembered the way he had looked that night in Gertie's, a clean, neat, city gentleman, unlike the western men she had known all her life.

Yet, there was something about that man. She recalled vividly how he had come gayly to her aid in Gertie's, how he had twice knocked Jasper Kincaid down and fought off a whole room full of men on her behalf. Yes, he was different and she had to admit to herself she had thought more about him during the past weeks than any man since Billy Kincaid. And that had been years ago. Hadn't she reached the conclusion her life would always be alone, as far as any special man was concerned? She had determined that it was a complete waste of time for her to ever think there could still be a romance in her life. No one, not even a lonesome cowboy, wanted a thirty-five-year-old, old maid.

Then, she recalled the tramp at the barbecue at Kincaid's. The man had then looked like something the cat had drug in, a big bluish knot on his head and not appearing in the least the type to find out anything about cattle. She wondered if the man had ever thought of her after the wagons had pulled out. Probably not. Why should he? He had been back East, and no doubt, had known many real ladies, not plain old ranch-women. It rather embarrassed her to admit to herself the time she had spent thinking about him.

How she hoped he had not been hurt by those horses. She had seen her father go through years of pain and suffering from what a horse had done to him and she certainly did not wish that for any other human. Even more, she hoped he had found the answer to what was happening to their missing cattle. The thought of her father having to give up all he had worked so many years for, was hard for her to even think about.

As she worked, her glance often went out the north kitchen window. That was the direction she expected the men to come from. Two other women hurried about the kitchen helping her, Mrs. Vigil, Manuel's wife, and Christine Kincaid, Kate Kincaid's seventeen-year-old daughter. Actually, Marian knew

Christine had come more in the hopes her brother Claude would get to spend a day or two of his lay over at home, and she would get to see him, than to help with the work. The two young people were exhibiting all the signs of love and Marian would never stand in the way of true love. That sort of thing had passed her by and she did not want to see anyone else with the aching heart she had carried for so many long years. Actually, she liked the girl, enjoyed her company and hoped she and her brother did fall in love. Christine was Kate's daughter by a former marriage but had taken the Kincaid name.

"They're coming!" Christine shouted, returning from the long porch which extended across the east side of the house and where they had set the long tables and benches for the men. "I can see the dust of the remuda."

Marian hurried to the back door and stood on the small platform and steps on the west side of the kitchen. Yes, she could also see the dust of the horses. She hurried back inside to put the rolls in the oven and check to make sure the dinner was in proper readiness.

Every few minutes, the woman would hurry to a window and look out. She saw the running horses as the men turned them into the corrals. Then, she saw the three wagons disappear behind the barns and sheds where they would park and set up camp.

Minutes later, she could hear the men gathering outside the screened in porch awaiting her call to come inside to eat. As usual, the men were anxious to get to sit at a table and eat food prepared by women. They always looked forward to that treat.

Marian walked past the long tables to the screen door. Opening this, she looked out over the crowd of hungry men, looking for one face in particular. It was not hard to spot the remains of that ridiculous beaver hat with a whiff of his dark wavy hair protruding through a hole in the crown.

"Mr. Archer!" she called and saw he was already watching her. She waved and watched him return the wave, his carefree smile on his lips. She wondered that he seemed so relaxed, as she stood on her tiptoes to call loudly, "Your things came, Mr. Archer. They're in the bunkhouse."

He waved his thanks and turned quickly to walk away from the crowd toward the out buildings. He really wanted to talk to the woman, but knew better than to disturb her while getting the meal ready for all these men. His appearance bothered him, too, for he knew he looked even more like the hobo tramp than when she had last seen him. Even from where he had been standing, he could tell she was looking as neat and pretty as he remembered her.

She now turned to speak to her cousin, who was leaning against the house near the door.

"Is he still riding the rough string, Eben?" she asked.

"I'll say he is. That man's got more pure guts than anyone I've ever known, Marian. I have no idea how many times he's been throwed, got up and got back on those horses and made a ride. Bart, the cook, put something in his coffee that made him sick as a dog and he still rode those horses. I'd say you're mighty lucky to have him looking after your interests, although I don't think he's found out much. I know for sure, he kept an eye on everything Shadrow's done."

"You sound like he's won your respect," she commented, watching the man's face keenly.

Eben pushed his hat forward until it all but covered his eyes. Then, he turned his head up to look up under the brim at his cousin. "Yes," Eben said lazily in his high, tight voice. "Archer's one man I've come to even like."

"Well, that certainly does speak well for Mr. Archer," Marian said, turning to go back inside. "It will be ready in just a few minutes."

Inside the bunkhouse, Dean found the war sack he had used many years on Arrowhead Ranch, filled almost to the bursting point. Beside it was a big burlap bag of riding equipment and a wooden box. He eagerly pulled the strings from the bag and drew out his saddle, the one Foster Saddlery in Pueblo had made especially for him. It had been freshly oiled, and oh how good it looked. As he thought of those friends on the Arrowhead, again remembering how very special they were to him, he let his fingers slowly trace the pattern of the hand tooling on the skirts and stirrup fenders. A new lariat rope was fastened to the fork, a gift from his old boss, he felt sure.

Also from the bag, he withdrew the Navajo blanket and hairpad he had left so many years ago. These were followed by his batwing chaps, bridles, hobbles and other gear.

From the war sack he drew out the neatly folded Levi cowboy denim pants, work shirts and a wide leather belt. He immediately shucked out of the patched remains of those city clothes and pulled on those cowboy clothes. Never had any clothes felt so good to him.

From the wooden box came his Stetson hats, one so new it had hardly been worn, the other sweat stained but still with lots of wear in it. It looked like a cowman's hat. By golly, it was a cowman's hat. The beaver hat went flying across the room and he put the sweat stained Stetson on, immediately feeling better. There were also two pair of handmade, high-heeled boots, one of them slightly worn and the others did not look like they had ever been on his feet. He had forgotten how new they were, when he left them. Quickly, he unlaced the shoes, taking them off, to pull on the used pair of boots.

The final touch was the large rowelled, silver-mounted spurs his old boss, Clay Hamilton, had given him years ago. He quickly buckled these on his boots. He stomped his feet just to hear them jingle. By God, he could put his feet in the stirrups now and his biggest fear of the rough string was gone. When he stood up, he was no longer the tramp from the East, but the old Dean Archer, cowman.

The last man was just entering the porch for dinner when Dean arrived, his spurs ringing with each step. That was music to his ears. He now entered the porch, tossed his Stetson on the pile near the door and found a place on one of the benches. He knew they were all looking at him. Those rough cowboys would never admit that clothes made the man but they would all have admitted that this man now looked the part of the cowman. The slender man proudly wore those clothes as the badge of his profession.

"I must say they changed your looks," Marian whispered as she passed behind him while serving the table.

He turned to smile up at her, his dark hair falling in waves across his forehead. For the first time, she realized he was really quite a handsome man. His thin face was now sun bronzed except where his hat had protected his forehead. He had completely lost the pale look of the Eastern city dude. He now looked what he really was, a vigorous and healthy cowman.

The next time the woman came near him, he asked softly, "How about that horseback ride?"

"Not today but maybe tomorrow," she replied, leaning between him and Eben to put a fresh platter of meat on the table. "Come to the kitchen later and we'll discuss it."

"I will, if I can," he promised, feeling the warmth of her arm through his shirt sleeve. That touch made his blood race through his veins. He couldn't believe the woman could make him feel like this.

The men had not eaten from a table or off china plates for weeks. How they all fell to that meal. Everything seemed extra delicious to them and they all ate with relish and enthusiasm. The pies and cakes that followed the main meal were the first desserts the men had eaten since the start of the roundup and they made short work of them, Dean not being the only one who overate on those pastries.

Immediately after the meal, Shadrow led the men to where the cook and his helpers had set up camp some distance from the main ranch buildings and hidden from sight of the ranch by the corrals and sheds. This cook was here under protest, for he had signed on to cook for Summers' middle wagon and had been forced by Jasper to change with Bart. This man directed some of the men in unloading a wagon load of supplies and transferring them to the chuck wagon. Shadrow stopped Dean after he had carried a case of canned tomatoes to the wagon.

"You, Hugh and Hessey, come with me," the captain said. "You get the job of helping the ropers and blacksmiths with the horses," he told them.

At the big corrals, Ed Ward and Les Boyd roped horses and turned them over to the three men, who led them to where three blacksmiths had set up their forges. The men helped hold the horses while the smiths trimmed their hooves and put shoes on those they felt needed it. This country was so sandy that many of the horses were never shod.

Most members of the rough string refused to let the smiths pick up any of their feet and these had to be thrown to have their feet trimmed while lying on their sides and backs. This was hard work and took time. Dean wanted in the worst way to go see Marian, but could not leave as either Shadrow or Boyd seemed to be ever present, as though watching for him to try to leave.

It was almost supper time when Dean finally finished with the horses and could get away to go to the house. Marian was again busy preparing the evening meal for the crew.

"Sorry I couldn't get here sooner," he apologized, his hat in his hand as he stood on the back steps by the door. "Shadrow wouldn't let me leave."

"Well, I've got hungry men to feed again tonight," she said rather tartly, in her abrupt manner. "The roundup cook will take over in the morning, so this is the last big meal I have to prepare. I've got no time to talk, now."

"How about later, after supper?"

"Give me time to get the dishes done and then come to the house and we'll see what happens. Dad wants to talk to you, anyway."

Dean returned to the bunkhouse and took his turn at the galvanized bath tub. Although he had shaved that morning, he shaved again and then took his turn with one of the men who did the barbering for the group. Most of the men liked their hair well trimmed as it was much easier to keep clean. It had felt good to have a real bath with warm water, even though the facilities had been primitive. It was sure better than trying to wash off what he could in the little creeks or occasional lake they had come to.

That evening at the supper table, Dean found that Claude Shelly had indeed come to spend a little time at the ranch. He could instantly tell that the boy and Christine Kincaid were sweet on each other. He enjoyed watching the two exchange their feelings across the room every chance they got to look at each other.

Dean caught himself looking at Marian Shelly. The woman's face was flushed from the heat of the stove but her trim figure showed how neatly she cared for herself. The woman was completely unlike many of the ranchwomen he had known, for she kept herself neat and attractive, rather than letting the hard life grind her down. When she came close to him while serving coffee, Dean caught not only the aroma of the coffee but also that of her perfume. Dang it, he thought, I'm acting as silly as that kid across the table. Marian Shelly would certainly not be interested in exchanging moon-eyed looks across the room.

Later that night, he went to the house and was greeted warmly by Marian and led into the parlor where they joined Herman Shelly, Claude and Christine. The rancher shook his hand warmly and Dean took a seat in a large rocking chair and was pleased when Marian sat on a straight-backed chair next to him. Herman Shelly was anxious to know what he had found and came right to the point.

"Claude tells me he's not been able to pick up any sign of misbranding on his wagon, or any other reason why we would be short of cattle," the rancher said, his expressive face empathizing his disappointment. "He saw Manuel Vigil a few days ago and he said the same thing about the east wagon. Have you found anything?"

"I hate to add to your troubles, but I've found absolutely no evidence of any wrong doing," Dean said, meeting the rancher's eyes. "There have been at least four of us watching every move Shadrow has made and have not turned up one thing. I've not seen one calf carrying a brand different from its mother. I have found the other reps to be honest cowboys, always trying to look out for their outfits and have seen nothing to make me think any or them are stealing your cattle."

"Dang, I was so in hopes you'd know something by this time. I guess it was too much to expect. Any ideas?"

"No, but there's got to be an answer somewhere," Dean said. "I doubt they'll start misbranding between here and the Arkansas, but I guess that's still possible. We've worked lots of your cattle lately, too. I really can't see why you shouldn't be able to have a respectable beef gather. They must someway be taking cattle between the time this roundup ends and the beef gather starts. My only idea is to ride as much country as I can, after the roundup ends, and see what I can find that way."

"God, if you haven't found anything yet, I'm afraid it'll be too late to find anything after roundup," Shelly said, his face showing how disappointed he was. "I've been so sure whatever was happening was done then."

"Do you have a better idea?" Dean asked.

Shelly shook his head sadly.

"All the wagons meet at La Junta," Marian spoke up. "Why don't we plan to meet Dean and Claude there and see if anything has happened? If not, we can come back here and he can take some horses and a small pack outfit and see if he can find anything we've all missed."

"I guess that's all we can do, but you and I'll have to be back for the Pool meeting at Kincaid's," Shelly said. "All the reps are supposed to stay with the wagon until they get the horses and equipment back to Kincaid's. I guess we can take someone to replace Dean. At least that way, he can immediately start checking for any sign of anything happening that is not connected with the roundup. By God, we're really going to be in trouble, if we don't have a good beef shipment this fall."

They visited for a while and Herm gave Dean permission to leave any of his extra gear in the bunkhouse, knowing the man would want to take only the essentials for the rest of the roundup. Marian and Christine talked a little about things at the Kincaid Ranch. Dean was surprised to learn both Mac Kincaid and his daughter-in-law, Kate, were away from the ranch for most of the summer and the girl had been there alone for some time.

"It must be kind of lonesome there with just you and old Unk," Herm said.

"Oh, Unk's gone too," the golden-haired girl said quickly. "Each year, about this time, Unk goes off for a month or so on what he calls a reunion with some of his old buddies. Some of them come to the ranch for a few days and then they all go off for over a month. I don't know where they go, or just what they do, but there's lots of talk about wagons, horses and roundups whenever any of them are there. Right now, there's only the cook, a couple of farm hands and me at the ranch. It is lonesome. That's the main reason I love to come over here."

"Unk's probably just talking over old times with those men," Shelly said. "After all, he's been a cowman around this country for a long time and has ridden with a lot of men. He was the one that started the Resolis Pool and he ran it for years. Those men are probably some that rode with him on those early roundups and they just like to get together and talk about old times."

"I'm sure that's all there is to it," Christine said and straightened her skirt as she looked sideways at Claude. "Unk does talk to those men about Jasper and some about Billy. Apparently he thought more of Billy than he does of Jasper."

"Who's Billy?" Dean asked.

"Billy Kincaid was Jasper's younger brother," Claude spoke up, a gleam in his eye as he looked at his sister. "I remember Billy. He wasn't like Jasper, at all. He was a heck of a good rider, too. Some folks called him a fancy Dan and I do remember how all the girls were crazy about him and his riding. Rode a slick-horned saddle, one of the very few I ever saw. You'd ought to get you a slick-horned saddle to ride the rough string with, Dean. You'd have all the girls in the country swoonin' over you."

"Claude, that's enough!" Marian said firmly.

"Oh, heck, Marian, it's been years. Billy always did enjoy a good story and a good laugh. He'd probably enjoy seeing you blush, now, if he were here. He was a fun person to be around."

"That he was," Marian said primly and Dean could see that, in truth, her cheeks were slightly pink. "But, you exaggerate things so much."

"Well, I'm not exaggerating when I tell Dean you were one of the girls who had a crush on Billy," Claude said, enjoying tormenting his sister. "You used to love to watch him ride. I even remember you and him racing your horses over west of the ranch where Dad couldn't see you."

"Oh, Claude.... So we raced...I usually won."

"Let's change the subject," Herman suggested uncomfortably. He knew his daughter was being embarrassed by this talk. Sometimes, Herm wished Marian had married Billy Kincaid. He hated it when he thought of her getting this late in life with no interest in any man. Billy had been the only man Marian had ever shown any interest in. To change the subject, he turned to Christine. "I don't like for you to be at the ranch alone, or with just hired men, Christine. You should stay here with us."

"I'd like that," the girl said gayly. "However, I must stay there in case Mother gets back. Last year she didn't come back until the roundup was over and Jasper was home."

"Several things might have been different, if Billy hadn't been drowned," Claude said, his eyes still on his sister's face. "I think Billy would have been a heck of a lot better roundup boss than Jasper. Would sure have been better for me, if my brother-in-law was running the outfit."

Marian now stood up rather quickly, catching Dean's eye and turned toward the kitchen.

"Let's go make some popcorn," she said. "Claude needs something to keep his mind on while he talks."

Dean arose and followed the woman. Once outside the parlor, the ranch house was quite dark and he felt her hand reach for his in the darkness. He let her lead the way through the dining room and into the kitchen. A moment later, she let go of his hand and a match flared as she lifted the lamp chimney to light it. He was disappointed. The touch of her hand had sent his blood tingling.

"I never thought I'd want to see that stove again tonight," she said, setting the lamp on a shelf above the big range. "Claude was talking too much. Besides, you may not like popcorn, anyway."

"It's been so long since I had any, I think I've forgotten what it tastes like," he said, after a quick laugh. "They always told me I'd never be a cowboy if I ate popcorn or drank pink lemonade."

"And, I suppose you wanted to be a cowboy so badly you never tasted either one?" she guessed, knowing cowboys. "It's really more like ice cream weather, as it has been hot lately, but we have no ice and we do have popcorn."

"Another thing they always told me was to make do with what you had," he said.

He took over building up the fire in the stove as she brought a jar of popcorn from the pantry and took the popper down from where it hung behind the range. Dean let his eyes go over the woman as they waited for the stove to get hot enough. Marian's dark eyes met his briefly and he noted again the twin streaks of gray at her temples. The simple house dress she wore still managed to set off her slender figure and he thought how womanly she looked. She was actually quite a striking person.

"Were you engaged to Billy Kincaid?"

"No." Her abrupt answer was firm and blunt. "We went together some but he never asked me to marry him." She turned to look squarely at the man, his dark hair again waving down over his white forehead which contrasted so sharply with the bronze of his lower face. "It doesn't matter, anyway. Billy's dead. He was a good boy, a fancy Dan perhaps, but he was a good man."

"He was drowned?"

"Yes, in a cloudburst and flash flood on the Big Sandy.

That old creek gets full of quicksand during high water and has trapped many a person. Billy had been here to see me and was on his way home. He met Jasper somewhere between here and their ranch, so they were together. Jasper said he tried to get Billy to go up to the safe crossing above their home place but Billy insisted on crossing a few miles east of the ranch. That was so much like Billy, he was quite reckless. Jasper said Billy's horse went down in the quicksand about halfway across. He thought Billy got caught in the rigging. Anyway, we never found any trace of him or his horse."

She did not say anymore as they popped enough of the corn to fill two large bowls. Marian seasoned these with butter and salt and they each carried a bowl to the parlor. Marian went back to the kitchen to return with a number of smaller bowls and they were all soon enjoying the treat.

"Boy, Dad, we've sure seen a lot of nester places starting up," Claude said around a mouthful of the corn. "A few are fencing their land and some of the men say if they get much thicker, we'll have to give up the open range."

"Oh, it'll never come to that!" Shelly's expressive face plainly showed his nonacceptance of this idea. "There'll always be open range. Only cowmen can use all of it."

"I wish I was sure of that," Dean said and felt all eyes turn to look at him. "We've seen some homesteaders moving into the country our wagon covered, too. Some of the older hands say there must be forty or fifty new places in the past year. Give them a few years to fence their land and plow it up and it'll be hard to drive cattle through the country."

"I just don't think they'll last that long. God never meant for this country to be plowed and farmed. Most of them people will give up long before they can prove up on their land. Them that do, will be glad to sell out to any cowman and then, we'll own it," Herm insisted.

"And, what will you cowmen use for money to buy those places with?" Dean asked, and watched the startled look come across the rancher's face. "Most of you are having a heck of a time making a go of it on free grass. How will you ever do it if you have to put out money for the land and then pay taxes on it? I rode for the Arrowhead Ranch for years. It's almost all private land, too, originally a Spanish land grant. I'll bet Clay's having a heck of a time making a go of things, and he's one of the smartest cowmen I ever knew."

"Well, I'm not going to worry about nesters forcing me off the range," Herm said and snorted his disgust at the thought. "They'll never be strong enough to do that, and besides, I've got enough trouble without them."

"They could well be a part of your problem, Herm," Dean said. "You take a few hundred nesters scattered over the territory covered by the Pool, and with each family eating a beef or two a year, that could amount to a part of your missing beef."

"Now, that could be true," Marian said, looking sharply at Dean.

"They probably do help themselves to a cowman's beef when they get the chance," Claude said. "Most of the ones I saw, looked like they were half starved to death, especially, those that came out last fall and spent the winter. Some of them have really had a rough time to survive the blizzards and now the dust and rattlesnakes."

"Speaking of snakes, I hear the men killed a big one this afternoon," Herm said. "We haven't seen many close to the house for years, but some of the men said tonight they'd gotten a big diamond back at the sheds this afternoon."

"I hope they killed it before Les Boyd got hold of it," Claude added. "They tell me he likes snakes and that he'll catch one and play with it for hours. I guess he knows just how to catch them so they can't bite him."

Herm's rubbery face expressed his dislike of even the thought. "The only way I like a snake is very dead," he said.

It had been a long time since Dean had enjoyed an evening as much as he had this one. It seemed to him Marian Shelly had now accepted him as a friend and he had to admit being thrilled at the easy way she had in speaking to him. She was a very open and frank person and he felt she would be one to pointedly let him know, if she didn't like something. He finally decided he would have to leave.

She went to the door with him. For a moment, he held his hat in his hand, not knowing just what to say. "It's been pleasant, Marian," he leaned toward her to whisper.

"Much more so, than when we first met," she whispered back and her smile gave meaning to her words.

"How about that horseback ride? I'll race you in the back pasture, but I doubt you'll win."

"Well, I'll show you," she teased. "I'll be ready about middle of the morning. Meet you at the corrals."

"You sure will."

He walked away from the house in the darkness, feeling an elation he had not known in years. Wouldn't it be a funny turn of events if he found he had chased a pipe dream all the way to Ohio, when what he really wanted had been right here in the West he loved so much? What a woman Marian Shelly was. A ranchwoman who knew the hard work and hard times of ranching, yet kept herself looking like a lady. You would go a long way and not find another woman of Marian's ranching knowledge and background, things he respected. Come to think of it, he had gone a long way looking for something which may have been right here, all the time. She was such a contrast to the pale, sweet young thing he had followed to Ohio and thought he had wanted. What had been wrong with him?

There was enough moonlight to let him roughly see to find his way around the corrals and sheds and across the prairie to where the wagons were parked. He could make out the gray beds scattered around the wagon. Eben's would be the furthest away, near the saddles.

His bedroll was still lying by the bed wagon where it had been laid when the other riders had gotten theirs. Something stopped him a few feet from the bed as he sensed, rather than saw, movement near it. His instinct told him snake! As he stood frozen in his tracks, something thudded on the ground close to his feet. He jumped back instinctively. It was a snake!

He had heard no warning rattle, his hand went to his hip before he remembered he had not taken his gun to the Shelly house that night. He struck a match and saw the reflection of the twin red dots of the snake's eyes as it coiled and readied for another strike.

Dean ran to the chuck wagon and got the shovel the cook kept near the fire. Returning with this in hand, he lit another match, located the snake's eyes, and with a sharp jab of the shovel cut off the serpent's head. He tried to flip the dead writhing form away from his bedroll. He could not. Every time he tried, the snake's body was drawn back to the bedroll as though tied to it.

Sure the snake was dead, he returned to the chuck wagon and got the cook's lantern and lit this. When he brought this back to his bedroll, he found the snake was actually tied to the bedroll with a piece of stout string. Someone had cut the rattles off the serpent and tied its tail tightly to his bed. It was a big snake, over three feet long. Someone had deliberately done this hoping the snake would bite him and perhaps kill him.

Anger was something this slender man seldom displayed but it now welled up inside him and seemed to explode in his brain.

FIFTEEN

Dean chopped the string in two with the shovel and picked the snake up by the string. He now carried this toward where he thought Hugh Loring's bed would be.

"Anything wrong?" Hugh called from the darkness ahead of him.

Dean carried the snake closer, holding the lantern so that Hugh, now sitting up in his bed, could see it.

"By God, that's a big one!" Hugh exclaimed. "It's dead, isn't it?"

"It is, now, but it wasn't when it was tied to my bedroll."

"That damn Les had one about that size this afternoon, playing with it," Hugh said. "Him and Shadrow got some whiskey somewhere and was both pretty drunk by bedtime, but Les was still playing with that snake the last time I seen him."

"Well, this is the last straw," Dean said, his voice calm but his anger pushing him. "I'm going to shove this snake down somebody's throat. You want to come watch?"

"You bet I do," Hugh said, rolling out of his blankets.

While Hugh pulled on his pants and boots, Dean went back to the bed wagon and got his pistol from his war sack and shoved this in the waist band of his pants. With Hugh now following him, he made his way to Les Boyd's bed. He leaned down to pull the canvas cover back far enough to reveal the man's crooked face, in a deep drunken sleep. Hugh reached down and picked up the pistol the man kept near his head.

Dean lifted the blankets and threw the snake on the man's naked belly.

"Snake!" he yelled. "Snake!"

He sat the lantern down and straddled the man's shoulders and head, holding the blankets tightly around the man's neck. In the lantern light, they could see Boyd's eyes open wide. For a moment, he stared stupidly up at the light, then his body sensed the reptile moving on his stomach, for the snake still writhed in its death throes. A look of sheer terror replaced the stupid one in the man's eyes. Boyd's face twisted in horror and he tried desperately to throw the covers back. "You like playing with snakes, Les? Let your friend play with you for a while," Dean snarled as he held the man down.

"Let me up!" Les cried, his face twisting in his terror and his deep voice pleading through his twisted lips. "Damn you, Archer! Let me up!"

The little man twisted and fought in fear, striving with all his might to roll Dean off his shoulders but Dean had wrestled too many calves those past weeks and his strength was too much for Boyd.

"Enough, Archer! Enough!"

"I'll tell you when you've had enough!" Dean shouted at the man beneath him. "When he bites you, that'll be enough. I want you to remember this, the next time you cut the thongs on my saddle."

"Don't blame me, Archer. Shadrow made me do that! For

God's sake, get off me!"

Hugh was watching closely. When Boyd's thrashing finally tore through the canvas covering of the bed and his naked leg flashed out, Hugh had his pocket knife ready. He grabbed the flashing leg and made two quick jabs, using only the sharp point to make two little punctures high inside Boyd's exposed thigh.

"He bit me!" Boyd screamed and Hugh jabbed again.

The little man kicked and fought in sheer terror and Hugh jabbed in the most sensitive area, pleased with each new scream of fright from the man.

At last, Dean let the man up. Fear made the little man stand naked before them, looking down at the little marks and the blood on his leg.

"My God, I'm going to die!" the man moaned.

"Sure looks like it," Dean told him calmly, as Ed Ward came to see what was going on. "You're the one that asked for this, Les. You tied him to my bedroll, hoping he would bite me. Far as I'm concerned, serves you right."

"Get me to a doctor. I'm going to die!" yelled the little man in his big voice. He cheeks twisted grotesquely as nerves made his face twitch.

"There ain't no doctor for fifty miles," Hugh told him. "You'll never make it."

"Maybe your friend Shadrow'll lend you a horse," Ed Ward said. "He wasn't too keen on letting the flunky have one, but maybe he'll even send somebody with you."

Dean carefully unrolled the blankets to where part of the snake's body could be seen in the lamp light.

"He sure got you, Boyd," Hugh said. "Why, you can see the fang marks there on your leg."

Boyd looked down again at the little marks on his leg and fainted.

Dean got the snake and lifted the man's head to coil it several times around the skinny neck. "Maybe he'll faint again when he wakes up and feels that."

"Ol' Ben didn't even wake up to take part in the fun,"

Hugh said, looking at the bulky bed of the wagon captain. "He'll be sorry he missed this."

The next day, Dean finally got his ride with Marian. He borrowed a gentle horse from Shelly, so he would not have to ride one of the rough string. It was a warm beautiful day. The prairie was green with new grass and the air was filled with the song of the little lark buntings which some of the cowboys called bob-o-links. These little birds flew up in front of their horses and darted away while making their distinctive call. They usually flew in short quick spurts for only a short distance before landing on a bush or soap weed.

Marian was a good rider, much better than he had expected. Since her father could no not ride, she did much of the checking on their land and cattle and spent many hours horseback each week. Again, Dean was impressed by the neatness of her trim figure. He knew how hard the woman had worked to prepare the two meals for the roundup crew. Yet, last night and again today, she looked fresh and neat in her trim riding habit with divided skirt which allowed her to ride astride. He could not help but again feel the great contrast between this woman and the girl in Ohio who would never have lived like this woman. Had she ridden, it would have been only on a side saddle and for a much shorter time.

They rode west of the ranch for some distance, the prairie rolling endlessly before them. In the far distance, they could just make out the white top of Pike's Peak as it rose glistening in the center of the Front Range, some seventy or eighty miles to the west.

"You can't quite see the Spanish Peaks from here," Dean said, looking at the horizon far to the south of Pikes Peak. "To me, those are the prettiest mountains in the world."

"We can see them, when we go to La Junta," Marian said. "Even though they're still a long ways off, I'll admit they stand out real pretty, like twin sentinels."

"When a person has lived in their shadow for as many years as I did, those old peaks someway get into your blood and you never want to leave them." He was not looking in the distance now, his eyes were following the smooth line of her neck. He thought, how pretty she is. What a woman.

"That's where the Arrowhead Ranch is located, isn't it?" she asked.

"Yes. The Home Ranch is in the foothills of the East Peak on the Santa Clara. You would like it there, Marian. It's beautiful country with tall pine trees on the upper end. The winter country runs out onto the open country a lot like this but has some piñon and cedar breaks for shelter."

"Are you going back there someday?"

"Probably...after this job's over. However, I may only get to make a short visit. I was foreman when I quit. That was the only job I ever really wanted. I'm sure Clay has long ago replaced me. There may not be any opening for me, now. Oh, maybe a cowhand's job, but nothing more."

"You don't like it here?"

"I have to admit I don't see too much future here," he drawled, looking intently at the woman. "I think we're about to see the end of the open range and these big Pool operations. I have to admit I kind of hate that, for these are the real cow outfits. However, the homesteaders are going to come in with fence and plow. To survive, I think the cowman will have to learn to operate on his own land. He's got to develop better cattle, too, and especially use better bulls for his own cows. He'll have to feed his cattle through the winters and not let them drift with the storms. We're just now catching up with cattle that were driven out of the Big Sandy country with those last storms. The worst thing is, the whole country is getting way overstocked."

"I'm afraid Dad can't see the open range ever ending," she said, meeting his gaze, her dark eyes searching his clear blue ones. This man talked as no other man she had ever known and his ideas intrigued her.

"Well, I think you dad's dead wrong on that. There will be lots of homesteaders coming out here, urged on by the government. To compete with them, the rancher will have to compete for ownership of the land."

The woman drew her horse closer to his. "For whatever it's worth, I feel you may be right, Dean. I just hate to think of all this natural cow country being turned into farms and I seriously doubt many of them will survive."

"They won't have to survive, to ruin the open range," he said seriously, a sad tone in his voice for he, too, did not like what this meant for the cattle country he loved. "They just have to be here long enough to plow things up. Oh, the land may come back someday but it will take years and who knows who will own it by that time?"

"We're certainly pessimistic today, aren't we?" she asked, turning her face away from him for a time, her mind telling her he was more than likely right.

"I admit I'm pessimistic about the cowboy's future," he said, in spite of the fact he was enjoying the feeling of being close to her. They let their horses walk slowly side by side. "I think it's mostly because I haven't been able to find the answer to what's happening to your cattle. I hate that. I've tried and tried to think of some answer and just can't seem to come up with a single idea."

They ate the lunch she had prepared, in the shade of a cottonwood tree beside a small spring. Their talk drifted from one subject to another, both enjoying getting to know the other better. Dean was impressed with the keenness of the woman's mind. She was a very open and frank person, deeply religious, and greatly concerned about the people around her. She and her father had worked long and hard to bring churches into the area, hoping someday to replace the circuit riding preachers with permanent pastors.

Her abrupt and probing questions sometimes amused him and he delighted in trying to give answers that did not tell her all his thoughts, just to get her to ask more questions. The woman also felt herself drawn to this slender, seemingly carefree man. She was now realizing his ideas about this country, the cattle industry and its future, went far beyond those of the average cowboy.

After lunch, they rode leisurely back to the ranch, enjoying each other's company greatly and also the beautiful day. It had been a fun day for them both, one neither would ever forget. They did no racing, although she teased him about it.

"Come to the house for supper," she invited as they reluctantly dismounted at the corrals. "Be your last chance at a home-cooked meal for quite a while."

"I'll be there," he promised, taking the reins of her horse so that he could unsaddle both.

"Claude will have to go back to his wagon after supper."

"Do you think he and Christine Kincaid are serious about each other?"

"Yes, I think so. However, they're both too young."

"Some people wait too long," he told her and gave her his carefree grin as her face frowned at the implication of his remark.

"Sometimes, it takes a long time for the right person to come along," she said, not wanting to end the spell he had cast over her.

"Maybe what I'm trying to say is, I think I'm glad you waited," he said rather shyly.

She looked at him keenly before turning to walk swiftly away, disturbed by his remarks and also by the feelings he had stirred in her innermost emotions. She admitted she really liked this man, this rider of the rough string. He was so different. She greatly admired his determination and pride, those were things she held very highly.

Dean unsaddled their horses and walked to the roundup camp, carrying his saddle. He checked all his gear and washed the dirty clothes he wanted to keep. He draped these over some brush to dry and threw the rest of his once fancy clothes, including the beaver hat, on the fire to burn.

Some of the men were playing cards around a blanket on the ground near the chuck wagon. He drifted over to watch. The cook was busily preparing the evening meal.

"I won't be here for supper tonight, cookie," Dean told the man. "I've been invited up to the house."

"Don't like my grub?" the man asked, his beady eyes

looking sharply at Dean. He had not liked having to change to this wagon. He wiped his whiskery face with the back of his hand. "I understood you was the reason I'm here."

"That may be, but you just can't compete with the lady at the house," Dean said evenly.

"Hell of a note," the man grumbled, turning back to his work. "Ben and Les are too drunk to eat and you're too sober."

"I'll watch your bed better tonight, Dean," Hugh said over his shoulder as he dealt the cards.

"Thanks, Hugh. Les get over his snake bite?"

"He took enough snake-bite medicine to kill a horse. I don't know where he and Ben got the liquor, but they're both drunk. Didn't offer to share with any of us, either."

"We'll make up for it in La Junta," Ed Ward said.

Dean waited until his clothes were dry. He folded them before putting them away in his war sack. He added the carpet bag valise to the fire, glad to be rid of it. He thought once of leaving his pistol in camp again but, remembering last night, decided to wear it.

Marian greeted him warmly at the kitchen door.

"You're a little ahead of time," she told him, as he entered the kitchen.

"Maybe I can tease the cook," he said with his cheery grin. She liked to see him smile and realized she seldom saw him without one. "A friend of mine always said to be early with a woman. He said that, if he came home late, all his wife ever gave him was hot tongue and cold shoulder."

She laughed pleasantly at this. "Dad used to say something like that," she said. "Go on in the parlor, Dad and Claude are in there."

"I'd a whole lot rather stay here," he said lightly, honestly. "You're a whole lot more interesting to look at than they are."

"I could even say the same for you."

They bantered easily as he watched her put the finishing touches on the meal. Christine came at her call and helped her put the meal in the serving dishes and carry them to the big table in the dining room.

It was another pleasant evening and Dean found himself constantly looking at Marian. He could not keep his eyes off the woman. Everything she did and said attracted him more. He thought again how odd it was to see a woman her age still single and attractive in this country. The cowboys around here must be retarded or something, he decided.

At last, Claude had to leave. The gangling youth disgustedly got up and walked to the front door, saying his good-byes to Christine more with his eyes than with words. Dean knew the boy wanted to be alone with the girl. At the door, Claude leaned forward to whisper something in the girl's ear. She smiled and nodded her head.

"Well, I'd better go, too," Dean said as the door closed behind Claude. Marian followed him to the door, where he picked up his hat and gun from the little table.

"I'll look forward to seeing you in La Junta," the woman said softly, directly. Her dark eyes seemed to sparkle especially for him tonight.

"Thanks for everything, Marian. I enjoyed the great food and especially that horseback ride. Good night, Mr. Shelly, Christine."

Marian followed him outside and across the screened-in porch to the front steps.

"Good night, Dean," she said softly. "We Shellys do appreciate your staying on and trying to find out what's happened to our cattle. Dad tells me that if you hadn't taken this job, the bank would have already foreclosed on us…so we're in your debt."

"I only hope I can turn up something by the time I see you in La Junta."

"Oh, I hope so, too, Dean." She closed the screen door after him but stood there looking through the screen.

"Good night, Marian," he called softly from the foot of the steps. "We'll ride again, or do something even more exciting, the next time."

"I'll be waiting."

He turned and walked away into the darkness. A moment

later, Claude rode past him on his way back by the house. Dean turned to watch as the boy reined his horse close to the porch steps and saw the golden-haired Christine was now standing on the top step waiting for him. Claude leaned down and the girl's arms went around his neck. When the boy straightened in his saddle, he put spurs to the horse and let out a loud yell of sheer exuberance, as the horse dashed around the corner of the house. A moment later, the sounds of straining wire, snapping posts and the boy's scream of terror came to Dean.

He turned to run back toward the house. He saw Marian come outside and both women were running along the house toward the corner and the sounds. Dean caught up with them just as they rounded the corner. It was dark, but they could make out Claude's horse, thrashing wildly about on the ground. They could not tell too much in the poor light, but Dean could hear the wire staining as the horse kicked.

"Claude!" Marian called, trying desperately to see what was happening.

The only sound was the wild thrashing of the horse in its struggle to free itself and regain its feet. Dean reached out to hold Marian back.

"Don't get tangled in that mess. What in the world did he hit?"

"The clothes line!"

Dean felt his way carefully to the one post still standing. Some of the wires were still attached to this, and he felt his way down these toward the horse. He could now make out the animal's head and front quarters. It was up on its front feet but its hind ones appeared to be tangled in the wire and it could not stand up.

It was hard to see in the darkness. Was that Claude lying beneath the horse's hips? For a split second, the memory of Clyde dying under his horse, came to his mind. No, that was part of a post. Where was the boy? Dean tried to catch the horse's bridle to calm the animal, but in its pain and fright, the horse reached out, trying to bite him. He struck the animal's nose a hard blow as he jumped back, once again saved by the reflexes developed by his battles with the rough string.

"Damn!" he exclaimed, tripping over a wire and falling heavily. He was up in an instant. "Go get a lantern so we can see!" he called to the women. "I can't tell where Claude is!"

"Run, Christine, run!" Marian yelled savagely. "Get Dad and a lantern. I'm coming to help you, Dean!"

By this time, Dean had managed to catch the bridle reins and tried to steady and calm the frightened animal by pulling lightly on them.

"I don't see how in the hell he could get so tangled!" he exclaimed as the horse continued its struggles to get up. "Thank God it's smooth wire!"

"Do you see Claude?"

"No. Go around behind me, Marian, maybe he's on the other side. Don't go near that horse, though, whatever you do! He'll bite or kick you."

He felt the woman pass behind him and then saw her light-colored dress showing in the darkness.

"I think I see him lying alongside the horse!" she called a moment later. "Claude! Can you hear me?"

"Yeah," came a hoarse whisper.

"Is the horse hitting you?" Dean called, as the horse continued its struggles.

"No!" Claude managed to call back. "But every time he kicks, he pulls me closer to him."

"Say the word and I'll shoot him."

"No, don't do that!" Claude yelled. "He's a Pool horse. Besides, it's my fault, I forgot that damn clothes line."

"Lovesick boys do stupid things," Dean said between gritted teeth, now pulling for all he was worth on the bridle reins trying to hold the horse away from the boy.

Christine came running with a lighted lantern. Shelly followed her as fast as his crippled foot would allow.

"Get something we can cut this wire with!" Dean called, and Shelly almost fell in his haste to turn back toward the house.

The horse whinnied in fright and lunged to get up on its

back feet. Dean jerked savagely and the horse went all the way down, flat on its side. Like a cat, Dean jumped on the animal's head to hold it down, careful not to get his hand close to those teeth.

Marian ran toward her brother, hit a wire she did not see, and sprawled very unlady-like, head first to the ground.

"Are you all right, Marian?" Dean called.

"I guess so," she said, getting to her hands and knees. "What a mess you made, Claude."

Claude did not respond and she could now make out the boy was waving his arms frantically. She got to him as quickly as she could, to find one of the wires was looped around his neck. When Dean had jerked the horse down, it had drawn the wire tight and was now choking the boy.

"It's choking him!" she screamed and tore at the wire with her slender fingers. She got a little slack and loosened the loop slightly as Claude sucked in a deep breath. The horse kicked and lunged and the loop tightened again in spite of her utmost effort to prevent it. Even in the dim light, she saw the terror on her brother's face.

"Dean, the wire's around Claude's throat. I can't get it off and it's choking him to death!"

Dean pulled his pistol and shot the horse behind the ear. He quickly jumped across the dead animal toward the woman's light-colored dress. He could now see the wire. He placed the muzzle of the pistol against the wire about two feet from Claude and pulled the trigger.

"That did it!" Marian cried as she unwrapped the wire from around Claude's neck.

For some moments, the boy lay gasping for his breath. It had been a close call. By the time Shelly arrived with wire cutters, it was all over. Dean stripped the saddle and bridle from the dead horse and carried them to the porch steps. Claude was now up and able to walk. He came to where Dean stood by the steps and picked up the bridle.

"I'll have to replace that horse, Dad," he said hoarsely. "That was a Pool horse."

"Take Fox," Shelly said, as the boy headed for the corrals. "Tell the men at the wagon what those shots were. And for God's sake, Claude, ride straight to your wagon and don't do anything else foolish."

The two women were looking at the havoc the horse had done to the clothes line. Marian was sad about the horse. Dean walked over to stand quietly beside her, as she contemplated the scene.

"Sorry about the horse," he said in an effort to console her.

"Oh, it was the only thing to do," she told him in a steady voice, her manner again frank and abrupt.

Shelly called for them to come back to the house and Christine ran ahead with the lantern. As Dean walked beside Marian, he let his arm go around the woman's slender waist. She made no protest as they walked slowly toward the porch steps and a thrill went through him. He felt his heart tighten in his chest.

"You seem to always be around to rescue me," she said, turning her face to look up at him in the poor light. "It does seem that something exciting happens whenever you're around."

She held her gaze up at him, her dark eyes like deep pools in the soft light of the lantern coming from the porch. He leaned to kiss her quickly, hungrily. He felt her body tense but she did not push him away, even responding ever so gently. Then, he was gone. For some moments, she stood looking after the man as he melted into the darkness.

"Back to waiting," she said to herself and went into the house, cherishing the memory of his soft lips on hers. She had felt the hunger of his kiss and wondered if he had felt the hunger in her response.

As dawn broke over the eastern horizon, Marian stood looking out the kitchen window toward the west, trying to see what she could of the roundup crew's morning activities. Most of the camp site was hidden from her view by the barns and corrals. She watched as the wrangler brought the remuda into the big ranch corrals, not using the rope corral when having the solid ranch corrals available. One by one, the men began roping their horses for the day.

Then, she saw a man ride into the corrals and snub a big black horse to his saddle horn. That would probably be one of Dean's rough string, she thought. Her face grew tight as she strained to see what was happening. The man on the horse led the black out of the corral and around behind the sheds where she could not see them.

At last, she could make out the shape of a rider's head and shoulders over the top of the shed. A moment later, another man's figure was in her view, as he had mounted the black horse. Her heart leaped into her throat as she saw the big horse and rider shoot up to where she could see them plainly over the top of the sheds, behind the other horses and corrals. Even from where she was, she could tell this animal was bucking viciously. She watched the man bob up and down above the ridge of the shed and her heart pounded as she hoped the man would be able to stay on his mount. The rider lost his hat but was still in the saddle when the horse bucked around the corner of a shed and was completely hidden from her view. She could still make out the man's head a time or two as it bobbed momentarily above the roof line at the peak of the horse's pitch.

Although she had been a long way from the action, she felt as though she had taken the pounding of the horse herself. From her own experience, she knew the rider was taking tremendous punishment from any animal that could buck like that horse was doing. Her heart went out to the man, knowing he was largely taking this risk for her and her family.

Yes, there was something very special about Dean Archer. He was cut way above the average man and she knew it. This man had stirred her emotions so strongly last night and the memory of the way his lips had hungrily, yet so tenderly, clutched at hers, was uppermost in her mind. She had lost the only other man who ever interested her to the flooding Big Sandy. Now, she prayed she would not lose this one to a horse in the rough string.

Dean managed to ride Poncho all the way that morning. Having his own saddle and being able to put his feet in the stirrups had helped greatly. Before mounting that morning, he had debated whether or not to continue to tie the old jumper roll across his saddle fork. Now, he was glad he had. The big black had used its days of extra rest, not only to recoup its energy, but also to think of new ways to buck. The horse had tried several new tricks that morning, but in spite of them, Dean had managed to stay with the horse. As usual, he had a gushing nosebleed by the time the horse had quit bucking. He now circled the horse back toward camp where Hugh was waiting with his hat.

Dean now rode directly to where Ben was trying to get on his horse. The big man was in no condition to be in command of anything this morning, as he fought his hangover. He heard Dean ride close and turned to look up at the slender man on the big horse, wiping his nose with a bloody handkerchief.

"Boyd admitted last night he was the one that has been cutting the strings on my saddle, Ben," Dean said evenly, his temper under strict control. "He said you told him to do it."

Shadrow stood there looking up at the man in his stupor.

"If it happens again, Ben, I'm going to hold you responsible and shoot you."

The wagon captain shrugged his heavy shoulders and turned back to climb awkwardly into his saddle.

"Let's move out," he managed to say, his eyes never meeting Dean's, and knowing that the entire crew had heard Dean's threat. For the first time, the man felt a twinge of fear.

A short time later, they left the ranch, the horses strung out ahead of the wagons. Les Boyd rode on one wagon beside the wrangler that morning, too sick to ride his horse. All knew he was allowed to do this only because of his friendship with Shadrow.

As they left the ranch, Dean looked back, thinking about the black-haired woman. He would never forget that first kiss. To heck with the memories of the girl back in Ohio. He now knew he had found the woman he wanted, and again, wondered that he had been so foolish as to chase a pipe dream. Cowboys could sure be dumb, he thought.

SIXTEEN

The crew was soon back to their normal routine. One day followed another. Dean was riding the rough string better now. He knew just how each horse would act. No two were alike and each responded differently. He was still thrown occasionally but not nearly as often. Dean was not the same man he had been when he came fresh from city life just a few short months ago. He was now as hard as nails, his muscles and reflexes toned and trim from his constant battles with the horses and flanking the calves. He was not a big man, medium height and slender build, but his drive and determination to do as much as anyone else made up for any lack in size. All the men were accepting him now and most respected him quite highly.

Shadrow said very little to him and Boyd avoided any contact he possibly could. Dean worked with both men, always trying to do his job, but he did not try to hide the fact he had no respect for either man. Dean, Hugh and Ed now arranged their beds each night so as to be handy to the other, should the need arise. Eben Hessey always camped alone, near the riding equipment.

These four continued to watch very closely every calf that was branded and they still could find no attempt to alter a brand by anyone. A few questions of brands came up, but each time was settled to the satisfaction of the reps involved. Dean thought about Shelly's missing cattle each night before he dropped off to dream of Marian. Also, each night, he realized he was no closer to the solution than he had been the day he joined the roundup.

The days grew warmer as July neared and the wagons moved farther south toward the Arkansas. It was hot, dry, dusty work and the flankers would be wet with sweat long before the end of their shift.

As they neared the Arkansas, they saw more and more evidence of the influx of homesteaders. One morning on the far edge of Dean's circle, he still rode the farthest of any of the riders, he met a young farmer returning from a trip to Limon. The young man seemed interested in the roundup wagons and stopped to chat with the cowboy for a little while. He was one of those inquisitive young men who had come west to win his place in the world.

"Your one wagon is sure quite a ways behind the others," the man said. "I wonder why you have the one so far behind?"

"Are you sure it was one of our wagons?" Dean asked, his curiosity immediately aroused.

"Well, I sure thought it was a part of your bunch. I ain't heard of any other wagons working in this country. It was rigged out just like your outfit, which I seen this morning. I saw it a few days ago, quite a ways north of here. Big bunch of cattle with it and moving in this direction. I've been riding mostly straight south ever since I left Limon."

"What direction would you say that wagon was from right here?" Dean asked, watching the man closely.

"Due north," the young farmer said. He turned in his saddle and pointed behind him. Dean immediately saw the man was pointing much more west than north. Limon would be to the northeast of there.

"Did you happen to talk to anyone on that wagon, hear the name of the captain or anything?"

"No, sir. They were holding quite a herd of cattle and I just rode around them, not wanting to get in their road. I'd say there was fifteen or so riders." The man looked questioningly at Dean. "It was your wagon, wasn't it?"

"It was probably our middle wagon," Dean said easily, not wanting to let on that the man did not know where north was, pitying the man's ignorance. Typical cowman, Dean had little respect for these farmers moving into the country, anyway. "That wagon must have gotten a little behind us," he added as he turned his horse toward camp.

He shook his head as he rode away. If a man didn't know where north was, how could he know one wagon from another? Besides, if he had been pointing in the direction of a wagon he had seen, it could not possibly have been one of theirs, as they had no wagons west of the one he was with. It could even possibly be that some other outfit was running a roundup in the country west of where they worked. Because of his distrust of the man's ability, he put the incident out of his mind.

A few days after that chance meeting with the young farmer, Shadrow turned the wagon in a southeasterly direction and three days later they joined Summers' center wagon, which had been somewhat behind in covering their territory. The following day, Masterman's east wagon arrived. They were now only about five miles from the Arkansas and they turned all the horses together into a fenced pasture which the Pool rented for that purpose each year.

Jasper had the men line up at Summer's chuck wagon where he sat at the extended tail gate table with a stack of greenbacks and three tablets of paper in front of him. Each man was advanced thirty dollars against his wages from the ranch hiring him. After getting his money, each man signed his name on the tablet for his wagon.

"You going right to town?" Dean asked Hugh as he put the money in his shirt pocket.

"You bet. The whole outfit normally goes together," the youthful cowboy said cheerily. "I've been waiting for this since last year. Come on, let's go have ourselves some fun."

There was a lot of commotion around the three wagons as the men saddled horses and made ready to go to town. Dean saddled the gray horse, Ute, who had developed into one of his better mounts, as long as he used the hackamore with the wires. That afternoon, the gray gave a few halfhearted bucks when Dean first mounted, but then acted as though it wanted to go to town, too.

The men from all three wagons rode toward town together, Jasper leading the way, as always, the center of attention. The fifty or so riders did make an impressive sight. There was much old comradeship among the men, as most of them had not seen each other since the start of the roundup. Good-natured bets were made as to who would get the first woman, who would drink the most or win the most money and who would have the most fun.

Dean rode at the rear of the group between Hugh and Ed Ward, his mind on the woman he hoped to meet, not really interested in the other riders' conquests. He wondered if Marian had even thought of him since their parting. Occasionally, he grinned that carefree smile at some remark from the high-spirited Hugh.

The riders had passed the first few houses on the long, narrow street leading into town, when a sharp explosion suddenly came from just behind the last riders. Dean thought it had been right under Ute's rear feet. Horses jumped and snorted wildly, running into those ahead of them, as suddenly alert riders jerked the slack out of their reins. Dean's first thought was that someone had fired a gun. That explosion was all it took to send Ute into one of the gray's bucking spells. By now, Dean was always alert to such a possibility and was not caught off guard.

The gray outlaw bucked between several horses, sending them running, bucking and jumping out of his way. This made the horses hit the horses ahead of them, sending them all into frightened running or bucking. Ed's horse struck the one ridden by Les Boyd, knocking the horse to its knees and the rider over its head, the little man rolling several times before coming to a stop.

Several more explosions came rapidly and several horses joined Ute in bucking. There was great excitement and real confusion among the men and their mounts. Several riders were thrown and found themselves sitting in the dust of the street while horses bucked and ran toward town with empty saddles. Other riders dashed wildly about, trying to control their own mounts or catch some of the free horses running down the street.

More explosions came, along with youthful laughter. Several young boys dashed from behind a house to throw more firecrackers behind the rear riders.

"Fourth of July!" Dean shouted, trying to pull Ute's head up. "I should have known!"

By now, Ute was bucking in earnest, pitching wildly through the rest of the horsemen and down the street toward the center of town. Dean pulled on the reins as hard as he could but found the hackamore was not having its usual effect on the horse and he was once again unable to exert any control over the animal.

Half bucking and half stampeding, Ute turned the corner and headed up Main Street. Both sides of the street were lined with wagons, buggies and horses tied to hitch rails. The town was extra crowded with people celebrating the Fourth and the arrival of the Pool wagons. Dean spurred and yelled but had little actual control over the horse, which now bucked and ran between the tied horses and the hitch rails along one side of the street. Dean was helpless as bridles and halters popped and broke and excited horses fought back to get out of the way. A team with a partially loaded wagon jerked one hitch rail completely off its supports and took off down the street, the wagon careening wildly behind them. Ahead of him, several horses managed to pull another rail off and they dashed after the wagon, kicking and bucking at the strange thing they were dragging between them.

People rushed from the buildings to see what was causing all the noise and excitement. From the doorway of the hotel, Marian and her father watched in open mouthed amazement as the man went flashing by on the wildly bucking gray outlaw. Loose horses were running in all directions. The woman gave a startled little scream and put her hand to her throat upon recognizing the rider. People were now pouring from the stores along the street and the shouts of running men calling vainly after their animals merely added to the general confusion. Well, Marian thought, hadn't Dean promised their next meeting would be an exciting one?

Finally, after freeing all the horses that had been tied along one side of the street for two blocks, Dean managed to get Ute's head up and under some control. He did not ride back toward town but circled until he located a livery stable. He rode into the long center alleyway, dismounted and quickly began to unsaddle. After putting the horse in a box stall, he checked the hackamore. It was the right one but someone had filed the sharp points off the wire in the knot and had loosened the wire on the nose band until it would not pinch the horse's nose when the reins were pulled. He cursed himself for being careless, again.

Some of the Pool riders rode up just as Dean finished telling the stable man how to handle his horse. Kincaid and the three wagon captains were cursing and grumbling but most of the men were now laughing. Their entrance into town had been the most spectacular they had ever made and would be remembered for a long time.

Dean waited near the big doors at the sidewalk until Hugh and Ed had put up their horses. Claude Shelly came out with them and it was plain the three had all thoroughly enjoyed the whole episode.

"That was some grand entry you made," Claude chided

Dean. "You practice that all the way down here?"

"Not really. By the way, I think I saw your folks at the hotel as I came by," Dean said easily. "You going up to see them?"

"Not now, no sir!" the young cowboy stated emphatically. "I'll see them tomorrow or sometime. Right now, Slim's taking me to a place he knows north of the tracks where he's going to fix me up with my first woman."

"How about Christine?" Dean asked with a slight lift of his eyebrows. He thought he knew what the boy's reaction would be.

"Oh, hell, I've never had a chance like this. Christine is a long way from here," the boy said, a little embarrassed.

"Just thought you might want to think of her," Dean drawled lazily, having known too many young cowboys to try to change this one's mind. It was really none of his business, anyway, but he had the feeling his lady would certainly not approve.

"You ready for that first drink, Archer?" Hugh asked. "I'm buying."

"Nothing I'd like better," Dean said. "However, I think I'd better report to the Shellys while I'm still sober. I've got a strong feeling they wouldn't appreciate a drunk cowboy."

"That Marian sure wouldn't," the lanky cowboy said. "I understand she's one of them women who don't approve of strong drink, strong language or much of anything else, for that matter."

"You'd sure better get a bath quick, then, Archer," Ed said with a wide grin. "If she don't like strong things, you sure hadn't better let her get down wind of you."

"Now, that's sure a case of the pot calling the kettle black," Dean said pointedly.

The four men walked up the street toward the center of town. They had gone only a short distance when two riders called to Claude and the boy went back to join them. On Main Street, they found men still trying to find horses and repair broken bridles and halters. The language some of them were using about those "wild cowboys," made the men feel they might not be too welcome in some circles that night.

Marian and her father had watched the excitement and turmoil in the street from the front of the hotel. Marian's heart had leaped into her throat when she recognized the man on the bucking horse causing most of the trouble. The last she had seen of him, he had gotten some control over the horse and had turned a corner off Main Street. In front of the hotel, the dust was still stirring in the street as men and animals still fought for either control or freedom. It was some time before the crowd settled down and a few began laughing.

Well, Dean was in town and she had to admit his entrance had been exciting. She had also gotten a glimpse of her brother, so knew the boy had made his first roundup in one piece. She and Shelly went back inside to get away from the dust. One of the hotel men shut the front doors to keep out the dust, and the heat was soon almost unbearable.

From where he sat in a big leather chair with his bad foot propped up on a stool, Herman Shelly watched as his daughter paced about nervously or sat for a very short time in another big chair. Funny, Marian had never acted this way. Could it be that her interest in Dean Archer was more than just wanting to know if he had found out anything about their cattle? Well, it was time the woman took an interest in a man…if she was ever going to, and Herm had come to respect this man, Archer.

They were both watching, as a buggy pulled up in front and a man got down to tie the team before turning to help a young woman step down. At sight of the golden hair, Marian let out a startled exclamation. It was Christine. Marian ran to the door and outside.

"Christine! Christine!" she called excitedly. "What in the world are you doing here?"

The girl whirled on her heel and hurried to throw her arms around the older woman. From the look on the girl's face, Marian knew instantly, her being here was more than just to meet Claude. The girl's face shown with excitement.

"Oh, Marian, am I ever glad to see you!" she exclaimed.

The man had gone to the back of the buggy and now sat a

valise on the sidewalk.

"You'll have to take your own things inside, Miss," he said rather nervously. "I'm afraid to leave this team and I've got to find Jasper."

"That's all right, Cal. Thanks for bringing me."

"What's he in such an all fired hurry to see Jasper for, that he can't even bring your bag inside?" Marian demanded in her direct manner, as she bent down to lift the girl's bag. "Yea Gods, Christine, you must have a floating library or a tombstone in here."

"Oh, it's not that bad, Marian. I guess I did bring almost everything I own."

Despite her slender figure, Marian was quite strong and she now carried the bag inside and up to the desk. The clerk was about to tell them he did not have another room but the determined look on Marian's face made him suddenly remember one of the rooms he had been holding back. Christine signed the register and he handed her a key.

"Hello, Mr. Shelly," Christine said cheerily as the man limped up to the desk. "I'd like Marian to come up to the room with me for a few minutes. I've just got to get some of this grime washed off and I have something I'm dying to show her." The girl turned to ask the clerk to bring her bag to her room. At his nod, she turned back to Marian. "Marian, I've got news you won't believe," she said excitedly. "Come on, I can hardly wait to tell you!"

"I knew it had to be something special to bring you here."

The two women went to the stairs and climbed the two flights to find Christine's room. The girl immediately began pouring water into the basin on a stand and dampened a rag to hold to her face.

"It's sure hot in this part of Colorado," she said.

Marian went to the window and lifted the sash. There was no breeze and it was a very hot day with higher humidity than she was used to. She looked out onto the street below and was disappointed when she did not see any sign of Dean or her brother.

There was a knock at the door and the clerk entered with

Christine's bag, which he placed on a chair next to the bed, before turning to leave.

"Now, what's all this exciting news?" Marian asked as soon as the man had gone.

"Well, I just don't know how to begin," the girl said and came to sit on the bed beside Marian. "I guess you don't know about the horrible cloudburst and flash flood at the ranch. No, you couldn't know about that. Well, anyway, there was a terrible storm. It seemed like there was a wall of water running in a big sheet off the country north of the ranch. It came right down through everything. It made a terrible mess at the ranch but was even worse farther west. It washed some of the sheds and corrals away at the safe crossing west of the ranch and really did a lot of damage up there."

"When did this happen, Christine?"

"Over a week ago, I don't remember for sure just what day it was," the girl said excitedly. "Anyway, after it was over, one of the men told me about the tremendous hole it had washed out at the safe crossing. So, one afternoon, I walked up there to see it. Cal, the man who brought me to town, was there, too, and was poking around in this big hole the water had washed out of the bank just below the crossing. Just as I got there, Cal let out a yell and began digging at some old bones that had been uncovered by the flood. One of them was a horse's skull."

"A horse's skull?" Marian asked quickly. "Well, I guess that's not so surprising. No doubt lots of animals have been killed in the quicksand all along the Big Sandy."

"This skull still had part of a bridle on it? There was some rotten leather straps and the bit was still between the jaw bones. Cal took one look at that bit and said he had to get word to Jasper right away. After he'd left, I went down in that hole and poked around a little for myself. It felt a little like being in quicksand, but I found a few more bones and something else."

The girl now went to her bag and opened it. She brought out an object wrapped in several layers of old newspaper. She spread the papers over the bed as she unwrapped the object. It was about four inches long, round and had one badly corroded screw dangling through one of the holes in the base plate. Marian instantly recognized it as a saddle horn. She reached out to take the horn, letting it roll across her fingers.

"I'm sure it's a solid brass horn, Marian," Christine said excitedly. "You can see it doesn't have the flat place on top where they would have fastened a leather covering. All the other old horns I've ever seen had that. They were all made of iron, too, not brass."

"Billy Kincaid!" Marian exclaimed.

"I'll bet anything that was his fancy brass horn Claude teased you about. I'll bet Cal recognized the bit and that's why he wanted to find Jasper so quickly. I believe he knew it was Billy's."

"If this is right, Christine, Jasper has lied about this all these years. He always claimed Billy had attempted to cross the creek way below the ranch. This means Billy had to have come up to the safe crossing with him."

"Of course it does! And, if they were both there, Jasper must have shot Billy or at least pushed him off into the quicksand. Naturally, all the time you folks spent looking for Billy was in the wrong place."

"I think this does mean Jasper did something to Billy!" Marian said, her mind racing at the shock of this discovery. She again looked intently at the horn in her hand. "Let's go show this to Dad. Does Cal know you found it?"

"No, I never showed it to him. When he said he was coming down here to find Jasper, I just insisted he bring me along." Christine dropped her gaze and her cheeks colored slightly. "I told him I was coming to marry Claude, just so he had to bring me. I'm a little ashamed I told him that."

"Oh, never mind that, now. It got you here and that's all that matters."

Marian was really excited now. She wrapped the horn back in a piece of the newspaper and led the way downstairs. The two women were walking toward Shelly when Dean came in the front door. His face carried that carefree grin she remembered so well, as he walked swiftly toward them. His eyes took in Marian's trim shape. She certainly had not disappointed him in the way she looked.

"Hi," he greeted lightly, managing to put the small bundle of clean clothes he carried under his arm, while reaching out to take each of them by the hand. This kept him from giving in to the temptation to take Marian in his arms and kiss her.

"Not every cowboy gets greeted by the two prettiest girls in town," he said lightly.

"Flattery will get you nowhere with us," Marian assured him as she squeezed his hand tightly, which told him what he wanted to know. "I do have to admit your grand entrance was as spectacular as anything you've done so far. What have you planned for later?"

"If you knew, it wouldn't be a surprise. Remember, I told you we'd do something exciting in La Junta," he said, thrilled at the warmth of her hand and greeting.

"Where's Claude?" Christine asked.

Dean hesitated a moment, he couldn't tell the girl the truth.

"Oh, I expect he'll be along shortly," he said, hating to lie to her. "I think he's still saying good-bye to some of the boys."

"Come on over here with Dad," Marian said, still holding his hand. She led him across the room to where Herm sat in the big chair where he could rest his foot on the stool. "Christine and I have something very important to show both of you."

"Hello, Mr. Shelly," Dean said and switched hands with Marian in order to shake the rancher's hand.

"Glad you made it, Archer." The rancher's face worked expressively as his eyes noted his daughter was not pulling her hand away from the cowboy. "Them bad horses didn't do you in, anyway."

"No, sir," Dean said and came right to the point he knew was the only real interest to Shelly. He might as well get it over with and he forgot, for the moment what Marian had been saying. "I regret to report I've found absolutely nothing, sir. No cattle have been misbranded, as far as I could tell, on the west wagon. I did see quite as number of your steers and dry cows which we should be able to gather in the fall roundup. It looked like to me, you should have a decent number to ship."

"Well, I'm not too sure of that, Archer," Herm stated flatly and Dean's eyebrows lifted in his surprise. "Marian, Everett and I covered a lot of country coming down here. We took several extra days and the two of them rode a lot of country while I drove. Very frankly, we did not see many of our cows, nor Holland's, nor Hessey's, either. We saw lots of Kincaid, DZ and the others."

"We covered enough territory to see where all of the wagons had camped at one time or another," Marian added. "We crisscrossed the country, trying to see some of all of it. However, it did seem part of the time, toward the south end, that one set of wagon tracks were much fresher than the others and moved across all of them. Was one wagon quite a ways behind the others, and seemed to be covering a wider territory?"

Dean looked sharply up at the woman. For the first time in days, he recalled his chance meeting with the young farmer.

"Which way were those fresher tracks heading the last time you saw them?"

"I would say mostly southwest. I really thought they kind of cut across some of the territory the other wagons had already worked. Why?"

"Well, I met a farmer who said he'd seen one of our wagons quite a ways behind the others and with a large herd of cattle. I thought he had to be mistaken, as he couldn't point in the direction of Limon, which he said he had come from." Dean's forehead formed a heavy frown. "Well, that settles it. I'll leave in the morning and have a look at those tracks and see if I can locate another wagon. If they went southwest, that would be away from our country entirely. Do you suppose it could have been Masterman's tracks you saw coming over to meet the other wagons?"

"Not unless Jasper's changed the way the wagons work," Shelly said. "The first time we saw the tracks they were too far north for that. Normally, Masterman don't swing west to join up until he has worked all the way to the Arkansas."

Dean shook his head in his disappointment. He had been counting heavily on a few days of rest, hopefully spending much of that time with Marian. It certainly did not appeal to him to think of going right back out on the range.

"Forget the cows a minute. They might not be as important as the news Christine brought," Marian said, her excitement again showing in her face and voice. "Here, Dad, see what you make of this." She extended her hand with the paper wrapped object.

"What is it?"

"Unwrap it."

The rancher's hands fumbled a moment with the paper, the horn rolled across his palm and fell to the floor. Dean let go of Marian's hand and bent swiftly to pick it up. He rolled the horn over in his hand before handing it to Shelly. His eyes were now intently on the rancher's expressive face. Shelly examined the horn with little interest.

"Saddle horn," he said at last, and for once, his face was expressionless. "A horn off somebody's old saddle, been buried where the ground was wet, I expect."

He handed it back to Dean. The cowboy took out his knife and scraped some of the corrosion away.

"What's so special about this particular horn?" Shelly asked, his face again expressing his feelings as he looked up at the women. "It could have come from anywhere. There are lots of old saddles around that have been discarded and buried."

"Solid brass," Dean said softly, his eyes now intently on Marian's face. "Not a leather covered horn…a slick horn. Never been many of them in this country."

"What!" Shelly exclaimed, reaching out quickly to take the horn back. "Are you sure?"

This time, Shelly really examined the object. His expressive face plainly showed them he now knew what it was. Where Dean had scraped the corrosion away, the brass shone brightly.

"Billy Kincaid!" the old man breathed. "So, they finally found him!"

"Yes, Dad, I think they found what happened to Billy, too.

One of the men found the skull of a horse where a flood in the creek had washed it up," Marian said excitedly. "The skull still had the bit in its mouth. The man has the bit and has taken it to Jasper. He didn't know Christine found this horn. I'm sure Cal was working for Kincaids when Billy was alive and I think he knew that bit had been on the horse Billy rode the night he was drowned."

"Did they find anything of Billy?"

"I don't think so, although there were several bones around there," Christine said. "I wouldn't know if any of them were human or not."

"Well, it's too bad, but at least, we know for sure what happened to him," Shelly said, with a heavy sigh. "We all tried hard enough to find him."

"Yes, Dad, but we were all looking in the wrong place!" Marian exclaimed. "They found the skull and this horn just below the safe crossing above the Kincaid Ranch...not below the ranch where Jasper always claimed Billy tried to cross."

"What! How could that be?" Shelly demanded, looking sharply at his daughter. "Jasper said Billy tried to cross miles below the ranch."

"Yes, Dad, Jasper said...I think Jasper lied," Marian said in her abrupt manner. "If he was with Billy, as he always claimed, then they both had to come to the upper crossing. Jasper must have killed Billy and shoved him and his horse off the crossing into the flood and quicksand. Jasper hated Billy for his attention to me. We've always known that. To throw the rest of us off, he made up that story about Billy trying to cross miles below there."

"Well, I'll be damned!"

"Dad, watch your language!"

"Oh, hell, Marian, don't you know where this puts Jasper?"

"Sure I do. He could face a murder charge."

"That's right. Now, how do we go about this?" Herm asked, his face now working at a furious pace. "Do we go to the sheriff here? The crime was committed in another county."

"I don't know, Dad, but we've got to report it. By the way,

Christine, what did Unk say about this? Surely Cal told him. Did he send for Mac?"

"Unk wasn't there. He's not back from his annual reunion with his buddies."

"Where's the county seat for the Kincaid place?" Dean asked.

"I guess it would be Kiowa," Shelly said. "I'm sure it's not in the same county as ours, Lincoln County. It must be in Elbert County. That's probably better for us, anyway, as the sheriff in Limon is a close friend of the Kincaids. I doubt you could get him to even investigate this."

"Well, I think you'd better get to Kiowa as fast as you can and get the sheriff out to see where they found these things, before Jasper can get there and destroy any evidence," Dean said. "Christine, you're sure Cal don't know you found that horn?"

"I never told a soul until I showed it to Marian a little while ago."

"Well, it's too late to do anything tonight," Dean said softly. "I'll go see if I can find Claude. I'll meet you back here and we can decide just what to do. Would you see if you can get Claude and me a room and put my things in it?"

He held out the tiny bundle of clothing to Marian.

"We've already done that," Marian said. "Do you want me to come with you?"

"No. Ladies ain't welcome where I'm going," Dean said with a wry smile, hating to have to turn down her offer. "Wait for me."

"Back to that," she said, more to herself than anyone else. It seemed all she ever got to do, was wait.

SEVENTEEN

Dean muttered to himself as he hurried along the street he hoped would lead across the tracks to the place Claude had mentioned. He did not like the idea of playing nursemaid to anyone. Yet, the thought of having to tell Marian where the boy was, or worse yet, having to lie about it, made him hurry a little faster. Dang it, he finally had the chance to spend a few hours with the most fascinating woman he had ever known and here he was traipsing around looking for a kid brother like a truant officer after a boy that had ditched school.

Why had Christine had to show up, anyway? No, he was glad she had, for she had perhaps brought the answer to what had happened to Billy Kincaid and he felt he knew Marian well enough that she might accept him better, if she knew for sure what had happened to Billy. Marian had looked so pretty, so womanly. That woman sure had a way of keeping herself.

The bawling of cattle came to him and he looked up in instant interest. There was a long string of cattle cars on the crossing ahead of him. Some cowman must be shipping awfully early, he thought. Perhaps there had been another roundup working west of them, after all. More than likely, some outfit going broke and shipping when they could. His curiosity aroused, he turned alongside the cars, trying to see through the slats. He could not see much but legs from the ground. At the end of the car, he caught the ladder and climbed high enough to look through the slats at the cattle. The car rocked violently as the cattle crowded away from him. Was that an X bar X brand on that animal? His mind came instantly alert. He crawled along the slats for a better look. The light inside was poor and he had trouble seeing brands in the darkness, as the cows crowded against each other, as far from him as they could get, afraid of the human.

Mostly steers and older stuff, he decided. He made out the brand of two more, they both belonged to Holland. There was another of Hessey's. Could any belong to Shelly? Had he accidentally stumbled on to some of the missing cattle?

"Hey, you! Get off that car!" a loud voice called from a few cars ahead of him.

Dean turned to see a burly railroad man hurrying toward him, a brakeman's club in his hand.

"Get down from there!" the man called again, belligerently waving the club over his head.

"Just checking to see if any of them were down," Dean called, hoping the man would think he was a cowboy sent with the cattle.

"You ain't one of the men assigned to this train," the brakeman protested loudly. "Get your butt down off there, or I'll shake you lose with this bat!"

Dean pushed himself away from the car and jumped to the ground. He managed to land on his feet, just as he had done so many times when forced to make a hasty dismount from one of the rough string.

The brakeman now turned toward the front of the train and raised his lantern in a signal to the engineer. From far up the tracks came the answering whistle and the sound of cars snapping their couplings as the engine pulled ahead.

"How about the loan of your lantern?" Dean asked as he approached the burly man, a pleasant smile on his face.

"Who the hell do you think you are, cowboy? Get off railroad property before I run you in!"

The man's eyes suddenly grew wide, for the smiling cowboy now held a Colt .45 pointed right at his thick middle. The man dropped the club and raised his hands quickly. "What is this?" he asked. "I don't have any money."

"I'm appropriating your lantern and that club," the cowboy said. "You just stand here like a good boy while I take a look at what's in those cars. You make a move toward me and I'll ventilate your middle."

The man offered no resistance as Dean took the lantern from his hands. The cowboy's gun never wavered as he stooped to grab the club and quickly ran to the ladder at the end of a now slowly moving car. He climbed to where he could put the lantern between the slats. After much maneuvering and poking with the brakeman's club, he made out several more brands, the animals belonging to Holland and the Hesseys. Then, he found three steers carrying the Shelly brand. He had indeed found cattle he was sure their owners knew nothing about shipping. Two more cows with Shelly's 2 slash S brand.

By now, the train was picking up speed. He climbed down to the last step of the ladder. Just as he threw the lantern and club away, he saw the burly brakeman coming toward him over the tops of the cars. Looking for a soft spot, he jumped, missed his footing and sprawled in the dirt and cinders of the roadbed. He got up slowly, shook himself and made sure his pistol was still in its holster. He'd been thrown much harder by many a member of the rough string. However, the prairie sod had not done near the damage to his clothes and skin as the cinders had done.

He brushed himself off as best he could and walked back

alongside the tracks and moving cars to the street he had been on when he had first seen the train. All the cars had cleared the crossing when he got to it and he turned up the street. It was getting dark now, and he looked for a building which could be a saloon or rooming house. Ahead of him, a door swung open and a cowboy came out, apparently feeling quite good. The man was a Pool rider but one he did not know.

"Must be the place," he muttered under his breath, and went into the building.

For a moment, he stood by the door letting his eyes grow accustomed to the dim light. Indeed, it was a saloon.

"There you are, Archer!" Hugh Loring's voice called and Dean saw the tall rider waving to him from across the room. "Come on!" Hugh called and raised a full glass above his head.

Dean saw Claude Shelly was sitting at a table next to Hugh's, with a young girl of the evening on his knee. Claude's two friends also sat at this table, one with a woman on his lap and the other with his arm around a tall, thin blond woman standing by his chair. She looked tired and worn. All three women wore heavy make-up.

Dean walked around the crowded tables to Hugh and accepted the glass the cowboy offered him but did not sit down, although the cowboy pushed a chair toward him. He took a sip of the whiskey as he felt a feminine hand touch his arm and he looked around into the eyes of a tired painted face.

"Maybe something more than a drink, cowboy?" the woman asked hopefully.

"No, thanks, ma'am. I'm a happily married man with five kids," he said with a wry grin. "Came to get my oldest boy, here, and take him home before his mother beats the hell out of both of us."

The woman grimaced her disappointment and moved away.

"What's wrong, Dean?" Hugh asked, for he could tell Dean was not interested in drinking. "I thought you'd come to join the party."

"Maybe later," Dean said, letting his hand drop to Claude's shoulder.

The boy turned to look up at him. On recognizing who it was, he shrugged the hand off and returned his attention to the girl on his lap.

"One more and we'll go upstairs," he told her, patting her rump affectionately. She swayed her body on his knee and reached out to pour his drink.

"He's already had enough, ma'am," Dean said politely and softly. He pushed the girl to a standing position. "Claude, Christine's at the hotel, waiting for you."

A stupid expression came over the boy's sun-bronzed face as he looked up at the thin rider. "Christine?" he exclaimed incredulously. "Christine's here?"

"At the hotel. Now, I don't like being your nursemaid anymore than you like me being one, but I kind of think it would be a good idea if we was to head up that way kind of quick like."

"Now, don't you try spoilin' Claude's first fun, fellow!" one of the cowboys said from across the table. "I don't know who you are, but you got no call to spoil the kid's first time."

"Like I just explained to the lady, I'm taking my oldest boy home to his mama," Dean said softly but firmly, wanting to get Claude out of there without trouble, if possible. He knew how these men could be after a few drinks. He turned to the girl who had been on Claude's lap. Reaching into his shirt pocket, he pulled out a bill, which he handed to her. "Here, young lady, all you really wanted was the money, anyway. Now you don't have to work for it."

"Oh, damn!" Claude stammered as the girl tucked the money down the front of her dress and walked away. "You're sure spoiling everything."

"Yeah, yeah, I know. Thanks for the drink, Hugh. I owe you one. If you see Ed, or any of the Holland men or the Hesseys, tell them I've found their missing cattle," Dean said, pushing Claude to his feet and toward the door. "Tell them to see me at the hotel as soon as they can."

"Can't it wait 'til tomorrow?" Hugh asked, with a laugh. "You're too serious, Dean. Tonight's the time for some fun."

"This is serious, Hugh."

The man across from Claude now stood up so quickly the woman on his lap missed her footing and fell to the floor.

"You can't take Claude!" the man shouted, as the woman scrambled to her feet. "Not after what Slim and I done to set this up for him."

"Hate to spoil the fun, boys, but duty calls," Dean said easily and pushed Claude away from the table.

"Duty, hell!" the man exploded, his hand near his pistol. The whiskey was beginning to have its effect on him.

"Sit down and shut up!" Hugh said in a strained voice. "That's Archer, and them three Hesseys at the far end of the bar, and me will back him up, if you start anything."

The cowboy looked at Hugh's face, thought a moment, then turned to look at the three men in black hats at the far end of the bar. He well knew the Hessey reputation. He sat down. Dean raised his hand in a salute to Hugh and turned to follow Claude outside. Once out the door, Claude turned angrily to face him.

"Damn it, Archer, why'd you have to mess that up? Is Christine really here in La Junta or did my sister have you tell me that, just to get me out of there?"

"Christine is at the hotel," Dean said evenly. "I don't like doing this, believe me. If you want to play around with some barroom gal and pick up a disease you can pass on to your bride, that's your business, as far as I'm concerned. But, for your sister's sake, I came for you. They don't have to know where I found you."

"You sound just like Dad and Marian."

"Maybe that's because I've seen a few more cowboys make fools of themselves than you have."

He sent the boy on to the hotel while he turned on the street just south of the tracks and followed it until he found the depot. After a little friendly persuasion, he got the night agent to send two urgent telegrams for him.

When he finally got back to the hotel, he found all the others waiting in the lobby. They were planning to all go to dinner together.

The way the man hurried up to them made Marian instantly realize he was excited and had something he wanted to tell them.

"Boy, do I have news for you!" he said eagerly, as he rushed up to again reach out for Marian's hand. Even in his excitement, he noticed how neat and pretty she was in her high-collared blouse and skirt. He also knew he looked even worse after his fall in the cinders of the railroad bed, than he had before.

"Herm, I found some of your missing cows," he said and watched the expression change on the rancher's face. "They're on a train that just went through town on its way back east somewhere."

"Well, bless my soul! How can that be?" Herm demanded, his rubbery face working frantically to display his emotions. He was plainly startled. "I thought you just told me you had found nothing!"

"At the time I told you that, I was no closer to finding the answer than the day I met you," Dean admitted with one of his shy grins. "I still don't know all of it, but when I went to find Claude, I found a lot more. There was a cattle train parked on the street crossing. It had to be loaded at Rocky Ford, or some place west of here. Anyway, I climbed on a couple of the cars and found it had some of your cattle in them, Herm, as well as some of the Holland and Hessey brand."

"The hell you say!" the rancher exploded.

"Dad!" Marian admonished him. "You never use language like that!"

"How in the world did our cattle get on a train?" Shelly demanded, his face now working extensively. "Who put them there? Kincaid?"

"I have no proof of who did it," Dean said. "I did send a telegram to a man I think will be able to find out for us."

"Just how do you have it figured, Dean?" Marian asked, her dark eyes looking at him sharply. "I know you've got a theory of some kind."

"Well, I met a homesteader a week or so back who said

he'd seen one of our wagons quite a ways north and maybe some west of the rest of us. I thought he must have been mistaken and that he probably had seen the middle wagon, which I think was a little behind ours. I should have tumbled when you said you'd also seen tracks that looked like a wagon had been behind the rest of us, too, but I didn't. Now, if you put it all together, Jasper must have been running another wagon behind the three regular roundup wagons. I'll bet that wagon was gathering cattle from you, the Holland and Hessey outfits, to ship. If anyone saw them, they'd think, like the farmer did, that it was one of the regular wagons just a little slower than the rest."

"And since Jasper would know just where each of the wagons would be, he could keep any of you from seeing the wagon behind!" Herm said, his face plainly showing his understanding of what had happened.

"I'd guess that wagon took the cattle across behind us and west to Rocky Ford and loaded them. Jasper probably laughed about sending them right through La Junta, while all his riders were getting drunk and glad to forget things like cows."

"I still don't see how they could sell the cattle, though, surely some brand inspector would stop them, if not when they loaded, then surely someone would check those brands when they got to the stock yards back east."

"Did you ever give the Pool your authorization to sell your cattle for you?" Dean asked.

Herm's face took on the expression of a man who had just been reminded of a most unpleasant memory. Marian was watching intently.

"By God, of course, I did!" Herm said. "Years ago, all of us gave Unk Kincaid authority to sell our stock and sign for our brands. We did that so he could ship cattle at the rail head after the fall roundup. He sold all our cattle for us for a number of years. Later, we began to sell our own stuff again but I never thought to get that paper back. I hadn't thought about that paper in years."

"Well, I'll bet somebody is still using it," Dean said

meeting Marian's keen look. "That paper probably would get them by any inspectors."

"Well, if Jasper got those papers from Unk, he would have no problem running a fourth wagon behind the rest and no one would ever know it. It's beginning to make sense."

"What do we do, now, Dad?" Marian asked.

"Don't forget, you have another problem," Dean said. "Remember the saddle horn? I don't know just how much you want to say in front of Christine, either. After all, Jasper's her step-father."

"I hate the man," the golden-haired girl said emphatically. "He's made Mom miserable, so I say, make him pay for stealing your cattle and make him pay for killing his brother."

"Well, it will take a day or two to get the answer to my telegram," Dean said. "About all we can do is wait for that."

"Who the heck did you send that telegram to?" Herm asked. "We've got to get those cattle stopped before they can be sold."

"I sent it to my almost ex-father-in-law," Dean said. "He's a director on the Santa Fe Railroad as well as a big lumber dealer and an Ohio state senator. I'm sure he has enough influence to get the cattle impounded at whatever stock yard they were sent to."

"We've got to get someone to the sheriff at Kiowa, too," Marian said.

"If Cal has shown Jasper that bridle bit, I'll bet he's already on his way to the Big Sandy," Christine said. "You'll never catch him."

"There's also the Pool meeting at Kincaid's on the ninth," Herm Shelly stated. "Marian and I have to be there. She's secretary and I sure want to tell them what's been happening to our cattle. They've all thought me and Holland were just belly aching."

"But, you won't have any proof until Dean gets the answer to that telegram," Marian said.

"If you and Marian leave first thing in the morning, you should be able to get to Kiowa, find the sheriff and get to

Kincaid's before the ninth, Herm," Dean said. "I also sent a telegram to Homer Reid at the bank in Denver. I look for him to meet us at Kincaid's."

"Heck, I forgot to tell you, Reid's here in town, Dean. I saw him go upstairs a little bit ago," Shelly said. "Christine, you should go with us, too. After all, you're the one who found that saddle horn."

"Yes, Dad, you must take Christine with you," Marian now said. "Her testimony may be needed and she can show the sheriff just where she found that horn. I'd suggest you take Mr. Reid with you, too, as he may be able to back you up with the sheriff and also at the Pool meeting."

"What about you, Marian?" Dean asked.

"I'm going to wait for that telegram with you," the woman said defiantly.

"I don't think you realize what you're saying, Marian," Dean objected. "If that telegram don't get here for several days, I'll have to make a heck of a ride to get it to you folks at the Pool meeting on the ninth," Dean objected. "Kincaid's is well over a hundred miles from here, no ride for a woman. Besides, you should be with your dad."

"No, I'm staying with you. I can make any ride you can."

"Marian, you'll come with me!" Herm Shelly stated flatly.

"Dad!" The woman said, turning to face her father, her hazel eyes blazing, "Let me remind you, I'm, no longer your little girl. I'm staying with Dean, and that's all there is to it!"

Shelly shook his head but knew when to accept defeat. He had raised a headstrong woman.

Dean looked sideways at the beautiful woman beside him. Man, he thought, here was one real woman, the woman he had always dreamed of. He knew she thought she could make the ride he planned. He couldn't have been more proud of her, or more disturbed, than he was at the moment. He sure wanted her with him, but he knew all too well the ride he might have to make. He doubted Marian, or any woman, could make it.

But, like her father, Dean had already learned when not to push the black-haired beauty.

EIGHTEEN

Early the next morning, Herm, Homer Reid and Christine left La Junta for the trip north. None of them had been able to persuade Marian to go with them. The woman was determined to stay with Dean and would listen to none of his protests, either. It was plain Christine hated to leave Claude, as the boy stood manfully between his sister and Dean as all waved their good-byes. After the buggy was out of sight, the three returned to the hotel.

As soon as the stores opened, Dean purchased a few new clothes and changed into these. He also got a real barber haircut. He was enjoying the luxury of a bath every day with running hot water in a tub in the little bath room off his room. He had heard some of the hotels were installing such modern conveniences, but this was the first time he had ever stayed in one. It was pretty fancy living for a cowboy.

He checked the depot, but there were no messages for him. His one telegram had been answered by Homer already being in La Junta. Fearing his original message to the senator in Ohio had not reached his party, he sent two more to the senator at different places in hopes one of them would reach the man. There was nothing else to do but wait.

Claude soon left them to return to his friends and Dean could only hope the boy would not give in to the temptation to be unfaithful. He knew the boy would come under a lot of pressure from the riders he had been with all summer. Well, a man had to make those decisions for himself.

After Claude had left them, Dean and Marian spent much time walking the streets and looking in all the store windows at the goods on display. They now held hands openly as they walked and Dean was surprised at how much this simple act thrilled him.

When he mentioned this, she said, "You have no doubt held hands with a lot of women, Dean. I seriously doubt holding hands with an old maid can be much of a thrill to a man of your vast experience."

"Well, now, I'll admit I've held a few hands in my time, but I've never enjoyed it as much as holding yours," he said, looking down at her with his smiling clear blue eyes.

She squeezed his hand warmly. The real thrill to him was that she seemed to want his touch as much as he did hers. He felt a great temptation to ask her to return to the hotel with him and let him make love to her. However, something held him back. He knew her well enough, by this time, to know she would never really forgive him, even if she gave in to his desires. Besides, damn it, deep down in his own heart, he didn't believe in that kind of living, either. Surely he was a bigger man than that kid had been last night. He was certainly old enough to know better. You had to stand for something in this world, he remembered his old friend, Clay Hamilton, telling him.

That afternoon, after checking again for an answer to his

telegrams, they met the three Hesseys on the street. All three were somewhat the worse for wear but were glad and amazed at Dean's news about their cattle.

"What can we do?" Eben asked, as they were about to part. The man was quick to note his cousin's hand in that of the cowboy. "We sure want to back your play."

"Well, there isn't much any of us can do, right now," Dean said. "I sure want to have the answer to my telegrams at the Pool meeting for Herm to show them all what's been happening. I want to see the look on Kincaid's face."

Neither Dean nor Marian said anything about Herm going to the sheriff at Kiowa. They both thought it best to let that part of Jasper's problem be kept secret, until they found out what the sheriff would do.

"There's one thing you could do, though, Eben," Dean said. "Unless I get an answer before the ninth, I'll have to make one heck of a ride to get the information to Herm in time for that meeting. I'd like to have the two buckskins out of the rough string to make it on. They're the best circle horses in the remuda and have more stamina than any two horses I ever rode."

"They'll be at the livery in the morning," Eben promised. "Normally, the wagons stay over two days and leaves the morning of the third, that'll be the seventh. If you're still here, we'll see that you leave the roundup in good shape. If you've left before then, we'll cover for you."

"Dad brought Everett to take Dean's place, so there should be no trouble in his leaving," Marian said.

"You can never tell about Ben," Eben said tightly. "But, hell, since Dean found some of our cattle, I'd like to see Ben, or anyone else, stop him from making that ride. I only hope you get the answers and can get them to the meeting. I know Dad will be there and Shelly can fill him in. He'll back you and Herm. We'll see Ed Ward and the rest of the Holland boys, too, so they can back you."

"I'll need my other hackamore and a couple of halters," Dean said, not wishing to go back to the camp.

"They'll be with the horses," Eben promised.

After the men had gone to the livery for their horses, Dean and Marian walked slowly back to the hotel to sit in the lobby and wait for the answering message. They both enjoyed the visit as they learned more about each other's background and beliefs. The more they learned, the more they felt sure of themselves in their decisions. It was amazing how they thought alike on so many things.

The weather was hot and sticky and there seemed to be little breeze to cool things off. That night, after eating supper with Claude, they all went upstairs to their rooms. Dean felt sure Marian would have volunteered to kiss him good night, had Claude not been with them.

In his room, Dean stood in just his underwear for some time by the open window. It was hot and not a breath of air seemed to be stirring. He wondered how people lived in this heat all the time. Yet, La Junta and the farming areas along the Arkansas seemed to be swarming with people. They were irrigating much of the land close to the river. He drew a glass of water from the faucet. God, it was awful, no wonder stains were already forming on the new tub. He guessed the water must have lots of iron and other minerals in it.

He finally laid on the bed, not pulling the sheet over him and thought about the woman in the other room. He wondered if she could be wanting him as he was wanting her. It seemed funny he now acknowledged so openly he was in love with this woman. Not many months ago, when he left Ohio, he had been swearing he would never look at another woman.

Big Ben Shadrow opened his bloodshot eyes and looked around the little room. He did not know where he was. He did not know how he got here. He rolled over and felt the warmth of the woman's body next to him. He raised himself on one elbow, and for a long moment, looked closely at her. He could not even remember having seen her before, and right now, she did not appeal to him in the least. She must have looked better last night, he thought.

Slowly, trying to avoid moving his head, the big man got

up and pulled on his pants. The woman rolled over, looked up at him, smiled and went peacefully back to sleep. Good, he decided, he must have paid her last night. Otherwise, he felt sure she would have awakened enough to demand her money. He was in the act of strapping on his pistol when a soft knock sounded at the door.

Ben very gently placed his hat on his head as he crossed the little room to the door. Outside, in the still morning air, stood Les Boyd, his red eyes and lined face showed he had also spent several hard days and nights.

"You ready, Ben?" the little men growled.

"We've got just about time to get something to eat before we meet the men," Shadrow said, stepping outside and turning to look back at the shack. Another unkept little shanty stood a few yards away, where Les had apparently spent the night. "How the hell did we find this place? I sure don't remember meeting that woman, or coming here. Man, my head feels like a tub of guts."

"You're not alone there. I don't rightly remember where you found those women, either," Les said, in his deep voice. "All I remember is, you brought them to the saloon last night and they brought us here. Man, I need a drink to sober up on."

"I don't think we'd better start that. Summers and Masterman are sticklers for the rules. Even if Jasper ain't here, they'll be wanting to head out for home."

"Wonder where that damn Archer's been?" Boyd asked as they walked toward town. "Sure ain't seen anything of him since his horse tore things up when we got to town."

"I'll bet he's been hanging around that Shelly woman. I think he's sweet on her. Why else would he have stayed on the roundup and taken what we've dished out to him?" Ben asked, as they neared a cafe where they could get some breakfast. "I never in my life seen a guy who would take what we done to him. If you get a chance, cut his latago or cinch this time. To hell with just cutting the strings on that jumper roll or the wires on them hackamores. I'd still like to see one of those horses do him in."

"Jasper sure wasn't very happy with us, when he was still on the wagon when we got here, but you did everything you could to make him quit," Les said. "Besides, that stuff Jasper gave Bart to make Archer sick, didn't work any better than what we done."

As soon as they had eaten, they walked to the livery stable, where they found several of the Pool riders waiting for the wagon captains to show up. Some of the men had already caught their horses and had them saddled and tied in front of the stables. Ben noticed Archer was there, standing by the stall with the gray outlaw but was making no move to saddle the horse. Probably waiting for the captains to show up, he decided.

The big captain went out into the corral and caught his own horse, leading the animal back inside to saddle. His head was in no condition to think of anything but what he was doing. More men were coming now. Few were in much better condition than the wagon captain and many had problems catching their mounts and getting them saddled. Most were trying to act in good spirits to show what a good time they'd had. Some of the more sober ones seemed to enjoy teasing those in the worst condition. There was much talk and loud laughter, neither of which helped the big man's head.

Masterman and Summers arrived together and immediately went to get their horses, as other men arrived in various stages of sobering up. There was much confusion in the stables and corrals as the men got their horses and equipment ready.

"All your crew here, Ben?" the bullet-headed Masterman asked, as he came back into the stables from tying his horse on the street. This man acted as boss in Jasper's absence.

"Hell, I don't know," the big man said, his eyes going around the faces crowded near the door.

"Well, you'd better check. We may have to hunt a few men," Masterman said.

"Usually do," Summers said in his taciturn manner. He was a very somber man, known as a good cowman and a hard driver.

As he turned back from studying the men near the door,

Ben noticed Dean was still quietly standing beside the stall and had made no attempt to saddle the gray horse. The big man's anger boiled instantly.

"What the hell's your hold up, Archer?" he demanded hotly. "Can't you even saddle that horse here in a stall without somebody to snub him up for you? Get that horse saddled!"

"I'm here to replace Archer for the Shelly outfit," the older cowboy, Everett, spoke up from behind Ben and stepped away from the door a little.

"That right?" the big man asked, turning to look back at the Shelly rider. "I thought it was funny you was here."

"That's right," the older cowboy said. "I'm to take Archer's place back to Kincaid's."

"Well, I guess you know he's been riding the rough string, Everett. If you're taking his place, you'll have to ride his horses. That gray's one of them, so get your saddle on him and let's go."

"Oh, no! I'm no bronc rider! You'll have to give me some decent horses."

"Now, wait a minute," Masterman cut in. "Rules are rules, Everett. The ranch has a right to replace a rider but the rules plainly state that man has to ride the horses assigned to the man he replaces. Hell, Shelly knows that. That rule's been in effect ever since the Pool started furnishing the horses."

"I rode on the Pool for several years, but they never gave the rough string to a regular ranch rep before, either," Everett said slowly, as his glance went to Dean as though asking for help.

"Well, whether you like it or not, Archer rode those horses down here and, if you're replacing him, you'll ride them back. Hell, it'll only be for a few days, anyway," Shadrow said. "It ain't like being on roundup."

"Not on your life, Ben," the cowboy stated flatly, not in the least ashamed to admit he could not ride the rough string.

Ben turned slowly back toward the slender man standing by the stall. Dean met his eyes squarely.

"I guess that means you ain't relieved, Archer," the big

captain said, a sneer slowly spreading across his heavy face. "Since you ain't been replaced proper, saddle that gray horse and let's get going. We're late enough as it is."

"Sorry, Ben, but I'm not going with you," Dean said, speaking in a soft voice. "Sure funny, you've been trying to get rid of me all this time and, now you have the chance, you tell me I have to go back with you. I'm not going and I'm keeping three of my string with me."

"You can't do that!" Ben shouted, his anger rising with each word. "Nobody takes a Pool horse without approval from the wagon boss. Them's the rules and I say you can't take them."

"I don't give a damn about your rules, Ben," Dean said, his voice deceptively mild. "This is kind of Pool business, anyway, as I'll need them to take a message to the Pool meeting at Kincaid's."

"The hell you say!" Ben exploded and looked to the other two captains, wanting their support. "What the hell message can you deliver? Anyway, you ain't takin' no Pool horses!"

"Summers and me'll have to back Ben on this, Archer," Masterman said firmly. "That's a Pool rule."

"Like I said, I don't give a damn about your rules," the slender rider said evenly. "Make some new ones. I ride for Shelly and I'm taking those horses to get a message to him for the big meeting."

As he spoke, Dean moved a few steps away from the stall to the center of the long alleyway which ran the length of the stable. He had already checked to see that none of the riders were still behind him. The men now stood behind the captains, near the big double doors, some having gone on outside. Dean crouched ever so slightly and his hand was close to his pistol.

Shadrow was quick to note the man's manner. While he felt sure of his ground on the rules and was afraid of no man in a fist fight, he was not sure he really wanted gunplay over enforcing them. Knowing the determination of the slender man before him, and seeing the way he was acting, it could well take gunplay to solve this. Some of the men on the street outside the barn now crowded closer around the doors and two windows to see what was going on inside, many expecting a fight and all wanting to see it, should it happen.

Ben peered at the slender rider through his bloodshot eyes. Everything he had done to rid himself of this man had failed. Maybe this was his lucky day.

"Personally, I'll be damn glad to be rid of you, Archer, but you ain't breaking any Pool rules and you ain't taking any Pool horses!" He said flatly. "All these men will back me on that."

"You don't seem to hear too good this morning, Ben," Dean said, crouching a little lower. He tried to keep his eyes focused between Ben and the other two captains so he could catch the slightest movement any of them made. "I'm keeping those horses."

Little Les Boyd was standing directly behind Shadrow, as he usually did, completely hidden from Dean's view by the big man's body. Boyd now pulled his pistol and stuck it around Ben's side to fire blindly in Dean's general direction.

At the shot, Dean dropped to one knee, his pistol now in his hand. The bullet had missed him by over a foot and he thought Shadrow had someway drawn his gun without him seeing the man's hand move. Dean's first shot took the big wagon captain in the shoulder as the man dove sideways, clawing at his own gun. As Ben fell to the side, Dean could make out the little man behind the captain, and the smoking pistol in his hand. Boyd suddenly realized he was no longer hidden and snapped a shot at Dean which went over the man's head. The little man was turning to flee when Dean's second shot dropped the man in his tracks.

Pandemonium broke loose as men dove for cover behind stalls, piles of hay, and a mass exit was made through the open stable doors. Two men dove out the windows and several sobered on the spot. Masterman almost ran over Summers as they both tried to get behind a feed box. There was much cursing and shouting. Ute kicked the wall of his stall with both hind feet. That sounded like two more shots had been fired and made the fleeing men move faster. The horse whinnied wildly and then stood nervously to let long, loud snorts roll through its nostrils, in the stillness that followed the shots.

"Don't none of you move!" Eben Hessey hissed from the doorway, as he stepped back inside with his pistol drawn. His two brothers and Hugh Loring quickly followed him, all with weapons in hand. "You wagon captains aren't the only ones who will back people. We're backing Archer!"

At this turn of events, the two wagon captains came from behind the feed box with their right hands raised shoulder high and went immediately to kneel beside Shadrow's prostrate form.

"Send for a doctor!" Masterman said, in the silence that now settled over the group. "These men are both hurt."

"How about the sheriff?" Dean asked.

"We don't need him. This is roundup business," Summers stated in his flat tone.

"Your friend, Boyd, almost got you killed, Ben," Dean said, as he also came to kneel beside the big man. His bullet had hit the man high in the right shoulder. He did not think the big man was badly hurt. "I'd feel mighty lonely with a friend like that."

Boyd had been hit in the upper left arm and Dean felt relief neither man had been killed. He did not really wish to kill any one. As they waited for the doctor, Dean and Eben Hessey explained a little more to the other captains, but did not tell them anything other than a message was coming to Dean that would explain about their missing cattle. Although neither captain would say anything about the situation, they decided it best to accept the fact there was nothing they could do to stop these men. Neither man felt the cause worthy of more gunplay. They would report all this to Jasper, when they got home, and let him handle the matter.

When the doctor arrived, he gave emergency treatment to the two wounded men. He decided Shadrow could probably ride the wagon back home but he felt he should keep Boyd for further treatment, as the man's upper arm bone had been shattered.

After all the men had left, Dean supervised the feeding of the three members of his rough string, as well as Marian's horse. From this animal's appearance, he thought the woman had ridden a good mount.

They waited for the message that seemed would never come. Those two days in town alone and close to the woman he knew he loved were the hardest days Dean felt he had ever lived. Marian now not only accepted his kisses but openly responded to them. After their evening meal and a walk around town, they both went to their own room and to bed. It was still very hot and Dean slept but fitfully. Between the heat and thinking of the woman in the other room, he got little rest.

He had hoped they would get an answer in time to make an easy ride to the Kincaid place, but the evening of the eighth came with still no word. He had sent two more telegrams on the chance one would get through. Now, even if the answer came tomorrow, it would be almost impossible for them to get to the Kincaid Ranch in time for the meeting. He knew Shelly and Homer could stall the members only so long.

Dean awoke before dawn from force of habit. This was the final morning. If they did not get their message early today, it would be impossible for them to get it to the meeting. For a few minutes, he lay looking around the sparsely furnished room. It was still warm and no breeze came through the open window. At least, some of the Pool owners would stay overnight at the Kincaid place and, maybe they could still get it there before they all left.

He was about to roll off the bed to get dressed, when he heard noise in the hall and, a moment later, a knock sounded at his door. He quickly pulled on his pants and went to the door. It was the telegraph operator.

"Here's what you've been so anxious to get," the man said, holding out a yellow envelope.

Dean took the envelope and thanked the man. He hurried back to the bed and sat on the edge of it as he tore open the envelope.

The message read:
YOUR TELEGRAM FINALLY PASSED TO ME.

STOP. SENATOR IN EUROPE FOR SUMMER. STOP. PRESIDENT OF RAILROAD HAD ATTORNEY STOP PAYMENT ON CATTLE IN CHICAGO UNTIL OWNERSHIP PROVED. STOP. HAVE YOUR ATTORNEY CONTACT H. YATES, PRESIDENT, CHICAGO STOCK YARDS. STOP. COMMISSION FIRM YARNELL AND SMITH CLAIM THEY HAVE SOLD CATTLE FOR SAME MAN FOR MANY YEARS WITH POWER OF ATTORNEY FOR ALL OWNERS. STOP. MAN'S NAME JASPER KINCAID. STOP. MONEY ALWAYS DEPOSITED HIS ACCOUNT STOCKMAN'S BANK PUEBLO, COLORADO. STOP. YARNELL AND SMITH OLD TIME COMMISSION FIRM WITH GOOD REPUTATION. STOP. HOPE ARRANGEMENTS SATISFACTORY. STOP. WIRE IF YOU NEED ANYTHING ELSE. STOP. RUTH AND I MARRIED MAY ONE. STOP. YOUR FRIEND, TED BAKER, SPECIAL ASSISTANT TO SENATOR CRAWFORD.

There it was. The proof they needed. He quickly shaved and dressed in the new range clothes he had bought. Then he hurried to Marian's room. She answered his knock almost immediately, as she had also been awake.

"Morning," he greeted as she opened the door slightly. For a moment, he thought about teasing her about the message but decided against it. He merely handed her the yellow paper.

He watched her face as she quickly read the message. He thought, she's even pretty in the mornings.

"So, it's what we suspected!" she exclaimed. "Jasper!"

He looked away from her and spoke softly. "I'll have to ride like heck, if I'm going to get to Kincaid's even by dark tonight. This is the day of the meeting. I wish you'd reconsider and not come. It'll be a heck of a ride at best, and to make it, I won't be able to hold back for you."

"Well, you can bet your sweet life I'm coming with you," she stated firmly. "I want to be there when you show this to

Jasper. I wouldn't miss that for the world. I won't hold you up."

"I'll go down and order some breakfast and see if the cook will make a few sandwiches."

"Order ham and two eggs for me. I'll be down by the time they pour the coffee."

The woman was as good as her word. The waiter had hardly taken Dean's order when she sat down across the table from him. She wore a divided riding skirt and a white blouse. He was quick to notice she had on her riding boots and silver mounted spurs.

"Who's the man who sent you the telegram?" she asked, sliding the message across to the table to him, her eyes searching his face. "And, who is Ruth?"

He met her eyes and found her hazel ones were probing his.

"I told you, I went to Cincinnati after a girl. Ruth is Senator Crawford's daughter. She visited the Arrowhead Ranch one summer and I guess you can say I fell for her very hard, head over heels. She was so different from any woman I'd ever known and she fascinated me. I sure thought she was what I wanted for quite a while. She couldn't give up all she had back there and I sure couldn't fit into her life, so I finally got smart and came home. We parted good friends and I'm sure she'll be very happy with Ted. They have a great deal in common, including the senator. My only regret is that I wasted three years of my life and gave up the only job I ever really wanted to chase off back there. It was a mistake, a dumb thing to do, and I know it. In a way, though, I'm even glad now I did it. Otherwise, I'd never have come to this country and met you."

"Are you sure you're glad of that?" she asked in that direct way she had. "An independent old maid is not much of a catch, I'm afraid."

"Well," he drawled easily, enjoying teasing her. "Neither is a middle-aged cowboy who's long past his prime as a horseman, and probably anything else, but still dumb enough to try to ride the rough string. Personally, I think it is kind of wonderful that we two old has-beens and misfits finally got together. At least, I'm, real happy about it, Marian."

"So am I, Dean," she said, her hazel eyes full of her emotions. "So am I."

"When this is over and we get married, we'll find me a job someplace and start a home," he assured her, reaching out to grasp her hand.

They almost bolted their food, when it came, so anxious were they to get on their way. As soon as they had eaten, they hurried to the stables, carrying a small sack of lunch. Dean saddled her horse first, then Ute. He had repaired the hackamore and now made sure the wire around the nose band and in the knot under the horse's jaw were both in order. He did not want to leave town in the same manner he had entered.

He went outside into the corral and roped the two buckskins. He put the spare hackamore on Wrangler under a halter and the other halter on Button, tying both horses to stout posts in the corral fence. Marian mounted her horse and watched as Dean led Ute out of the barn and into one of the smallest corrals in the yard.

She saw the horse try to bite the man, as he made ready to mount, and saw he had been expecting this, for he hit the horse hard on its nose. He slid the blind up in place, twisted his stirrup and swung into the saddle. As soon as he let the blind slide down, the horse put its head down and tried to buck. However, the corral was too small for it to buck very hard and could not stampede at all. After a few disappointing bucks, the horse calmly trotted around the small space, stopping and turning as the man wanted. Dean made sure the horse felt the pull and pinch of the hackamore and felt it had to respect the rider's wishes.

A few minutes later, just as the sun was completely up, they rode from town, each leading one of the buckskins. They crossed Main Street and rode north toward the river.

As soon as they had forded the Arkansas, Dean settled the gray to a long, swinging trot, both riders standing in their stirrups, cowboy fashion. After perhaps a mile, he urged the horse into a lope. Ute instantly tried to run away but Dean managed to jerk him up with the wired hackamore. Marian stayed right beside him and they loped pleasantly along for some time before he drew the horses back to that trot. He had been pleased to note she rode the trot standing in her stirrups. He thought she sure made a handsome figure on the horse and he again admired her greatly, but could not help wondering if she could stand this ride.

It was already quite hot and the horses were soon showing sweat which worked into a lather across their shoulders and between their legs. Dean did not slacken the pace. Alternating between the long trot and an easy lope, they covered the miles swiftly and silently. There was no time for casual conversation. It was so hot Marian silently wished for a cloud to come overhead and cast a shadow for them to ride under, but nothing came between them and the sun. The morning continued beautifully clear and the sky was blue in all directions.

Dean did not follow the roads but cut across country, trying to remember it as best he could from the trip down. Having left from the Kincaid Ranch, he felt he would get back to it best by staying in the country the west wagon had worked.

When the sun was finally at its highest, they came to a small stream with a few cottonwoods and some heavy brush along its banks. Here, Dean pulled the horses to a walk and then stopped under the trees and swung down. He unsaddled the horses they had ridden and led them around a short time until they had cooled down, before he let them drink. He and the woman also drank from the stream and afterward each had a little time alone behind the brush.

They sat under one of the big trees and ate the sandwiches. Cowboys never carried a lunch but he was glad he had thought to bring one for her and had to admit it tasted good to him, too. It was at least a little cooler here under the trees by the water and it was a pleasant repast for the two riders. He felt they had made good time but still had so many miles to go that he allowed himself only a half hour before standing up and going to the horses.

"Hate to do it, but we've got a ways to ride," he said.

NINETEEN

After hobbling both Ute and Wrangler, Dean put her bridle and his own saddle on Button. He led the horse some distance away from where she stood near the other horses. He swung quickly on the horse and Button made only a few halfhearted attempts to buck before settling into his steady gates, working the reins well for Dean. Apparently, the hours being led had taken some of the buck out of the horse. Dean rode the horse in a large circle for several minutes and then rode to where Marian waited. He swung off and quickly pulled his saddle from the horse and put Marian's saddle on. He turned Ute and her horse loose and tied the two halters and the hackamore he had used on Ute behind her saddle.

He now saddled Wrangler and led the horse to about the place he had mounted Button. He turned the horse around several times before sliding the blind up over its eyes. He wondered if this horse would still want to buck after the miles it had already come. As soon as the blind went down, the horse dropped its head between its front legs and bucked in its usual high, twisting bucks, just as it would have done the first thing in the morning. The miles had made no difference to Wrangler. When he finally had the horse under control, Dean rode back to where Marian stood, Ute and her own horse standing a little distance away. Dean could see that Button was getting nervous at being saddled and not being ridden.

"Marian, if I get off this horse, I'm afraid I'll have another battle on my hands, he never wants to stand and he's sure not used to waiting around after I'm on him. Can you get on Button without my help?"

The woman stepped forward and Button drew back. Instinctively, she pulled back on the reins. The horse stopped, facing the woman, its head high and eyes alert.

"Whatever you do, don't let go of the reins," Dean said, trying to speak very calmly and not spook the horse or excite the woman. He kept Wrangler moving in a circle around them. "Walk up to him very slowly. See if you can get the rein over his neck."

She did as he instructed and managed to get the right rein over the horse's neck.

"That's it. Now, get right on him, just like you've been riding bad horses all your life," Dean told her. "If he tries anything, yell and spur him good and hard. Don't let him think you're afraid."

The woman did not speak but now twisted the stirrup, as she had seen him do, put her foot in and swung up. Dean turned Wrangler beside her and both horses moved off. For a moment, Dean thought they were going to make it, when Button suddenly bogged his head and began to buck. To Dean's surprise, the woman did not scream. She was holding tightly to the saddle horn, pulling on the reins and pushing her feet ahead in the stirrups, taking the jolts as well as any cowboy could have done. She even spurred the horse hard in the ribs each time it hit the ground. The horse made several pretty good, high jumps, then threw up its head and began walking away. Dean trotted Wrangler up beside them.

"That was great, Marian! You do ride well! Now that's over and you won, I don't think you'll have any more trouble with him."

After walking the horses a ways, Dean lifted them into their long trot. Marian was surprised at the smoothness of Button's movements. Even after having been led over fifty miles already that day, the horse moved out effortlessly, his stride long and smooth. Beside them, the rangy Wrangler also seemed to trot without effort.

She now found she had rubbed raw places on the inside of both knees, when Button had bucked with her. Standing in the stirrups, as the horses now trotted steadily, aggravated these raw places. She thought about asking Dean to stop to see if she could put a bandage of some kind on the places, but decided against it, feeling it would only cause them delay and perhaps give these two outlaw horses another excuse to go into their bucking act.

Again, Dean alternated their pace between the long trot and an easy lope. Not being used to the hours of standing in the stirrups, made her legs ache and she began to wonder if she had been rash, indeed, to think she could make such a trip. She knew the many hours and miles that still lay ahead of them. It helped when they loped, as the strain and rubbing of her legs was not so bad, when she could sit in the saddle.

The hours drug on. The horses never faltered. Never had she ridden a horse with the stamina and heart of the buckskin beneath her. Button was now sweating and drops of lather flew from his shoulders but his breathing was steady and strong and he never stumbled.

In the middle of the afternoon, they crossed another stream with brushy banks. Dean stopped and they dismounted. He held her horse so she could have a few minutes alone behind the bushes.

After leaving the stream, they walked and led the horses

for some ways to work the stiffness from their own limbs. She was rather sorry when, at last, they had to remount. Dean stood at Button's head while she swung up. The horse made no move to give her any trouble. He had to put the blind up on Wrangler before he could mount, but the horse did not offer to buck this time and they started off again at their long trot.

Several times during that afternoon, Marian thought she would have to tell Dean she could go no further. Each time, from somewhere deep within herself, she drew the strength and the will to continue. She wondered if he had not felt that same way often while he rode the rough string. She remembered her brag about never being left behind and that she could make any ride he could. Perhaps she had been a little overconfident. She had become so numb her knees no longer hurt.

On and on they rode, each mile becoming more agonizing than the last to the woman. The two horses were now breathing a little harder but neither slackened the pace. Dean, she thought, must be made of iron, for he rode with the same posture and form as he had started with that morning. If the ride was fatiguing him at all, it did not show on his features.

As the hours drug on, Marian had to often change hands on the horn and reins. She moved up and down in the stirrups to try to relieve some of the numbness in her legs. Dean never slackened the pace, although he was tempted to do so, because of the woman.

Marian recognized some of the country now, as they were not too far west of the Shelly Ranch.

"You could pull off here and go home," Dean told her, pointing a slender arm in the direction of the ranch. "I sure wouldn't blame you, if you dropped out."

"I don't drop out," Marian replied, with grim determination and hoped her voice didn't sound as though it came between gritted teeth.

The cowboy shrugged and lifted the horses to a lope. It was late afternoon, when they reached the more rolling country which indicated they were nearing the Big Sandy. Dean now let the horses lope up the easy south slopes and trot down the steeper north slopes. At last, they topped the highest rise they would cross and looked down on a wide, shallow valley. Down the center of this, they could see the cottonwood trees lining the banks of the Big Sandy. The cool green was a pleasant sight after looking at the hot dry prairie all day. Marian instantly recognized where they were.

"We've come a little too far west," she said quickly. "You can see the Kincaid place off to the right."

"Considering this is my first trip back to this country, we didn't do too badly," Dean said with a big sigh. "Now, if the Pool is still holding their meeting."

"I'm sure Dad has kept them there this long," Marian assured him.

They angled their horses to the right, cutting diagonally across the sloping country until they came to the crossing to the ranch. They could see evidence of the flood Christine had told them about and Dean remembered the buggy that had sunk in the sand of this crossing the day the roundup had pulled out. They crossed without incident and started toward the buildings.

Marian found Button was no longer pulling on the reins but that was the only difference she could see in the horse. Button would never quit while he had strength to put one hoof ahead of the other. She marveled again at the toughness of these two horses and noted Wrangler still showed spirit and pride in his carriage, despite the miles they had come.

"Surely these horses won't belong in anybody's rough string after today," she said.

"I'll bet you anything, Wrangler, at least, will buck when I saddle him tomorrow morning," Dean said. "However, if I can buy these two from the Pool, I intend to do so. They've worked their hearts out for us today and I'd hate to think of anyone else riding them and mistreating them."

"Well, we're almost there," she said, not sure whether she was relieved or not. She dreaded the meeting with Jasper, for she knew the big cowman would never give in easily. Perhaps the sheriff had already arrested Jasper. Wouldn't that be a blessing?

They rode past the corrals and toward the house. Dean's

heart sank. There was not a buggy or wagon in sight. Surely, had the Pool members still been here, there would be vehicles tied around the house. Were they too late? Wouldn't it be just his luck to have made this ride for nothing?

Dean pulled up at the yard gate and swung down to go to Marian's side as she attempted to dismount. As he feared, the woman's legs almost collapsed under her weight. He reached out to catch her. In spite of his weariness, the touch of her body against his, as he held her close for a moment, sent a thrill through him. It took a little time for her to get the circulation going in her limbs and was able to stand on her own.

He left her holding the two horses as he went through the gate and up the walk and steps to the front door. He did not know just what to expect and checked his pistol to make sure it rested correctly on his hip before knocking on the door. When no answer came, he knocked again. A few moments later, the door opened and Kate Kincaid stood before him.

"Dean!" the blond-haired woman exclaimed at seeing who it was. Plainly, she had not expected him.

"Where's Jasper and the Pool meeting?" he asked. "I understood they were to meet here today."

"Well, all I know is, Mr. Shelly and another man came here with the sheriff looking for Jasper. That was day before yesterday. Jasper was in Limon and not here, anyway. Mr. Shelly and Mac had a terrible argument about how Jasper was running the Pool. After the sheriff and the others left, Mac and Unk also went to Limon. Mac said he would notify the other Pool members they would meet in Limon, rather than here. Several of them still came here this morning, anyway, and I sent them on to town. I didn't understand all that was going on, but I did hear Mac say you were involved, in some way. He was terribly angry with both you and Mr. Shelly."

"Well, I am involved, Kate," he admitted. "Damn, we've ridden all the way from La Junta to be at that meeting."

"Tell me what's going on?" the woman asked, concern plain on her face. "Has Jasper been in anything wrong?"

"It looks like it, Kate, maybe more than one thing," he told her honestly, but offered no details. "Well, I guess we'll just have to go on to Limon and hope we get there before they give up on us."

"Knowing you, Dean, I know you wouldn't say Jasper was involved, if he wasn't, but I'm still married to him. I hope it can be worked out."

"Do you know anything about the bank account he has at the Stockman's Bank in Pueblo?" the rider asked.

"Jasper never banked in Pueblo, that I know of," Kate said as she wrung her hands in worry. "We bank in both Limon and Denver."

"Where's Christine?" Dean asked, as he turned to leave.

"She was with Mr. Shelly. She said she had to go with them, something she knew about Jasper."

"Well, we'll go on to Limon, Kate. I hope, for your sake, this don't turn out as bad as it looks right now."

Kate watched Dean stand at Button's head as Marian forced herself to climb back on the saddle. She had been so thankful the ride was over, and now this.

Dean thought he could mount Wrangler without using the blind, as tired as the horse must be. He reached for the stirrup and swung up. To his utter amazement, the horse promptly dropped its head and made three hard, twisting bucks, as though to let the man know it was still an outlaw and would always be one. Dean had been taken by surprise, for he had thought the horse would be too played out for such antics, and he was almost thrown. He managed to catch himself by the reflexes he had developed over the long months of riding these horses.

The golden-haired Kate watched the two ride from the ranch, then went back into the house to wait and worry.

Those last twenty miles seemed to take as much toll on their bodies as had the over one hundred miles they had already come to the Kincaid Ranch. They also both felt the discouragement of having thought they had reached their destination, only to find they had these other miles to ride. This tore at their spirits, especially Marian's. Just as he had done so many times during those past months, Dean forced himself to move ahead, despite the way he felt.

Now, as he rode, he looked often at the woman riding beside him. For the first time since he had known her, there was a smudge of dirt on her face. He thought it was a very pretty face, smudged and tired and strained as it was.

The two buckskins trotted on, never stumbling, never hesitating, moving their legs as though they were machines, not flesh, blood and bone. Marian again marveled that the horses could keep going and knew they were truly exceptional animals.

It had gotten quite dark when they finally rode into Limon. Lights were coming on in some of the homes and a big lantern showed the open livery stable doorway. Dean drew Wrangler to a stop at the door and swung down, still alert for the horse to kick at him. He hurried to Marian's side as she swung clumsily to the ground. He caught her as her legs again buckled. He held her close as he helped her walk those first few steps.

"I'll be all right in a minute," she managed to say, her arm still around his shoulder. "The ground never felt so good."

"Take your time, honey," he whispered in her ear. "I'm enjoying this, myself."

"You would!"

He held her gently and helped her walk until the strength returned to her limbs. Ron Hendricks came from the stable office. His baleful eyes went over the exhausted riders and the spent condition of the horses. He did not recognize Dean as the dude that had spent the night in his office a few months before.

"Want me to unsaddle your horses?" he asked.

"No, thanks, I'll take care of that," Dean said.

He led the horses inside, unsaddled them and put them in separate stalls. He brushed both of them vigorously on the back and shoulders, but made no attempt to brush their hind quarters.

"Let them cool off good before you feed or water them," he instructed the sad-faced Hendricks.

"That'll be two bits each," the man said.

Dean reached in his pocket and extended a bill.

"Feed them good again tomorrow. They've sure earned it. Do you know where the Resolis Pool's meeting?"

"I think they're at Gertie's," the man told them.

These last few days had been long, hard ones for Herman Shelly. After the grueling trip back from La Junta and on to Kiowa, he had found the sheriff none too anxious to take on the Kincaids. They had gone to the safe crossing, where Christine had found the saddle horn, only to find the hole had been filled by someone using teams and scrappers. At the ranch, they found Jasper had left a few hours earlier for Limon. The sheriff seemed relieved as he could return to Kiowa, without having to confront Jasper.

Shelly told Mac about Dean having found the train loaded with their cattle and accused Jasper of running the entire operation. Mac was furious and naturally assumed Shelly had brought the sheriff because of the cattle, as Shelly did not mention the corroded saddle horn. They argued for some time before Mac decided to move the Pool meeting to Limon, rather than risk bringing Jasper back here, where the Kiowa sheriff would have jurisdiction. He felt much friendlier toward the sheriff in Limon.

As soon as Shelly, Homer and Christine had left the ranch, Mac sent riders out with messages to the other Pool members to change the meeting to Limon and then he and Unk drove to town themselves.

It was late afternoon when the Pool members finally all arrived for the meeting. Several were most unhappy at having to make the extra miles to Kincaid's and back to town. Mac greeted each new arrival cordially, for he wanted all the backing he could get in this matter with Shelly. They all seated themselves around the large table Gertie had set up for them on the raised wooden floor in the dance hall part of the saloon.

"Well, since we're all here, let's call the meeting to order," Mac said. "Since Marian's not here, we will have to dispense with the reading of the minutes of the spring meeting and I'll ask Wade Harper to act as temporary secretary and keep some minutes of this meeting."

"You'll have to get me something to write on," Wade said and Mac called to Gertie's man who soon produced several loose sheets of paper and a pencil from behind the bar.

Jasper sat at one end of the long table, not taking much part in any of the talking, his mind on other things. His father had not told him about Shelly's accusations, wanting Jasper to hear them direct from the man. Mac ordered a round of drinks brought and Gertie's man hurried to do this.

"I guess we'll take up your complaint first, Herm," Mac said, eyeing the crippled man coldly. He noticed that Homer Reid stood away from the table at one corner of the wide doorway between this room and the main saloon.

"I'd just as soon wait," Herm said, his expressive face working to cover his real feelings. "Archer's supposed to be here with proof of what I'm going to say, and I'd as soon wait until he gets here."

"Archer!" Jasper snapped, becoming instantly alert at mention of that name. "What the hell kind of proof can he have? If he claims he found anything wrong with the way I run the Pool, he's a liar!"

"I have to admit, he found nothing on the roundup," Herm said, his face showing how much he hated to say this.

"Shelly, if you're going to make another accusation in your personal vendetta against the Kincaids, I'm for adjourning this meeting and going home," Horace Wagner of the Seventy-Six outfit said in disgust.

"That goes for me too," Carl Hardy stated flatly. "We've heard enough of your griping against the Kincaids."

"From what little I seen of this Archer at Kincaids this spring, I wouldn't put much faith in anything he had to say, anyway," Wade Harper added. He was so disgusted at this turn of events, he broke the pencil in two in his stubby fingers.

"Now, hold on, boys!" Ike Holland bellowed in that booming voice of his. "This time, it ain't just Herm. This concerns me and Hessey, too. That fellow Archer ain't only representing Herm, he's also representing us and the Denver bank that's holding mortgages on our places. We've got no choice but to listen to what he says, ain't that right, Mr. Reid?"

Homer nodded his head on his bull neck, his eyes peering owlishly at them through his thick glasses.

"Mr. Reid's from the bank, and he's here to see that our complaint is fully considered," Herm added, hoping the bank's weight would help him hold them there. "When Dean gets here, he'll have proof of what we're saying."

Rube Hessey sat next to Shelly and now squirmed in his chair. The big man plainly did not like talking or taking part in such meetings. He said nothing.

"When will Archer be here?" Wade asked.

"He was to be here today for this meeting. I had men out to head him off but he may have missed them and gone on to Kincaid's. I'm sure he'll be here," Herm said defensively.

"Well, hell, if you can't tell us any more than that, I'm for going home," Carl Hardy said. His ranch was backed by English money so the man from a bank did not impress him. He stood up, more businessman than rancher, he was not interested in any internal feuds.

"Now, hold on!" Shelly shouted, knowing he would have to tell them something to hold them until Dean could get there.

"Well, tell us what he found," Wade Harper demanded.

"All right," Shelly gave in. "He found a train load of cattle heading east as it passed through La Junta the night the roundup got to town. We know at least some of them belonged to Hessey, Holland and me."

"What?" Jasper thundered. "How the hell?"

"That's what we'll know, when Dean gets here," Herm said, his face showing his determination. "This is serious and I expect you to all wait."

"Do you mean to tell me those cows were loaded right there in La Junta?" Jasper stormed. "That's impossible without some of us seeing them!"

"Archer figured they were loaded at Rocky Ford," Homer Reid spoke up, not just sure how to play his part in this. "Dean saw enough brands to know there was cattle of those three ranches, anyway. When he gets here, we hope to know who shipped them and where they was sent."

"Well, I'll be hanged!" Carl Hardy exclaimed. "You mean there really has been someone stealing you fellow's cows, after all?"

"We've been telling you that for several years," Shelly said, sarcasm in his voice and disgust on his face. "Oh, I know most of you thought we were just complaining to get control of the Pool, but somebody's been stealing us blind and that has us in a real bind with the bank. I'm not saying who done it, until Archer gets here with what we hope's the proof."

"Well, this does change things," Horace Wagner said. "Let's go get some supper and then start the meeting again. Maybe Archer will be here by then."

They trooped across the saloon to the door of the cafe and entered single file. Shelly and Reid brought up the rear. They all seemed to eat heartily except Shelly. The man could scarcely force down a bit of the food. Time was running out. If Dean did not get here before morning, he knew he would have to let them all go home, he could not force them to wait longer. Everything now depended on Archer, and Shelly was not sure the man had even left La Junta!

The ranchers were returning from the cafe and trooping single file across the sawdust floor of the saloon toward the dance hall, when the outside door opened and the two riders came in. Herm immediately recognized his daughter. Even from across the large room, he could tell she was exhausted. The woman's face showed her determination, as well as weariness. He felt a swelling in his chest at the pride he had in her.

Gertie also watched the two enter. The big woman had placed her chair out in the big room close to the arch of the dance hall, the better to observe what was going on in both rooms. She now moved her huge bulk in the reinforced chair and got her feet under her to be ready to heave her tremendous weight to a standing position, if need be. She looked ready to pounce on the slender woman and Marian moved out to where she would pass the woman at a distance. Marian's hazel eyes met those little piglike eyes of the big woman squarely. Gertie could also read the determination in the black-haired woman's face and remembered well how that woman had thrown her to the floor.

"Where's the money you promised me?" Gertie demanded loudly.

"You'll get it," Marian said, staying well out of the woman's reach.

Herm moved to meet them, his crippled foot dragging through the sawdust with each step, as the other Pool members went on into the dance hall and took their places around the table.

"Did you get it?" Herm asked, his anxiety plain on his face.

"Yes, we got the proof we need on the cattle," Dean assured him. "What did the sheriff do about Jasper?"

"Nothing...by the time we got to Kincaid's, Jasper'd left for Limon. The sheriff from Kiowa won't come here, and remember, I told you the Kincaids are bosom buddies with the sheriff here. We didn't even go talk to him."

"Well, we may as well face them and get it over with," Dean said, pushing his tired shoulders back, his head erect. He nodded his head toward Homer as the banker still stood near one corner of the arch of the doorway.

As they had walked across the sawdust floor of the saloon, Dean had taken notice of the other men in the room. There were three tables of card players and several men standing at the bar. He had not recognized any of them.

Dean took Marian's arm, as they stepped up on the wooden floor. The Pool members were now all seated around the table and all eyes were on the slender rider of the rough string.

"All right, let's come to order," Mac said. "Marian, since you're now here, I assume you will take over as secretary. Wade, give Marian that paper and pencil."

"With pleasure," the rancher said and reached behind him

to get a chair and make room for her at the table. She was glad to sit down.

"I want you to keep very accurate minutes of this meeting, Marian," Mac said seriously. "Your father's been making some serious charges and I want it all down in black and white. Now, Herm, I want to see what proof Archer has."

"What have you told them, Mr. Shelly?" Dean asked, looking at the faces around the table. He noticed Unk Kincaid sat well back from the others, as though he were not a part of this.

"I told them you found that train loaded with our cattle and being shipped through La Junta. That you were waiting for a telegram to tell us who shipped them and where to," Shelly said. "That's about all. When did you two leave La Junta? Late yesterday?"

"About sun up this morning," Dean said and watched the surprised look come over several faces.

"You actually rode all that way in just one day?" Shelly asked, his face a wonder to watch.

"All the way to the Kincaid Ranch and then here," Marian spoke up. "Most of that way, we were on two members of the Pool rough string, too."

"Then you never saw the men I sent out to tell you to come here?"

"No, we saw no one."

"Well, go ahead, Archer," Mac cut in. "I'm damn anxious to know about this train load of cattle."

"The cattle were consigned to the commission firm of Yarnell and Smith in Chicago. That firm claims they've sold cattle for the same man for years with power of attorney to sell all the brands in the Resolis Pool. The money was always deposited to his account in the Stockman's Bank in Pueblo," Dean said, watching Jasper's face closely.

The big cowman said nothing but sat staring at Dean, unbelief and amazement on his face. There was not the faintest sign he knew anything about this, or had any guilt about it. Either the man was innocent or the cleverest man at covering his feelings Dean had ever seen.

"Who?" Mac demanded angrily. "Who is the man?"

"According to the telegram, the man's name is Jasper Kincaid," Dean said evenly.

"You lie!" Jasper thundered, pushing back his chair and standing up. Dean noticed the pistol at the man's hip. "You lie, damn you, Archer! I haven't shipped any cattle to anyone in Chicago, or anyplace else! I don't have a bank account in Pueblo, either! This is a frame up! Don't any of you believe any of this!"

Dean shrugged his thin shoulders. "There's no reason for the commission firm to lie. The president of the Chicago Stockyards is holding the money from this shipment for proof of the rightful owners. However, this has apparently been going on for several years, and that means there's been a lot of cattle stolen in the past, that there's no money for."

"Well, by God, I never had a thing to do with any of this!" Jasper yelled and stepped away from the table to face Dean. "I'll not take this, Archer!" Jasper's normally bronze face seemed ashen now under the lamp light. "You men surely aren't going to take the word of a saddle tramp like this against that of a Kincaid, are you? After all, we've been your friends and neighbors for years!"

"A neighbor you've been. I'm not so sure about the friend part!" Shelly shouted above the din of the others. "Besides, Archer's sure no saddle tramp. He knows cattle, and you can damn well bet I'll take his word! The bank will take it, too!"

"You don't have to take my word for anything," Dean said quietly, still watching Jasper's face closely. It puzzled him that the man seemed so sincere about not knowing anything about this. "Here's the telegram. The cattle have been sold, but the money's being held for proof of ownership. You ranchers can send to Chicago and get your money for these cows. That don't give you anything for past years, however."

"That's sure good news to me!" Ike Holland bellowed. "I'll take Archer's word, too. I guess, maybe, we'd better get the sheriff to hold Jasper, since that telegram does name him as the guilty man, until we can get a lawyer to press charges. We'll have to have someone else take over the fall roundup. Maybe we can get Archer to do that, too!"

The expression which now came over Jasper's face was of utter amazement and disbelief, and Dean thought the man was certainly a much better actor than he had thought possible. To look at that handsome face, you would think the man actually knew nothing about this. Dean watched as the big man now pushed the table violently away from him, so violently it upset onto the laps of the ranchers behind it.

"I'll not take that from anyone, Archer!" he shouted angrily, and threw his hat across the room. "I knew someday I'd probably have to kill you, if one of them horses didn't do it for me!"

His rush at Dean was that of an enraged bull charging its enemy. His head was down, his arms outstretched. Before the two could come together, however, Marian jumped out, almost throwing herself at Jasper.

"Don't make things worse, Jasper!" she cried. "This isn't all we've found! There's more—about Billy."

She had hardly gotten the name out, when the big rancher grasped her shoulders and flung her away from him, as though she were a rag doll. She spun against the wall of the room and her head struck the wall with a loud thud. She slid semi-conscious to the floor. Jasper continued in his rush at the slender rider he hated so much.

Dean met the man's charge with a stinging blow to the big man's face. It did not seem to faze Jasper in the least. Within a moment, the two were struggling and slugging at each other with all their might.

Homer Reid's glass case snapped shut and he slid it into an inner pocket. Gertie's man dashed through the archway from the saloon, a sawed-off shotgun in his hands. He was followed by several men from the card tables. They had obviously been listening and wanted to see the excitement. Before Gertie's man knew what had happened, Homer relieved him of the weapon and again backed against the corner of the archway where he could watch most of both rooms. He motioned for the others to stay back and out of the fight.

Dean instantly felt the drag of exhaustion on his body. Even the excitement of the fight could not seem to overcome his weariness, and he knew he would have to be at his very best, if he were to win this fight. He felt despair, as he hit out at the big cowman with all his might and nothing seemed to happen.

Then, just as it had happened so many times after being thrown by one of the rough string, from deep within his innermost being, came the will and determination to go on.

TWENTY

Jasper caught Dean by the arm, ripping his shirt half off and literally threw the smaller man through the archway and into the sawdust of the saloon floor. Dean landed on his back and slid several feet through a cloud of sawdust, before stopping almost at the feet of Dirty Gertie in her big chair. He was scrambling to his feet at the same time the huge woman was trying to heave herself out of the chair, when Jasper charged into both of them. They all crashed over the chair to sprawl in a heap of squirming flesh, flailing arms and legs. Gertie's screams now filled the air with filthy names for both men.

The men struggled up, swinging and ducking. They backed against a card table, tipping it over, sending money and cards flying into the sawdust. Jasper was finding he was not having much luck in hitting the slender cowboy, who dodged and ducked away, as he hit back at the big rancher with telling blows. The months of fighting the rough string, flanking calves and living in the open had hardened this slender man until he seemed tireless and as tough as a cedar post. The excitement of the fight seemed to temporarily overcome the fatigue of his long day in the saddle.

At last, Jasper quit trying to hit the man and managed to again catch Dean's left arm. The big man turned to use his hip as leverage to send the cowboy crashing against the bar. Dean's head hit a sharp corner and lights flashed before his eyes. Desperately, he tried to clear his head, as he fell to the floor. He could not locate Jasper as his mind seemed stunned. Then, he realized he was sitting on the floor with his back to the bar, and for a second, he could not seem to make his muscles push himself to his feet.

His vision began to clear and he made out Jasper standing a few paces from him, his feet spread wide apart, a gun in his hand. There was a loud noise and a searing pain burned across his left side. The big rancher had shot him!

Men were now scrambling to get out of range. Gertie moved her huge bulk quicker than one would think possible and threw herself behind the far end of the bar, where she was followed almost instantly by her man.

With the same grim determination that had driven him to pick himself up, time after time, and get back on one of the rough string, Dean forced himself to fight back. He drove himself to his feet and to one side, his hand streaking to his pistol as he moved. Jasper's second shot missed him by inches and splattered into the wood of the bar. Had he not been moving, he would have taken the slug in his chest. Still groggy from the blow to his head, Dean's thumb pulled the hammer back, cocking his pistol. He lifted the gun, thinking it must weigh a ton. When Jasper's big chest came in line, he squeezed the trigger. Swiftly, instinctively, he re-cocked the gun, pointed it and squeezed the trigger again.

Jasper went backward a step as though pushed by a large,

unseen hand. The big man seemed to trip over his own feet and sat down hard in another cloud of sawdust. He still had enough life to lift his gun with both hands but, before he could pull the trigger, his face went slack and his handsome head bowed as he toppled over backward and lay still.

There was the terrific roar of the shotgun as Homer fired one barrel into the ceiling.

"Everybody stay calm and out of this!" he shouted and backed toward Dean, facing the rest of the people.

Slowly, Dean moved along the bar, clutching at the pain in his side and his head finally clearing. He put his gun in his holster and leaned heavily against the bar, as the curious hurried to crowd around the fallen roundup boss.

"It's over," Dean heard Homer repeat several times.

Jasper lay where he had fallen. His father and uncle now knelt beside the body. A deathly silence had come over the place, as every person in the room watched the Kincaids.

"Get a doctor!" Mac's shallow, quavering voice called out.

"It's no use, Mac," Unk said. "I'm sure he's dead."

"This is terrible!" Mac cried passionately. "It can't happen. Now both my boys are dead!"

Unk stood up slowly, and leaning forward stiffly, walked over to face Dean, as the slender rider leaned heavily against the edge of the bar for support.

"You done quite a job of detective work, Archer," the old man said bitterly, his faded blue eyes searching the younger man's face. "I'll give you credit for finding out what was going on. You're a smart cowman, probably one of the best to hit this range in a long time, but.... you just killed the wrong man."

"You're the Jasper Kincaid that was shipping the cattle and getting the money," Dean managed to whisper. "I thought Jasper acted too surprised. I'd wondered if you weren't the one running the wagon behind us. You and your buddies on your reunion. You knew just where our wagons would be and how to work around us."

"Yes, I'm the one you was really after. Years ago, I started this Resolis Pool and I made it work, too. Then, Shelly and some of them helped Mac kick me out and take over. I had nothing. Hell, I taught Jasper everything he knew about the cow business. I knew every move he made, and it was easy to run the wagon behind him and pick up the stuff we wanted."

"That's why you could follow the wagons and not get caught," Dean said. "I guess I just don't understand why you did it?'

"Just to get even, mostly. Revenge, I guess you'd say. Shelly and Holland got the others to vote me out as president and roundup boss, after I'd started the Pool and made them all a lot of money. Well, I sure made them pay for that mistake. Without the Pool I gave them, they'd have gone broke years ago." The old man shook his gray head and pushed his Stetson to the back of his head. "As it was, we shipped train loads of cattle right by them, under their very noses, and they was too dumb to catch on. Hell, if you hadn't come along, Archer, and stumbled on to that train, we'd probably kept on for a few more years."

"It was a smart plan," Dean conceded slowly.

"It was smart enough to break the three of them, in another year or two. Hell, Shelly's broke now. Of course, if they'd turned the Pool back over to me, I'd have stopped their losses and we would have run things just like we used to," the old man said, running his blunt fingers through his gray locks, as the others gathered around to hear what he was saying. "I guess it was an old fool's dream, Archer, but I damn near made it work. If you hadn't come along, I think I could have pulled it off. Now, I've got a life I'll have to answer for and I doubt there's a man here who'll give a damn about me, anyway."

"Why didn't you step in and stop Jasper?" Dean asked. "You knew he hadn't shipped those cows."

"Hell, I hoped he'd kill you. If he had, you wouldn't be here to prove who'd done it. I didn't care if the rest of them thought he'd done it. That would have worked to help me get back in control of the Pool."

"Well, I may have shot Jasper for the wrong crime," Dean said slowly. "But, he certainly wasn't an innocent man. He deserved to be hung for what he apparently did to his brother. Show them the saddle horn, Herm. Tell them what we think really happened to Billy Kincaid."

"What the hell do you mean, Archer?" Unk demanded harshly, his old eyes keenly watching the cowboy's face. "You couldn't know anything about that. It happened long before you came to this country. Hell, we all know what happened to Billy."

Mac had also been listening. He now stood up and looked at the man leaning against the bar, still holding tightly to his left side. Kincaid's weak upper lip quivered under the heavy mustache.

"What do you know about Billy, Archer?" he demanded, and walked toward the man.

"The big flood you had a few weeks ago, apparently washed out a big hole up by the corrals at the safe crossing," Dean said.

"I know all about that, the men told me about it as soon as I got back from Denver. Jasper's already had that hole filled in." Mac came closer to the man now. "What did that hole have to do with Billy?"

Herm Shelly now limped to stand beside Dean. "Ask Cal about the skull of a horse he found in that hole, Mac," Shelly said, his expressive face working with each word. "That skull still had part of the bridle and bit on it. It was Billy's bit, Mac, the one he was using the night he drowned. Cal recognized that bit and took it to Jasper in La Junta. That's why he came back early from the roundup, so he could fill in that hole before anybody found anything else. He knew there was probably evidence in there that would incriminate him."

Herm held out the corroded horn and Mac took it in trembling fingers.

"It's Billy's slick horn, Mac. I'm sure of it. You can see the brass where we scrapped it a little. It sure wasn't a leather covered horn and I never knew anyone but Billy to ride a slick-horned saddle in this part of the country. It just has to have been Billy's. Cal didn't know it, but Christine found that horn after he left in such a hurry with that bit."

"But, Jasper always said Billy drowned miles below the ranch?"

"That's the whole point, Mac. Jasper must have lied about that because he killed Billy and pushed him and his horse off into the quicksand just below the upper crossing. Then, to throw all of us off on a wild goose chase, he told us that story about Billy crossing way below the ranch. No wonder we never found any trace of him. We spent all them days looking in the wrong place."

Mac slowly looked from the horn in his hand to the body of his oldest son lying in the sawdust. Finally, he knew what had really happened on that terrible night so many years ago. He sank down in the sawdust, his head bowed and his lips trembling. How could the boy he had loved and worked with so much have done this to him. Right then, life was a bitter taste in his mouth and he knew it would never leave.

Unk turned, as though to walk away, but was confronted by big Rube Hessey.

"I think you and me'd better have a talk with the sheriff, Unk," the big rancher said in a high, tight voice so much like Eben's. Rube was no longer bashful. He understood this kind of action.

Ike Holland loudly agreed and the three moved away toward the door.

Dean became aware Marian was now pressing close beside him and he turned toward her. As he moved, the pain in his side seemed to explode up into his brain and darkness settled over him like a soft blanket.

When he regained consciousness, he realized he was lying on top of the bar. His side and back ached dully, as well as his head. In the bright light of the saloon lamps, he made out the worried faces peering down at him.

"Well, by golly, I do believe the old boy's going to stick around to ride another rough one or two," Homer Reid said cheerily, his eyes smiling behind his glasses. "One thing for sure, Dean, whenever you and I get together in Dirty Gertie's, things do get exciting."

"I guess I earned that bonus the bank promised, didn't I?" Dean asked, trying to smile back at his friend.

"You sure did, old buddy. Jasper tried hard to cheat you out of it, though. His bullet ran along your ribs for several inches and then came back out. You'd lost a lot of blood, before we realized you were hurt and got a doctor to come sew you up. You'll be all right in a few days, he says."

"Well, I'm going to need that bonus money for a honeymoon, Homer, so get it here quick," Dean said, moving his gaze to Marian's face and lifted a hand to touch her cheek. "Now, Homer, if you're any kind of a friend at all, you'll leave me alone with the lady. I can talk to bankers any old time."

"I'm right here, Dean," the woman said softly and took his hand to clasp it tightly in both of hers. She looked down at him and her large hazel eyes held a look he would never forget.

"I'm sorry you made such a ride and then weren't able to stop the trouble," he whispered softly. "You tried. I sure never knew another woman like you."

"I used to feel kind of mad at God for taking Billy," she leaned down to whisper. "Now, I know he was saving me for a far better man."

He knew what she meant, for God had seemed to keep him waiting for this moment, and a far better woman, too. He lifted his arm around her neck to draw her face down and kiss her tenderly on the lips. Right then, it seemed like God must have known what He was doing and the wait hadn't been so darn bad, after all. Maybe waiting even made you appreciate things more.